THE CRUISE OF
THE *GULL-FLIGHT*

By

SIDNEY CORBETT

Illustrated by

BERNARD WESTMACOTT
and S. D. BROWN

THE "GULL FLIGHT"

LONGMANS, GREEN AND CO.

NEW YORK · TORONTO

1937

CORBETT

THE CRUISE OF THE "GULL-FLIGHT"

FIRST EDITION

CONTENTS

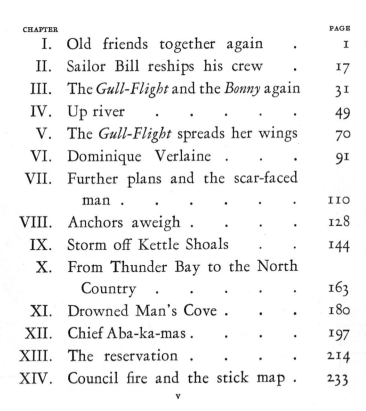

THE CRUISE OF THE *GULL-FLIGHT*

THE CRUISE OF THE *GULL-FLIGHT*

CHAPTER I

OLD FRIENDS TOGETHER AGAIN

SCHOOL HAD been out for nearly a week and it was a beautiful, bright, sunny, spring morning—late spring, toward the end of June. There were going to be strawberries for breakfast, and cream too—whole pitchers of it.

Katy had come down a few minutes early and was standing in the sun-bathed dining-room window bay, looking hungrily at the table and waiting impatiently for the rest of the family. For until they arrived breakfast would not begin. Afterward there would be nothing to do, and all summer in which to do it. Nothing tiresome, that is, like lessons, but heaps of other things, interesting things, really worth doing.

There was the old house in which they lived, surrounded by its waist-high iron fence and set a good ways back from the road. Out in front were the boat house and dock, and across the shining river with its burden of lake freighters, was the Canadian Shore—always a land of mystery. At this point it was visible only as a high bluff showing behind a sandy spur, thrust out at the upper end of an island which blocked the river mouth a mile or so below their house. Here the current split into two races of fast water, almost a rapids in fact; so that north-bound ships from Buffalo and other Lake Erie ports made heavy going of it upstream. On still nights you could hear the clang of ash-whips and the banging of shovels against steel doors in the fire hold, as the crew flung in extra coal to help beat up river under forced draught. And if there were any fog you slept uneasily to the blat of deep-toned whistles, snarling their warning to down-bound steamers to hug the right bank of the channel.

Some day, Katy thought, she too would like to sail up that river and through the little lake at its head, and then through the narrow swift St. Clair that emptied into it. And then on through the big lake that lay north of that, and maybe then through the "Soo" locks into the biggest lake of all, that stretched away to the cold North Country almost as high as Hudson's Bay, and as far west as Duluth and Superior where all the ore and grain came from.

But in that first big lake was a part called the North Channel and Georgian Bay, with narrow passages and deep sounds that slashed inland for miles and miles through wild rough country where you still used Indian guides so as not to get lost. And there were such queer names up there, half French, half Indian. Like Bay au Fin, which meant Narrow Bay; and Manitoulin, an island named for the Great Indian God. There were some Irish names for places too, like Killarney for example, which really wasn't a place at all but a lot of little islands that you could only go to in a boat.

Well, maybe they would make a trip like that some time and not just go to a camp as they did last vacation. Although once they all had gone to the seashore.

Katy remembered that summer two years before. The bright beach and the blue water on still sunlit days. And the same beach on stormy ones, all roily and dirty with bits of driftwood and seaweed flung high up beyond the wicked chop and surge of an angry sea. And how clouds of spray curled like smoke above the twin spikes of rock that marked the inlet a little farther down the shore.

She thought of the good sea food, the lobsters and clam bakes for their beach suppers. And how she always burned herself, raking away the coals over the sand pit where they had buried the wash boiler used to cook in. And the clouds of salty steam smelling of sea kelp, that arose as soon as they took the cover off. And the old smoke-blackened coffee pot full of melted butter.

Afterward just before going home they always went for a swim, wading out knee deep, and scooping up sand by the handful and rubbing it quickly up and down grimy shins and legs before the sea washed it all away. There's no better soap in all the world than that.

Katy sighed and looked at the clock and then back at the breakfast table. A quarter to eight—where are they all? she wondered, fidgeting up and down. Finally she pulled a chair into the window bay and resigned herself to a further wait.

Yes, they had all had a wonderful time at that far-off New England beach. And at the Bledsoe Farm, halfway between the seashore and a grassy back bay with clam flats at its lower end, showing all bare and black and shiny at low tide—what a wonderful place that was too. What fun they had, she and her brother and their three cousins. There was Cynthia Ann, whom they promptly nick-named "Spinach" because of the fuss she made whenever it appeared on the table, which it did, regularly, for supper every Monday, Wednesday and Friday. Spinach was thir-teen this summer, only a few months younger than Katy herself. And there was Morgan, the eldest of her uncle's three children, who brought with him his own nick-name of "The Raider." Just under seventeen, he was. And Teddy, the youngest of them all, whose frantic and seething rages blew up quicker than any thunderstorm upon the slightest reference to him by the others as "The Baby." Just turned eleven, he had, and hardly as yet a man of mature judgment.

There was Uncle Bill too, her father's eldest brother—a retired sea Captain who lived near New London where the Navy destroyers had their base. Not very far away, was New London. Close enough so that "Sailor Bill," as they promptly christened him, could come up every Fri-day night and spend the week-end with them. He had a son whom Katy had never met, for he was a Midshipman at Annapolis, and wouldn't get a vacation until the end of his second year. . . .

"Why, that is this summer!" Katy reflected.

My, hadn't they been excited when the expressman from the little resort town close by, brought around a receipt card for her father to sign, marked—"Hold for Captain Williams." That was on Wednesday she remembered, and all the next day they had pestered Father about it. "What was it? How big was it? Was it alive?" and so forth. And all Father would say was, "Ask your Uncle Bill. He'll be here tomorrow."

And Sailor Bill wouldn't tell them anything either, and would only say, "Now don't get excited. You'll know all about it in a day or two."

Then for two days they weren't permitted to go near the railroad station, nor toward Back Bay either. And how Sunday morning finally did come around, and how after church Sailor Bill collected "his crew," as he called them, and marched them all the short half mile to a little fisherman's landing that ran out from the shore to where the

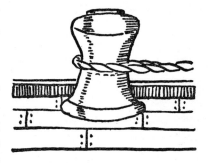

ONE OF THE SHORE BOLLARDS

water was about three feet deep, even at low tide.

And there fast to the dock, with a bow and stern line flung over two shore bollards was a little cutter, regular Navy style, with a main and mizzenmast and two sails furled neatly fore and aft—"Lug rig," Sailor Bill called them—"Dipping lug forward, and standing lug mizzen." And how then and there, he had taken them all for their first sail. "Time you got some salt behind your ears," he said, when the little cutter heeled over in the stiff afternoon breeze, shipping some water over her bows and wetting them all down with flying spray.

How nautical they had all become that summer, after the first four week-ends that is, when Sailor Bill felt it was safe for them to take the cutter out alone.

Bonaventure was the name they finally decided on for their little craft, and as Teddy couldn't pronounce it, *Bonny,* for short. "Means the same thing," said Sailor Bill, "only you've moved over to Scotland from France. 'Good'—that's what the first syllable means in either language. The adventure part's up to you."

Morgan, the Raider, was promptly chosen Captain as befitted his age and sex, and Katy and Spinach were Mates. Katy chose Teddy for her crew, and Brother was in the opposite watch under Spinach, carrying out orders smartly and on the run, as able seamen have done since the time when ships began.

Sailor Bill taught them the language of the sea as well as the art of ship handling, and before long the simple act of taking off one's clothes before going to bed was referred to as dousing our topsails. And the Sunday

THE "BONAVENTURE"

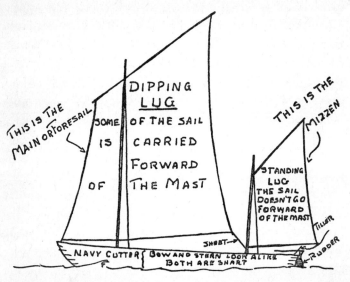

THIS IS THE MAIN OR FORESAIL

SOME IS OF

DIPPING LUG
OF THE SAIL
CARRIED
FORWARD
THE MAST

THIS IS THE MIZZEN

STANDING LUG
THE SAIL
DOESN'T GO
FORWARD
OF THE MAST

TILLER

RUDDER

SHEET

NAVY CUTTER BOW AND STERN LOOK ALIKE BOTH ARE SHARP

AND AS TEDDY COULDN'T PRONOUNCE IT
"BONNY" FOR SHORT

afternoon blueberry-muffin and cambric teas became, splicing the main brace.* Nobody ever went upstairs any more—they went aloft. And likewise, went below, for breakfast. The porch became the quarter deck, and one

---

* Whenever the crew of an old time Clipper Ship finished a hard job like handling canvas in a winter gale—grog (rum and water, either hot or cold) was served all hands. This they called, "Splicing the Main Brace."—KATY.

saluted smartly as he came up the companion ladder, which was their new name for the front steps.

They learned some of the customs of the sea too; the courtesy all good sailors show to each other, and respect for rank and authority. For instance Morgan, aboard and in command of the *Bonny,* was to be addressed as Captain Morgan, and never by his nickname. And Sailor Bill must be, Captain Williams, sir—if they ever went aboard his ship. "And maybe I'll take you some day," he said. "On a proper ship—big enough for us all to go on a long cruise."

Well that was all very nice but it was also a long time ago, and she hadn't seen her cousins since, nor her uncle, Sailor Bill, either. The good ship *Bonaventure,* with her masts unstepped and her canvas stowed safely away, had gone back into the crate and been returned to her home at the New London destroyer base. And now, what were they going to do this year?

There seemed to be some mystery about the plans for this summer. She couldn't pry any information out of her father, try as she might. Without asking too directly that was, and she didn't want to do that. Girls of fourteen weren't curious babies any more, and besides she had rather an idea the information would come of itself pretty soon. And it was much more fun to wait and see, and act grown up and dignified about it. Not like her brother who couldn't contain himself, but popped question after question at every meal the family had had together since he had come home from school two days ago.

Not that he had found out anything, for he hadn't. Father had been very bland, turning aside all questions in the most offhand manner in the world, and never giving a direct answer at all.

Then she heard some steps on the stair and here was Father, coming into the dining room and crossing to the window bay where she was, and taking hold of both her hands.

"Good morning, good morning," he said, kissing her on both cheeks and holding her off at arm's length, and looking her all over. "My, my—growing bigger every day. Soon a young lady, before we even know it, and a pretty one too, I'll bet. But what's for breakfast? Though I don't suppose young ladies ever go into the kitchen anymore to find out, and maybe steal a doughnut from cook?"

Katy had, but she wouldn't admit it for worlds.

And then Mother came in and took her place at the far end of the table. "Shall we start, Jim?" she asked, talking to Father. "Joey doesn't seem to be in sight anywhere, although I told him to stay near the house and not be late for breakfast."

"I suppose he's got a certain amount of exploring to do," said Father; "only two days home from school. There's a new calf next door, and this morning they're turning him out to pasture for the first time."

Father frowned a little as he said all this and Katy knew why, and smiled to herself. For Brother's name wasn't Joey at all, but James like her father's. And Father never would call him that, but always "Brick" on account of his having red hair. And this name stuck, and all the boys at school used it. Mother didn't approve of that, any more than Father did of Joey.

But anyway there it was, and neither of her parents would give in so that Brother never heard his own name except when they teased him, and called him Little James. And that made him jump up and down in a rage too, just as Teddy did when they spoke to, or of him, as The Baby.

Suddenly there was a furious barking out in back. It sounded as if it came from their neighbor's pasture which adjoined their own meadow lands lying behind the barn, and was separated from them by a high fence with barbed wire along the top of it.

"That's Gyp," said Father, referring to their little wire-haired terrier. "Brick and he are up to something."

They all listened for a minute. Then there was a slam of the back screen door and the sound of feet running up stairs, and presently Gyp came in to where they all were, looking pleased with himself and panting hard, and if his tail had been any longer he would have wagged himself right off his feet with it.

Father raised his eyes and looked at Mother.

"What's he doing upstairs?" he said. "Don't tell me that boy went up to wash, voluntarily;" and then, "Come here," talking to Gyp, leaning down and feeling his shaggy coat.

"Hot," he said, straightening up. "Been running. Now what, I wonder."

For a minute or two there was silence upstairs and then the sound of water, running from the bathroom tap. Then there was more silence—broken by the screech of a bureau drawer being pulled out and shoved in again.

"Getting out a fresh suit," said Mother, tracing her son's every movement by the noises he made. "Why would that be? He was fully dressed when I saw him a half hour ago."

"This ought to be good," said Father. "I have a great respect for imagination especially when it's in the family, and I haven't heard a new fairy story for a long time."

"He's so silly," said Katy. "As if anybody would believe the weird tales he tells."

"Ah!" said Father. "As you grow older, you'll find that in later life one refers to talent like your brother's as the 'Creative Urge.'"

Suddenly there was the sound of feet clumping rapidly down the front stairs, and Brick came into the room. He had changed his shorts and put on a fresh blouse. There had also been some liberal doses of soap and water for his hair was plastered down tight, and his face shone like the top of a cherry-wood table.

But running from the corner of his left eye was a flaming red scratch, and his right knee was skinned and bruised. There had been no time to switch shoes or socks, so the marks of green and dewy pasture were apparent to all. He bore himself lightly and went directly to his chair, hoping that the scratch, the bruised knee, the fresh blouse and shorts, and the grass stains wouldn't excite his parents to undue curiosity. He also glared at his sister in order to browbeat her into an awed silence. But it didn't work.

Father glanced at the clock ticking away on the mantelpiece. "Well let's have it," he said to his son. "I can see you have already done your good deed for the day. Who was the distressed damsel? And how come she got that way so early in the morning?"

"No," answered Brick, "it wasn't that exactly—it was that calf."

"Calf?" said Father. "That must be some calf—to scratch your face, skin your knee, and do I don't know what to the suit you first had on this morning. And all of this on its first day out of the barn."

"Well maybe it wasn't the calf exactly," said Brick. "I guess it was that bull."

"Ah!" said Father. "The bull. Haven't I told you bulls don't make good playmates? The place for a bull is on the other side of a fence—a high fence—one the bull can't climb."

"That's just it," said Brick. "I didn't have time to figure that fence right, and I kinda forgot the barbed wire on the top of it. Part of my pants is still there. That's why I was late to breakfast, I guess. You wouldn't want me to come down wearing a pair of pants with only one leg in them—now would you?"

Katy looked at her brother scornfully.

"That's not up to your usual standard," she said.

"Where's the dead grizzly bear? And there ought to be at least two Redskins biting the dust."

"Katy," said her mother reprovingly.

"What did Gyp do all this time," said Father.

"Good old Gyp," said Brick. "He ran right up to that ol' bull and barked as hard as he could and tried to grab him by the tail. And I guess maybe if it hadn't been for that little ol' dog, I never would have gotten to the fence in time."

"Oh, dear!" said Mother. "And only the third day of vacation too. I'll be frantic before we get these children away."

"Away?" said Father, catching her up as though hearing some news for the first time.

Brick, too, quickly interrupted, glad of the chance to get the subject changed. "Away?" he said. "Where? When? What are we going to do this summer?"

Katy pricked up her ears. Maybe now it was all coming out. But Father wasn't going to be trapped into any admissions. His air was very casual—so casual in fact that Katy knew something was up. And why was he staying so late at the table? On a week day too, when on all other mornings he was gone by eight o'clock?

Then just about as breakfast was over, there was a screech of automobile tires on the drive at the other side of the house, and in the hearty seagoing voice she was sure she would recognize anywhere, a great shout of:

"Ahoy in there! Get ready to repel boarders."

And then some other voices, not loud or deep but high, shrill, and excited, crying out:

"K-A-T-Y! — B-R-I-C-K!"

Then they both jumped up from their chairs, and Katy cried, "Why, it's Sailor Bill!"

And Brick said, "And Morgan the Raider, and Spinach. And Teddy too, I'll bet!"

Together they ran out of the dining room toward the side porch, and there in the drive was a long gray touring car. In the driver's seat was Sailor Bill, and beside him was The Raider looking all grown up in gray slacks and a blue jacket. And in the back seat scrunched up in a corner were her other two cousins, Spinach and The Baby. But right away Katy knew they couldn't call him Baby any more, for he too had grown up, almost as big as Brick.

And the reason both her cousins were crowded up in the back seat was that most of the tonneau, and the seat too for that matter, was piled high with regulation Man-of-War dunnage bags. Across one of them was stenciled the name "Cynthia Ann." On another she could see the letters that spelled "Morgan." And all the bags looked stuffed to the limit with what Katy was sure was their owners' deep-sea gear.

There would be sou'westers for rainy and squally weather, jumpers and knitted watch caps, and sweaters with pull cords at the neck to keep out chill night winds. She knew also that each bag contained a peacoat, which was really a Mackinaw, Navy style, blue—with a high collar, and black buttons engraved with an anchor running up and down the front. Plenty of room besides, there was in those sea bags, for underwear and bathing suits and camping clothes. Everything in fact that one needed for a whole summer aboard ship, or ashore either, for that matter.

The way you packed your things in a dunnage bag was to roll each piece separately, and secure it at either end with a length of white cord tied in a sea-going square knot. "Rolled and stopped before stowing," Sailor Bill called it.

Then the bag could be lashed to a rail or stanchion below, or chucked out of the way under a bunk—all without getting the things in it mussed or wrinkled. So that when you took them out again, there they were, all pressed as though a shore tailor had been at work on them.

Then her cousins jumped from the car—spilled out of the back seat all at once it seemed to her—and Spinach grabbed her by the hand. Together they pulled out the two top bags, and there underneath at the bottom of the pile, were two more bags just like the others. Only across one of them was stenciled Katy's name, and on the other was her brother's, painted in bold black letters.

By this time Sailor Bill had gotten down from the car and was around by the side of them. Katy half expected him to pick her up and swing her at arm's length as he used to. But he didn't.

Instead he stood in front of her for a second, erect and

almost at attention. Then he grabbed Spinach and put the two cousins side by side.

"Both my Mates grown up," he said. "I shan't want for First Officers now."

And then her parents appeared on the side porch.

"Well, come on in," said Father, holding open the screen door. "If Katy and Brick aren't told the summer's plans pretty soon, there'll be an explosion. You can't keep curiosity bottled up forever."

CHAPTER II

SAILOR BILL and Father led the way indoors, slapping each other on the back as brothers always do when, after a long separation, they meet again. By the side of her mother, and just ahead of Katy and Cynthia Ann who had paired off arm in arm, walked Morgan the eldest cousin.

The Raider, thought Katy, remembering his old nickname. I wonder whether he'll like being called that now?

Straight and tall, he carried himself well. At the side of his neat gray slacks, a white yachting cap swung easily from one hand. His head, topped by its closely cut brown hair was erect, and held squarely above the broad shoulders in the blue reefer jacket. Spinach noticed her cousin's appraising look and squeezed her arm proudly.

"Different, isn't he," she whispered, "than two years ago? He goes to Military School now—in their Naval Brigade. He knows lots about boats and engines, and everything. But he isn't stuck up a bit. He's just our old Morgan—Captain of the *Bonny*."

When they all reached the wide screened-in porch that

17

stretched straight across the front of the house, Sailor Bill turned to the five cousins.

"Up to now," he said, "we've been under Sealed Orders. We still are, for part of them, but Morgan knows most of the plans. So suppose you go over there and listen to his story. I'll be right here to answer questions as soon as he gets through."

Teddy and Brick piled themselves into a swinging bench that cut across the far corner of the porch, and Spinach and Katy sat each in an arm chair facing a large round table, behind which Morgan took his stand. Gyp, the little wire-haired terrier, didn't know quite where to go. He didn't want to miss anything, so he ran eagerly from one end of the porch to the other till he practically wore himself out. Then with his tongue hanging out and panting hard, he sat himself squarely between the two groups, looking all the while, first at the children and then back at their parents.

First Morgan uncapped a long metal tube and pulled out a roll of what looked like drawing paper. This he spread out on the table, face up; the cousins could see that it was a sort of map. A funny one though, for most of it looked like water and seemed but bound around the edges with land. The cities and towns were only indicated and roughly sketched in as though not very important, and that was right. The water was the important thing on this kind of map, and the land something to be avoided, for it was a sailing chart of Lake Huron and Georgian Bay, and the North Channel.

Morgan pegged the chart flat on the table by placing a book at each of the four corners. Teddy and Brick immediately jumped up to have a look at it, and Katy and Spinach almost fell out of their chairs craning their necks forward to be able to see the better.

Morgan grinned at them all and waved them back to their seats. "Time for that in a minute," he said. "Let's get the story started first."

"What story?" asked Brick.

"What are we going to do?" asked Katy. "What's that map for? Why are all those sea bags marked with our names? Why did Sailor Bill come way out here in that big gray car? And what's everybody so mysterious about?"

Spinach punched her elbow into Katy's ribs. "Sh-h-h," she said. "Give him a chance. He never can get started if you talk all the time and ask so many questions. We've got the most glorious summer ahead, and if you'll keep quiet you'll know all about it in a minute."

"That's right," said Teddy grandly. "You tell 'em, Sis'. The first thing every new crew has to learn, is to 'pipe down.' Let the officers do the talking. You'll find out everything soon enough, that way."

Brick glared at his cousin as though he would like to start an argument right then and there. But curiosity got the better of him, so he sided in with Teddy and took it out on his sister.

"Girls always talk too much," he said.

"Go ahead, Morgan," said Spinach. "Can't you see

they are all dying to know about it? Spin your yarn."

"Well," began Morgan, "you remember that summer at the seashore two years ago, when we got our first lessons in seamanship by learning to handle the *Bonny?*"

"Of course," said Katy. "When you were Captain, and Spinach and I were Mates."

"And Teddy and I were crew," put in Brick eagerly.

"And Able-seamen you were," said Spinach.

Morgan continued. "You'll also remember," he said, "how Sailor Bill told us that some day he would take us on a real voyage, on a proper ship. Well the time is now, here, this summer. And he says she's the finest little ship you ever saw. A real schooner with two deckhouses and a fo'c'sle below, and a galley, and a big cabin with three staterooms off that. One of them is for Katy and Cynthia, another for Teddy and Brick, and I'm going to be in the third with Sailor Bill's son, the Midshipman from Annapolis."

"What's his name, and what's he like?" asked Katy.

"Williams, of course," said Spinach. "He's Sailor Bill's son and he's like everybody else, only he's awfully sea-going, has just finished a trip half around the world in a battle cruiser."

"Silly," said Katy, "I know that. It's his first name I mean. Isn't he going to think us terribly young to be his crew?"

"Not a bit," said Spinach. "He and Sailor Bill came down to visit us for the Christmas Holidays last year, and we had tremendous fun. He rigged up a little iceboat and took us out on the bay, and he taught Morgan all about a compass and something about how to navigate. Then he showed us what a schooner rig was, and drew a plan of the boat we're going on this summer so that I feel at home on her already. And his first name's Robert— Bob, we called him right away."

"I'm beginning to like him already," said Katy.

"Where's the ship now?" asked Brick, who always got right down to cases and left all romance to his sister.

"Here," said Morgan. "Up the river a ways, that is, tied to a dock. Sailor Bill got leave for two of his old seamen, and together with Midshipman Bob they brought her up from Norfolk. Except for putting some stores aboard, we're ready to start."

"Start?" asked Brick. "Start where?"

"On our voyage," said Morgan. "Up the river first, and into Lake St. Clair for a day's practice cruise. Then, if everything goes right, it's 'Anchors Aweigh,' across Lake Huron to Georgian Bay and the North Channel. Once up there we're going to get an Indian guide, and camp and fish, and make side trips back inland."

"Oh, boy!" said Brick. "With a real Indian who can show us how to make a birch-bark canoe?"

"And put bead work on moccasins?" said Spinach.

"And teach us to weave baskets?" put in Katy.

"Yes," said Morgan; "but that will all be after we get up there. We've a long voyage first and there'll only be two grown-ups aboard, Sailor Bill and Midshipman Bob. We five have to run the ship. We're all the crew there'll be. I'm going to be Chief Engineer because I've been studying marine engines at school. Katy and Spinach will be the Mates, just as they were on the *Bonny,* only now they will be shipkeepers as well and take charge of the stores, and do the cooking too."

"What about us?" asked Brick. "What are Teddy and I going to be?"

"Able seamen," said Morgan. "Who ever heard of a ship without those."

"I know how to cook," said Katy. "But I've never tried it on a real ship's galley."

"I have," said Spinach. "Sailor Bill set one up in our summer kitchen last Christmas, and I've been practicing on it ever since. They call the stove a 'shipmate' and it burns coal, and you start it with little charcoal bricks. There's an oven and four top burners with a railing around them so the pots won't slide off when the ship heels over in the wind."

"She's pretty good," said Teddy. "Many's the meal we had off the shipmate."

"You'll get used to the galley in no time," said Morgan to Katy. "Ours should be a 'full feeding' ship."

"We'll do our best," said Katy.

"Fine," said Morgan, turning back to the table. "Now if you will all come up here, I'll show you where we are going to sail."

Then he took two other charts and laid them on top of the one he had pegged down with the four books. The

first one was the Detroit River, the whole thirty-odd
miles of it from lake to lake. There was Belle Isle at the
top where the head of the river opened from Lake St.
Clair, and Grosse Ile at the foot, where the river mouth
emptied into Lake Erie.

"What a funny map," said Katy. "What's that white
streak winding up the middle with the light blue on each
side, and the deep blue near the shore? And what are
all the little numbers for?"

"The white streak is the channel—deep water," said
Morgan. "The light blue is where the river begins to get
shallow, and the deep blue marks the shoals where we'd
go aground sure if we sailed into them. The little figures
show the depth in fathoms."

"Where are we now on that map?" asked Brick. "Our
house, I mean."

Morgan moved his finger slowly down the eastern shore
of Grosse Ile. Toward the lower end he stopped.

"Right here," he said, pointing to a black dot on the
chart near the river's edge.

"What a wonderful map," said Katy. "You can see just
where everything is. Look! There's where the road
turns back, and our boat house with the little island
in front. Why we can go anywhere with a map like
that."

"Don't be too sure," said Morgan. "These are narrow
waters. Wait till we're out of sight of land. It won't
be so easy then. That requires real navigating, and that's

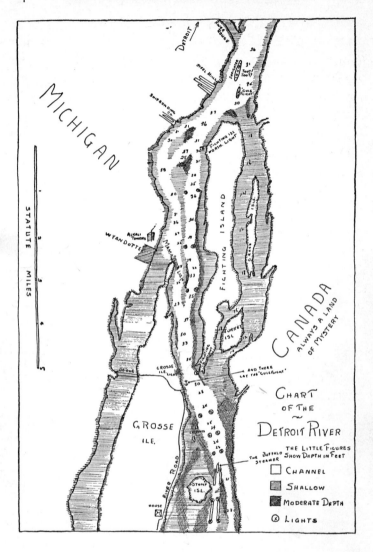

where Sailor Bill and Midshipman Bob come in. You've got to know lots to be able to tell where you are when there's no land to go by."

Then his finger traced slowly back up the shore line to where the deep water of the channel cut in toward the bank. At the upper end of the Island the chart showed just the narrowest trace of blue, with little or no shoal water. Also at that point was a little mark, where a dock and a pier ran out into the river. Right here Morgan's finger stopped.

"There's the ship," he said, lifting up his hand.

"Why I know where that is," said Brick. "That's Ferry's Landing at the Head of the Island."

"Yes," said Morgan, "and that's where we're to start from. The ship's only waiting for her crew to come aboard. Midshipman Bob is standing anchor watch, and tomorrow we begin loading stores."

Then there was a great shaking of hands and a slapping of backs, and lots and lots of questions. They all looked eagerly at the chart while Morgan showed how they expected to sail up the river on the first day out, and maybe anchor just below Lake St. Clair the first night so as to let Katy and Spinach try out the galley in quiet water.

"For you won't want to cook with your range on a slew," said Morgan. "At least not the first time."

Then the next day they would do some real sailing. "And that's where we will all come in," continued Morgan, "for getting up canvas is going to be an all hands' job on our ship."

While all this planning was going on, Katy could hear Sailor Bill and her parents talking in low tones at the other end of the porch. Sailor Bill was explaining something at a furious rate, and every now and then Father would break in and ask a question.

"No," she heard Sailor Bill answer. "They're to be scenery. Nothing else."

Then came another query—just a low-voiced mumble that Katy couldn't catch. But Sailor Bill's reply in a quarter-deck bellow was clear enough.

"They'll have nothing to do with that," he said. "We'll make the capture. They'll be nowhere near."

"But is it safe?" she heard her mother ask—and then Sailor Bill talked faster than ever.

"Now what?" said Katy to herself. For she knew from her mother's tone of voice that final permission for them to go had not been given.

"Those Sealed Orders," she thought, for Morgan hadn't said anything about those, nor had Sailor Bill. But suddenly she could tell that her father and uncle had sided together, and seemed to be pleading with her mother. And right away Katy knew everything was going to be all right, for nobody could hold out against those two.

But whatever it was, it seemed to be all patched up, and she heard Sailor Bill say, "Now don't you worry. There's little or no danger, and before the summer's over, we're going to be very proud of our Naval Auxiliary."

At last she saw her mother stand up and shrug her shoulders a little helplessly, and heard her say, "Oh, I suppose so, but they are only children after all. And for all summer, on such an errand."

Then Father put his arm around Mother, and both her parents stayed where they were, and watched Sailor Bill walk over to the cousins gathered about the sailing chart.

"Well," he said to Morgan as he came up. "Have I got a crew?"

Brick stood up, his red head coming just level with the third button on Sailor Bill's uniform.

"Yes sir, Captain Williams," he said. "Maybe I don't know much now, but I will before the summer's over."

"And we'll give you the best meals ever," said Katy.

"You'll never find two better ship's housekeepers," said Cynthia.

"And I'll try to be a real Able-seaman," said Teddy. "I'm strong enough to pull on any rope."

"I think I can handle her engine, sir," said Morgan. "And as for the outboard on the dinghy, well, there can't be many new kinks after the ones I've run against already."

"Fine," said Sailor Bill. "What more do we need? A Chief Engineer, two Mates who can be cooks and stewardesses as well, and a pair of very Able-seamen."

Then he fell to talking about other little schooners he had known, and voyages he had made in sail to the West Indies, and to the North again, past the surging tides of Barnegat and Bay of Fundy.

"Did you ever sail clear across the ocean?" asked Brick.

"Yes," said Sailor Bill, "on the Pacific. Both over and back."

And then he told about steering by compass and never seeing land for days and days. And of the schools of dolphins that played about their ship, and of flying fish that slapped into the sail and fell stunned to the deck, and how they cooked and ate them. And of the sweep of the mast across the friendly stars at night, and the cheerful glow of the binnacle light on a swinging compass card. And of the plash, plash of waves under the little ship's fore-foot, spreading out in creamy foam along her sides, only to lose themselves in a silvery wake stretching away behind them in the moonlight.

"Ah," said Sailor Bill. "Ships that drive by steam, and oil turbines have their place, but there's never a sailor lives who doesn't long for the days in sail."

Then he told about rough weather and storms. And how tremendous seas came in green over the bow and raced aft, slipping sullenly away again over the stern, foiled and angry at the helmsman still clinging to his wheel in the little cockpit. And how his shipmate came down sick after exposure to the fogs off Bering Strait and the bitter winds that howled down from the Arctic.

Then he broke off suddenly, putting aside his thoughts of that voyage long ago.

"But what about a doctor for our ship?" he said. "We must have one of those. What with colds and bruises, burns or a touch of sun, someone's bound to go to the sick bay."

Katy remembered her "first aid" lessons at camp last summer.

"I can help there," she said. "My best Christmas present was a wonderful medical kit. It's got everything in it. Bandages and plaster, iodine and mercurochrome, cough sirup, and even castor oil."

"Phaugh," said Teddy.

"Then that's that," said Sailor Bill. "But you're going to be a busy girl. What with being Mate, ship's housekeeper and cook, and now surgeon on top of that. But what about a mascot? No ship is going to have a lucky voyage without a mascot."

Katy looked around the porch and saw Gyp. The little dog had been sitting on his haunches all this while, with one ear cocked over and a wise expression on his face; just as though he understood everything they were talking about. When he saw Katy looking at him he gave a sharp bark, and thumped the stump of his tail against the porch railings.

"What's the matter with this one?" she said.

Sailor Bill looked down at the little dog and laughed. "Made to order," he answered.

Brick whistled Gyp to him. "Come here, ship's mascot," he said.

Then her father and mother came up and joined the group around the table. "So it's all settled," said Father.

"All but two things," said Katy.

"Let's have 'em," said Sailor Bill.

"What will we name the ship?" asked Katy.

"That's easy," said Sailor Bill. "We'll call her the *Gull-Flight.*"

"Of Grosse Ile," suggested Brick.

"Good idea," said Sailor Bill. Then to Katy, "What's the other?"

"Those Sealed Orders?" said Katy. "When we ship for this voyage, will the 'Port and Purpose' still be unknown?"

"For a little while longer," said Sailor Bill.

CHAPTER III

THE *GULL-FLIGHT* AND THE *BONNY* AGAIN

"NOW THE first thing to do," said Sailor Bill a little later, "is to have out those sea bags and look 'em over."

Brick and Teddy ran quickly out to the car, and in a few seconds hove around the corner of the house each with a bag slung over a shoulder, and dragging another along the ground by its pull cord.

"Hi," said Sailor Bill. "Here's lesson Number one for all able-seamen. Look at the bottom of those two bags you were dragging. There'll be no laundress aboard our ship. Everyone will have to scrub his own gear."

The boys looked a little sheepish, for the white canvas was green with grass stain. Maybe there was more to this business of being a sailor than met the eye.

"But never mind," added the Captain kindly. "We can fix it easily this time, here at home, where there's plenty of hot water and soap. But it's not so much fun afloat."

Then he turned to Morgan.

"Bag inspection," he said. "Show them how to do it."

Morgan loosened the fastenings on one of the bags.

Then he took a turn around the porch rail with the cord so it wouldn't fall over, and stretched out the neck. The first thing that came out was a sou'wester, a big oilskin coat, long enough to cover him from head to foot. This he spread on the porch floor. Then he started laying the other clothes out on it.

"That's right," said Sailor Bill approvingly, "things can't get dirty that way."

The rest watched Morgan, and when he had finished all his clothes lay in rolls, neatly stopped, and almost covering the sou'wester. The gear in each bag was the same, only for the girls there were pleated skirts instead of sailor trousers or shorts, and their white hats were smarter, with a black leather band. The jumper blouses were alike, except that those of the girls had two breast pockets, instead of one as the boys'.

"And that's only fair," said Sailor Bill to the Able-seamen; "each of you has pants' pockets. They don't make skirts that way."

Then he turned to Father and Mother and asked for suggestions. And of course this and that were lacking, for Sailor Bill never had had any girls—"mates or otherwise," as he said. There were no camp clothes, for his specialty was ship's gear, so all afternoon the five cousins were busy running around gathering things together. But by dinner time all was ready, and it was a tired, but happy and excited crew that gathered about the table.

And afterward, in the living room, it wasn't long either before yawns began to appear. Over in the corner where

Brick and Teddy were listening to Sailor Bill spin some of his sea yarns, two bright heads dropped oftener and oftener in sleepy nods.

Katy frankly gave it up.

"Who's for bed?" she asked. "Tomorrow's still another day."

So the four younger cousins trooped away upstairs. Tonight they rated the guest quarters on the third floor, two bedrooms, each with twin beds, opening off a little sitting room between. Before dinner they had carried up their sea bags and stood them at the foot of their beds. For in the morning they would have their first experience dressing out of a dunnage bag.

But of course they couldn't go to sleep right away. There were too many things to talk about and plans to shout from room to room, and everybody was too excited. Gone was the drowsiness of half an hour ago, and suddenly they decided to try on their new uniforms.

"I'll race you," shouted Brick to his sister. "Bet I get dressed first."

"Just you try it," Katy shouted back.

Brick and Teddy hopped out of the bed together.

"Open the bag," cried Brick, sliding out of his pajamas and into his underwear with two wriggles and a jerk. Pants, sneakers and socks were easy. But he struck a snag with the jumper. He held his hands up while Teddy pulled and tugged. Finally a red head emerged from under the folds of blue cloth. But something was the matter. The jumper came down all right, but the wide square collar wound up in front of his stomach; and the V of the neck just covered his spine where it went into the seat of his pants.

For the jumper was on wrong side to.

"What's the matter?" asked Teddy. "Can't you steer?"

"Steer," said Brick; "with that thing over my head, I couldn't even see."

But pretty soon everything was right, even to the white hat clamped down over one eye. And while the knot to the neckerchief wasn't exactly seagoing, it was a fairly regulation sailor that swaggered out into the sitting room. There was even a blue-water roll to his gait and a horn-pipe hitch to his pants.

But he wasn't first. Katy and Spinach were there ahead of him, fully dressed and inclined to be very scornful about it. Of course being girls, they could no more resist trying on their new things the minute they got upstairs than a cat could a dish of fish. So both of them had a head start on the Able-seaman.

And then Sailor Bill heard all the racket and stepped to the stair well below.

"Quiet between decks up there," he called. "It's time you were in your hammocks."

AFTER what seemed only a few minutes, and dimly through the great distance of deep sleep, came a shrill sound, almost a shriek. Brick struggled awake, to find it morning and the sun streaming in through the bedroom windows. Again came the sound, and this time he knew it for what it was, the piercing pipe of a bosun's whistle. And then a cry from below of—"Up all hammocks." He looked over at the other bed and saw Teddy still snoring away between the sheets.

"Hi!" he called, throwing a pillow at him. "On deck, there. Can't you hear all the fuss? Time to turn out."

And once downstairs and at the breakfast table, Sailor Bill outlined the plans for the day.

"You five," he said to the cousins, "take the car and go on up to the ship. When you get there, Morgan will introduce Katy and Brick to Midshipman Bob. The rest of us will be along later."

And when they all ran out to pile into the big gray car, there was Gyp, lying on the front seat and whacking his tail up and down on the leather cushions.

"Good old Mascot," said Teddy as the little dog sat up wriggling all over with excitement.

"He knew," said Katy.

"Just try and leave him behind," said Spinach.

"Which way, Sailor?" asked Morgan from the driver's seat, to Brick sitting beside him.

"Out the drive, and up the River Road. We've got about three miles to go."

The big car swung out from the house and along the shore. In a few minutes they had cleared an island lying between Grosse Ile and the channel cut, over on the Canadian side. And there was the river with all its traffic in full view. Two great freighters were coming down stream. A busy tug, puffing with fussy importance, was towing a huge scow. Suddenly over the stack of the nearest freighter appeared a plume of white steam, and soon they could hear the full deep blast of her whistle, warning the tug she was passing to port. Some cat-boats a little way off shore were tacking this way and that. First their white sails would be hauled flat as they pointed into the wind, and then as they came about, swung outboard, as they sailed free and clear before the morning breeze.

"Look! Look!" cried Spinach excitedly from the back seat.

Rapidly from behind the high banks of the channel cut, poked the black bows of the Buffalo steamer on her way to Detroit. Soon the white superstructure of her four upper decks came into view, and the heat waves over her three great stacks shimmered and danced in the morning haze. Little white dots that were her passengers lined the rails or moved to and fro on her decks.

"What a big ship," said Spinach in open admiration.

But Brick was inclined to be scornful. In order to show his cousins from the Atlantic Seaboard that salt water didn't bear all the big hulls in the world, he made light of the whole marvelous scene spread before them.

"Like riding on a ferry-boat," he said in a grand offhand manner; "not real sailors on a proper ship, like us. And when they get off," he added, referring to the passengers, "what do they do? Take a street car or a taxi. No wild back country for them, and no canoe nor Indian guide."

Morgan grinned down at his redheaded cousin.

"All right, Able-seaman," he said. "You tell 'em. But where is this Ferry Landing of yours?"

Hauled rudely back to his job of touring-car pilot, Brick looked quickly around. They had reached the upper end of the Island where the road turned, and just ahead of them a little lane ran off toward the river.

"Turn here," he said; "the dock's only a short ways."

And sure enough, the two spars of a sailing ship could be seen sticking up over the scrub trees and brush near the river bank. In a few seconds they came to the shore end of a dock, that ran out perhaps a couple of hundred feet to deep water. Morgan stopped the car and yelled at a figure in a midshipman's uniform sitting on a spile with his back toward them, and smoking a cigarette while he looked out over the river.

"Hi!" called Brick from the front seat, and Teddy from the back, both together.

"Your crew, coming aboard," said Cynthia Ann.

The figure on the spile got up, threw away his cigarette, and walked toward the car. Katy looked him over, for this was the first time she had ever seen her oldest cousin. She decided right away that they were going to be great friends. And why not? No one could help being friends with Midshipman Bob. Anybody that grinned the way he did, rated friendship. Especially so, if he happened to be one's own cousin and a future officer in the Navy, and with a very seagoing cut to his jib. Standing there spare and neat in his trim uniform and with a sparkle in his eye, he waited for them to tumble out.

"Who's who?" he asked Morgan, after the cousins had lined up on the dock.

"Katy and Spinach," said Morgan, introducing the girls. "Your Mates. And here are two very able seamen. —The one with the red hair answers to the name of Brick."

"And who's this?" asked the Midshipman.

"Who's who," answered Morgan.

And then they all laughed. For Morgan had forgotten to introduce Gyp, and the little dog was trying his best to remedy that. There he was, sitting up on his haunches at the end of the line beside Brick, and waving his forepaws in the air.

"Oh yes," said Morgan, "I almost forgot—Gyp—ship's mascot," he replied.

The Midshipman leaned over and took one of the little dog's paws, shaking it gravely. "A good crew for a trim ship," he said, straightening up; "but let's go aboard."

Together they all marched down the dock. And there, tugging gently at her spring lines, with her bow to the stream and nodding politely to the slap-slap of the little in-shore waves, lay the *Gull-Flight.*

She had a black hull and two black deckhouses, and a row of portholes bound with gleaming brass. Her sails were furled under tan covers, and up her foremast ran two ratlines so that her crew could handle her topsails from aloft. Amidship, on both port and starboard sides, two varnished boats hung in davits; and from the capstan on her fo'c'sle head to the burnished binnacle on her after-deck, everything shone and sparkled in the sun. And altogether she was as seagoing, shipshape a craft as any seaman could desire.

—AND THERE LAY THE "GULL FLIGHT"

A sailor in a white Navy uniform was busy on the foredeck coiling a line, and aft, a man in the blue double-breasted jacket and peaked cap of a Chief Boatswain's Mate, U.S.N., had a rag and a polish to the binnacle bright-work. As the crew, headed by Midshipman Bob crossed the little gangway that led from the dock to the ship, the Chief Bosun knocked off his work and came forward to meet them.

"A sort of reception committee," thought Katy.

The Midshipman went over the side.   The Bosun's

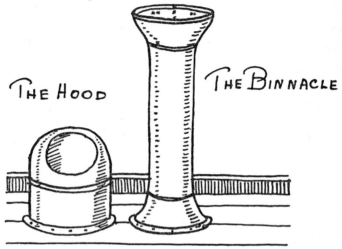

THE HOOD   THE BINNACLE

THE HOOD YOU USE AT NIGHT
TAKE IT OFF IN THE DAYTIME

hand snapped to a salute. Bob straightened up, turned aft to where the Colors flung out in the breeze, and saluted too. Then they both shook hands.

"Bosun," he said, "here are our two Mates, Katy and Spinach. And Able-seamen, Brick and Teddy."

The boatswain looked a little embarrassed. It was probably the first time he had ever run up against Mates that wore skirts.

"The Captain's nieces, eh," he said. "Knew your uncle

during the war. He was Navy Reserve then, and served under him in a sub-chaser. Lost track of him for a while when he went back into the Merchant Service. Later I heard he was ashore in some government department or other. Never knew quite what. Then about a month ago I gets a letter which asks, do I want to make a trip out of Norfolk on this schooner. 'Pick out another man to go along,' the letter says. 'And report to Midshipman Williams.' In two days me and Smith gets leave. The skipper fixed that in some way, I guess. Next thing I knew we're way out here to fresh water. Now I hear the Captain's coming aboard and we're to go back. What's up, I wonder?"

"Hm-m-m," said Katy to herself. "I wonder too.— Those Sealed Orders, I bet."

Then Midshipman Bob took the new crew in tow. First he led them along the port side of the deck and stopped abaft the forward deckhouse, pointing to a long-boat hanging in the davits.

"Meet an old friend," he said.

"Why it's the *Bonny,*" cried Katy and Brick.

Then they all climbed up to have a look. And sure enough, here was the little cutter that had given them so much fun at the seashore two years ago. Only now, instead of wearing a coat of dull gray paint, she had been scraped down to the wood and varnished and rubbed, and varnished and rubbed again and again, till she shone like a parlor floor.

"Why I'd never know her this way," cried Katy.

"And we've a dinghy too," said Midshipman Bob. "But come over here," he added, leading them straight across the ship. "Here's our visitors' gangway, and we'll use the forward deckhouse for a receiving saloon. Come inside and have a look."

"Hey! Not you."

This last was to Gyp, who had been following them around sedately enough, only stopping now and then to sniff suspiciously under this and that. But the minute Bob opened the saloon door he let out a yelp and dashed inside. A furious barking was immediately followed by a hissing and a snarling and then right past them all, and almost between their legs, ran a huge gray cat, chased hard by the frantic dog.

The cat cleared the deck in about four jumps and ran off down the gangplank, and up the dock. Gyp didn't go farther than just off the ship. There he sat down and watched the cat disappear in the distance. Then he came back, with his high opinion of himself pretty evident to all and an air about him which plainly said, "Now go on with your ship's inspection."

Morgan laughed. "That's it, old boy," he said, patting the dog. "Repel all boarders."

But Katy hadn't even watched the cat and dog. She was too anxious to see what the ship was like inside. So, when the rest came in, she had been all through the deckhouse. "Look," she said to Spinach, "a place up here to cook, with an icebox and an electric stove mounted on top. A regular breakfast nook."

"Sure," said the midshipman, "for hot-weather meals. So we won't have to run the big galley below. And when the Skipper comes aboard, he'll shake down here at night so as to be handy in case of a blow."

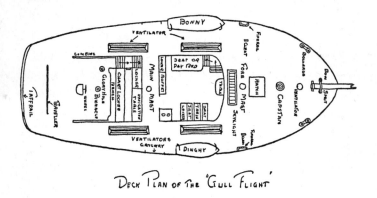

DECK PLAN OF THE 'GULL FLIGHT'

For the day bed which ran down the side of the saloon opposite the breakfast nook and icebox, could be changed into a regular bunk. And the front of the deckhouse was all windows backed by shining copper screens, so that there would be plenty of light and air.

"But go ahead and finish your exploring," said Bob, grinning at their wide-eyed interest.

Just forward of the Skipper's bunk were some wide, railed saloon stairs that led to the main cabin below. "Come on," said Katy, starting down with the others right at her heels.

And what a sight that main cabin was! What a place for a summer home! A long table ran almost across it, with an armchair at both ends, and a fixed bench on either side. Room for eight, there was at that table.

Brick plumped himself down in the chair at its port end. "Bring on the pie," he said.

"Out o' there," said Morgan, heaving him up. "That's the Captain's place. And the Midshipman's at the other end. Mates and crew are along the sides."

Katy was looking around, all eyes. Suddenly she spied a door leading forward from the starboard side of the cabin. On it was fastened an engraved brass plate, and she went up to have a look. "Spinach! Come here!" she cried. "It says, 'Mates.' That's us. What's in here?" she asked the Midshipman.

"Go in and see for yourselves," was the answer.

And they did.

And when the door opened, there was a stateroom, absolutely designed and made to fit the needs of two girls. First there was a space with a big open porthole to look out of, and then along the side of the ship an upper and lower bunk. On the top one was tacked a card marked KATY, and on the other was the name CYNTHIA ANN. At the forward end was a shower bath and toilet, and lockers for clothes and bed linen and things like that.

Not that this was the only stateroom on the ship, for it wasn't. Brick and Teddy had one that opened aft from the main cabin on the starboard side, and Morgan and Bob had another, also aft, but on the port side.

"Go look in the galley," said Midshipman Bob, who had followed them into their stateroom and was laughing at their shrieks of delight. "That's one part of the ship that's 'Mates' Country' exclusively. You're boss in there."

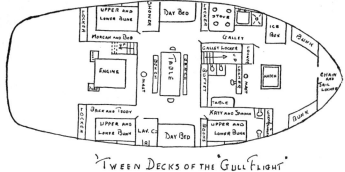

'Tween Decks of the 'Gull Flight'

And what a sight that was too. First the range, the little Shipmate, with its railed top burners and oven below. Then the gleaming sink, and the great icebox that Katy could almost stand up in. And the pantry lockers with their rows of shining pots and pans, and stores of all sorts. Cans of this and that, and a dozen different kinds of cereal each in its proper box, and bins for potatoes and beans and onions, and canisters marked salt, pepper, sugar, and all the other condiments.

"We've only to ice up and put the fresh things aboard," said the Midshipman. "That's Mates' job. You and Spinach should make out the lists tonight so as to be ready to get them first thing in the morning."

"Why can't we stay aboard when the rest go ashore?" asked Katy. "We could get dinner and check the stores afterward."

"You can," said Bob. "I haven't had a good meal for a week. But come on now, all of you. The Skipper will be aboard soon and Sailor Bill, as you call him, is a swell uncle. But he's also had command of his own quarter-deck, and when he makes an inspection—well—things had better be shipshape."

"What will we do first?" demanded the five cousins, almost with one voice.

"Mates below," said the Midshipman. "Put the cabins in order as well as you know how, and then try to do it twice as well as that. Able-seamen, on deck. Look for Irish pennants. Clew up all you find. He's death on those."

"What's an Irish pennant?" asked Brick.

"Any loose rope's end, hanging from the rigging or not coiled on deck," said Bob. "Morgan, you're for the engine room. There's lots to do there. We've a great motor, nine knots or better when she's opened up, and purrs like a kitten. You had better look into the light system and the pressure pumps as well. Hurry now. We've only an hour or two."

Then there was a great scurrying around. Katy and Spinach swept and dusted, straightened up and put away, and wiped up this and that. Brick and Teddy coiled and clewed up until there wasn't even a bit of yarn blowing loose in the breeze. Morgan dived into his cabin and re-appeared a minute later clad in dungarees, which is the sea name for overalls. With a ball of cotton waste in one hand and the plans of the ship's wiring in the other, he went mysteriously here and there. Smudged across the nose and with a swipe of grease under one eye, he was as busy as could be, and happier even than that.

By one o'clock the ship sparkled and shone in the sun, and, bright and clean as she had looked when they came aboard, now there wasn't a spot on her anywhere. They finished just in time too, for a car was coming down the road and turning in to the dock.

"Quick," said Midshipman Bob to the cousins, "line up on each side of the gangway. Mates opposite each other and next to the rail. Then the Able-seamen. Morgan, you're inboard. Bosun, get ready to pipe the Skipper over the side."

By the time Sailor Bill got to the dock edge, his crew in two parallel lines were ready to receive him aboard, and the minute he stepped over the side they all came to a salute—and held it. All but the Bosun. He stood in readiness with a silver whistle in his hand, holding it to his lips, and the minute the Skipper's foot struck the deck, started a shrill series of pipes. These he kept up until Sailor Bill passed through his line of side-boys and turned aft, saluting the Colors.

All the crew's hands came down smartly in time with the Skipper's, and Midshipman Bob said, "Your ship, sir."

"Very well," said the Captain. "Suppose you take us through."

Father and Mother fell in behind, and together they went from stem to stern. They saw the cabin and they saw the staterooms. They looked at the galley and they went into the engine room with Morgan. Sailor Bill showed them his bunk in the forward deckhouse. "I'll be here," he said, "when everyone else is below. On deck for any emergency whatever."

Then he took them to the after-deckhouse where the chart room was, with its table and compasses, ship's chronometers, and all the other navigating gear. And then still farther aft to a protected space on the ship's quarter-deck where the steering wheel and binnacle were. "See how the combing curves down from the charthouse roof," he said. "Forms a sort of cockpit, even though we are flush decked."

Afterward they all had something to eat in the saloon, Katy and Spinach serving. Rather a sketchy meal, but with sandwiches and tea and some cold drinks too, enough for everybody including Gyp, who got most of the leavings and a bone raked up from somewhere.

Then it was arranged that Morgan and the Able-seamen should go home with the grown-ups that night. For in the morning there were all the sea bags to get together, and there were just bound to be odds of this and ends of that to be looked after at the last moment.

"Do you think you will be able to keep house aboard tonight?" asked Father of the two Mates.

"Why not?" said Katy. "There's only five of us to look after."

"It will be good practice," said Spinach.

"You'll get plenty of that," said Father.

CHAPTER IV

UP RIVER

KATY OPENED her eyes suddenly, wide awake, but taking just a second or two to remember where she was. A soft breeze was blowing through the open port at the head of her bunk. Splashes of sunlight from the ripples on the shining river danced across the cabin ceiling and chased each other down the white walls.

Not a sound from the bunk where Spinach lay. For tired as they were the night before, neither of the Mates had gotten to sleep very easily. There was too much to talk about on their first night aboard; but what had really kept them awake were the strange river noises and the little friendly creaks the ship had made. Just as though

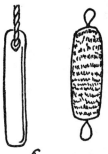

FENDERS
BETWEEN THE SHIP'S SIDE
AND THE DOCK.

she were trying to talk to them and welcome them aboard. There was the soft squeak of fenders between the dock and the side of the ship and the rattle of slack hal-

49

yards against the spars as the *Gull-Flight* rolled gently to the waves made by the passing of other ships. Away over on the Canadian shore a dog had barked, setting Gyp into a frenzied response until she had called him down from the deckhouse and let him into their stateroom where he now lay, curled up and asleep on the soft carpet. There was the puff-puff of a tug working upstream, and the sound of oar-locks and the splash of oars from a rowboat going out to a yawl anchored a couple of hundred yards from where they were.

BELAYING PIN
WITH
LINE BENT UPON IT

But now it was time to turn out, for over her head she could hear feet moving around and the rush of water sluiced along the deck, where the sailor and the Bosun were washing down. A minute before she had heard the Midshipman slam the door of his cabin, and run rapidly up the companion stairs, through the charthouse and out on deck.

Then Katy remembered all there was to do this day, and sticking a bare foot over the side of her bunk, lowered herself to the stateroom floor, a little gingerly though, for it was quite a ways. Of course she woke up Spinach, who rolled a sleepy and questioning eye in her general direction.

"Stay where you are," said Katy. "I'll go to the shower first."

By the time she was through, her brother, or rather sister Mate was out of her bunk too.

"How was it?" said Spinach.

"Cold," said Katy, shivering a little; "but we mustn't mind that. Think what it's going to be like when we get up north."

Midshipman Bob had breakfast all ready for them, and they had it on deck, for it was too glorious a morning to stay indoors anywhere, even to try out the breakfast nook.

"Thought I'd help you out this first morning," said Bob. "With all you've got to do. Are your lists ready?"

"Yes," said Katy.

"Then off to the store with both of you. See if you can get them to send the supplies down right away. While you're ashore, the Bosun and his man can get their things over the side ready to leave for Norfolk the minute our regular crew arrives."

But before the Mates got back the big gray car hove in sight, piled high with sea bags and lots of other things too, Brick and Teddy riding on top with Morgan at the wheel. Bob showed them where to stow their gear, and by the time the store truck arrived with Katy and Spinach holding down the load, all were ready to turn to and help get the supplies aboard.

First there was ice for the galley box, great hunks of it, covered with sawdust just as it came from the icehouse where it had been stored since the winter before.

"Here," said the Midshipman to Morgan, throwing him the ship's tongs. "Bend a line on one of the handles and give each piece a tow in the river before you lower it aboard. We don't want sawdust all over the ship. Able-seamen Brick and Teddy can lend a hand. Get the deck hatch over the box open first. We load from the top. Watch your fingers though."

Katy and Spinach started immediately to carry eggs, butter, fresh vegetables, meat, and other things from the grocer's truck to the ship.

"Wait a minute," said Bob, holding them up. "Where are the manifests? You're in charge of those. Check everything in as we load it aboard, and off again as we use it up. That way you can keep a running inventory and know just what to order whenever we make port."

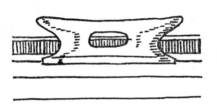

CLEAT

Meanwhile the Bosun and the sailor had gone back aboard and were busy too. For it wasn't only with stores and housekeeping that you got a ship ready for sea. Tidy and smart as the *Gull-Flight* had looked yesterday, Katy could see that lots had been done with the rigging and running gear, since last night. And it seemed as though there were more yet to do before Sailor Bill came aboard, let alone being ready to cast off. Every line must be un-bent from belaying pin and cleat, and given an experi-mental tug to see if it were free in the block. The falls on the davits that held both the *Bonny* and the dinghy were cleared and then put back again, the lines neatly re-coiled and hung from their pins along the rail. The anchors were chocked inboard the hawseholes, and four or five fathoms of chain laid out on the foredeck. It was then fed carefully back to its lockers so there would be no chance of fouling when the anchors were let go.

On the after-deck over the engine compartment was a round brass plate, something like a man-hole cover in a city street. This was called the "Glory Hole." It was here that Morgan was spending most of his time, out of sight maybe, but certainly not out of sound. For the cover was off now, and through the opening came a weird series of thumps and bumps as he tested out the engine connections by tapping on them with a hammer. Also there arose some rather bad language for so young a member of a strictly non-professional crew. This, and the horrid stinks of gasoline and oil, succeeded in raising the lurid blue haze always found over engine-room hatches of every vessel that sails the seas, salt water or fresh.

But Morgan had his check-up work to do as well and pressed Brick into service to help him out. Together they could be seen moving around the deck; to all the standing and running light connections, snapping them on and off to test them out. Then they brought up some oil emergency lanterns—red, green, and white.

"Here," said Morgan to the Able-seaman, "trim the wicks. Clean the glass, and see that they are all filled. When you get through, hang them on the inside of the engine room bulkhead where they'll be handy."

By noon, everything was ready. Bob came out of the after-deckhouse where he had been busy most of the morning laying out charts, quadrants and dividers, and the other navigating instruments. He took the hood off the binnacle, so that the compass card would be visible to the man on steering trick. Then he looked carefully around the deck, and up aloft at the mastheads and rigging. Everything shipshape there. At last he seemed satisfied that even Sailor Bill could find no fault when he came aboard.

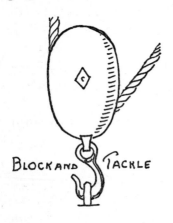

BLOCK AND TACKLE

"All right," he called. "Able-seamen on the dock. Cast off the midship lines and carry them aboard."

Brick and Teddy jumped over the rail, and pulled the loops of the two middle mooring lines off their spiles where they had been flung when the *Gull-Flight* first tied up. Then they carried the lines over to the side of the ship and flung them on deck without letting them fall into the water.

"That's right," said the Midshipman. "No use starting out with wet shore lines. Only have to dry 'em out before we can stow them away."

This left only a light bow and stern line holding the ship to the dock. The *Gull-Flight* stirred a little at her release, settling back finally as though she were on her mark, eager to be off. It was just about this time that the two Mates came up from below, finished with their checking and storing of supplies. Katy looked around.

"This looks like business," she said to Spinach.

And it was business too. For a car was coming down the dock, and in it Sailor Bill, ready to come aboard; and Father and Mother to say their last "Good-byes." Katy went ashore to meet them.

But first the Captain took the sailor and the Bosun aside and talked to them in a low voice—so low a voice that Katy couldn't catch what he was saying. Orders, she supposed, about their return to Norfolk. For presently both piled their bags into the big gray car, waved their hands in farewell, and drove off up the dock.

Morgan was leaning over the rail watching the proceedings.

"Well," he said. "It's good-bye to the salt-water crew. From now on, it's up to us."

Katy had a little scared lump in her throat. But let anybody see it? Not much!

"We'll manage," she said bravely to Morgan.

And the lump didn't go away either when Mother came up and put her arms around her, hugging her tight.

"You may be Mate aboard this ship," she said. "But to me, you're just my little girl. Be careful, oh, do be careful!"

Then Father picked her up and kissed her good-bye, and after putting her down, shook hands with Brick. But that wouldn't do at all for Mother, who picked Brick up, too, and gave him a great resounding smack, much to the embarrassment of that Able-seaman.

"Ready aboard," said Sailor Bill.

And then the children crossed the gangplank that would cut them off from Grosse Ile and home, and all that it contained, for the whole long summer.

CAPTAIN WILLIAMS went to the wheel and gave it an experimental twist or two. Then he turned to Morgan who was standing by.

"Kick her over," he said; "so she'll warm up. We'll go up the river under power."

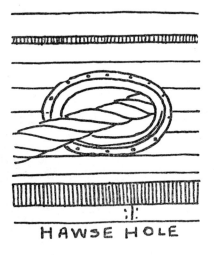

HAWSE HOLE

Morgan dived below, down the companion stairs. Then they heard the slam of the door that led from the main cabin to the engine room. Soon there was a rumbling and a grinding, as the starter turned the big flywheel. This was followed by a cough and a grunt. And then the engine caught; its first roar settling quickly down to the quiet purr of steady power. Sailor Bill listened for a minute. Satisfied that the motor was warming to its work, he stepped to the wheel. Then he turned to the

Midshipman.

"All right, Mister," he said. "Cast off."

Bob jumped for the dock and threw off the bow and stern lines, climbing back aboard over the bowsprit. Katy and Spinach hauled the mooring lines in through the hawseholes. Teddy and Brick coiled them flat. Slowly the current carried the *Gull-Flight* away from the dock. A strip of blue water appeared alongside, widening as they drifted clear. Morgan came back on deck and stood ready at the clutch-control lever.

"Half speed forward," said Captain Williams.

The ship quivered and shook as Morgan threw in the lever. `Water boiled from under her stern. Slowly she gathered way.

"Full ahead," said the Skipper, twirling the wheel and heading out toward the channel.

They were off.

"TAKE the wheel," said Captain Williams to Morgan, a minute later.

The Skipper went into the charthouse and reappeared in a second. As the *Gull-Flight* drew ahead, he looked quickly around, sizing up his position. They were passing through a row of buoys and fixed ranges that stretched up and down stream, marking the channel. Then he walked over to the helmsman and took a squint down at the compass.

"North by West," he said. "By a half West"—giving Morgan the course.

Morgan spun the wheel, throwing it hard over. Katy

moved closer so as to be able to see. The *Gull-Flight's* bow began to swing upstream. The points on the compass card also began their swing. East . . . East by North . . . East-Northeast . . . Northeast by East. . . Northeast.

The helmsman eased up on the wheel. The compass card swung more slowly . . . North. Up came the

THE COMPASS

wheel to center . . . North by West . . . a half West. The little line at the back of the bowl showed the true course.

"Dead on, sir," said Morgan.

"Keep her there," said Captain Williams.

Katy let out her breath in a long sigh. She had been holding it, standing there tense and rigid, watching the ship come up on her course. "So that was how it was done."

Sailor Bill stood by the wheel a little longer, glancing first down at the compass and then up and around at the river, keeping one eye on the traffic and the other on the shores slipping smoothly by and dropping quietly astern. Soon the Grosse Ile Light fled by them to port, and when the Fighting Island South Light bore hard on their starboard beam, the Skipper gave Morgan a new course.

"North by East," he said ". . . a little East. Stay toward the right bank of the channel, near the Canadian shore. You know the rules of the road. Answer the whistles from down-bound steamers. They have the right of way. Brick, come back here and help Morgan out. When he tells you to blow an answer, either once or twice, there's the lanyard. Lean on it. Don't be afraid."

The redheaded Able-seaman took up his post in the sheltered lee of the after-deckhouse. He stuck his head over the side into the wind, saw a clear channel ahead, and sighed with relief. Nothing to do for a minute anyway.

—Soon The Great Bluff Bows of a Freighter.

Pretty soon the great bluff bows of a freighter appeared up ahead. From the deck of the little schooner she looked as big as a house. She seemed to be minding her own business and bearing well away from them. But suddenly her bows swung in toward them as she followed a bend in the river. Then a cloud of white steam flung up over her funnel, followed by two warning growls from her whistle.

Brick was very much interested, but not at all concerned. After all, he was neither at the wheel nor in charge of the ship. But a sudden silence seemed to settle over everything—and why was everybody looking at him. Sailor Bill stiffened, all Ship's Commander now.

"Well?" he said sharply.

"The whistle, Silly," said Katy. "Answer the freighter."

"Two pulls," said Morgan from the wheel.

Brick woke up. His face flamed till it about matched the color of his hair, except that it grew a shade redder. He gave the lanyard a sharp pull.

"T-O-O-T," went the compressed air whistle on the *Gull-Flight*.

"Once more," said Morgan.

"That's the boy," said the Skipper. "Eyes and ears open, and your mind on the race. No other way to stand watch."

On they went. Past Mamajudy Light, and the tall towers of the Alkali Works above Wyandotte. Abeam of Fighting Island North Light, the river turned a little.

"Follow the channel," said Sailor Bill to Morgan. "Keep working her farther over toward the Canadian shore."

Detroit's lower city came into view. On the ways of a shipbuilding company, the gaunt ribs of a giant new freighter stretched nakedly to the sky. A little farther on, blast furnaces of the great steel companies lined the river bank, and through the murk and gloom of their open sheds came the flash of white-hot molten metal. On the parade ground of old Fort Wayne, a company of soldiers was drilling; and from the top of the tall flagpole, the Colors flung out in the breeze. As she went by, the *Gull-Flight* dipped her own Colors in salute.

Soon they passed under the iron lacework of the Ambassador Bridge, swung high over their heads from the graceful arch of its cables. The river traffic grew more dense—cross stream, as well as up and down. Huge car ferrys and their smaller passenger sisters scurried back and forth between the American and Canadian shores. A little steamer, yachtlike as to trimness of line, but with a very business-like air about her, put out from under the skyscrapers of downtown Detroit.

"Watch this," said Sailor Bill to the cousins, who were all seated about the fore-hatch.

"Watch what?" asked Katy.

"That little black and white steamer just putting out from shore. Marine Post Office. The only one in the world. She has some mail for that red, down-bound freighter."

The mail steamer, towing a rowboat, headed out into the river. When she was about in mid-stream, a man in the uniform of a mail carrier climbed over her stern and dropped into the small boat. The towline was immediately let go, and the tender swung around and headed back to shore. A few hundred yards off, the bell in her engine room clanged "full stop," and she lay there drifting idly with the current.

The red freighter kept on down stream. The man in the rowboat sized up his position, and gave a few pulls on the oars so as to be squarely under the freighter's bows. Then he sat there, quite undisturbed by the towering mass bearing down on him.

"Won't he get run down?" cried Cynthia.

"Wait and see," said Sailor Bill.

It certainly looked as though he would be. But just at the right instant, when the freighter was almost on top of him, he gave a quick jerk with the oars so as to carry his little boat a trifle to one side. He was safe and clear, and the bow wave from the freighter swept him along her high steel sides, but so close as to almost scrape the paint off the rowboat.

A man in a brown derby hat and red suspenders was leaning over the rail, looking down as though waiting for something. He did not have long to wait. A coil of line flung up to him from the rowboat. This he made fast, and then on the end of another line, passed a bucket down to the mail carrier. Some envelopes, a package, and some rolled-up newspapers were put into it and hauled quickly up. The man in the brown derby freed the towline and tossed it back. The rowboat drifted clear. The carrier in the uniform waved good-bye, and picked up his oars. Over on the tender the bell clanged again, and a swirl of white water appeared under her stern as she got under way to pick him up.

"Boy!" cried Brick. "I'd like to get a letter that way."

Midshipman Bob came up from below.

"It's five o'clock," he said to the Skipper. "By the time we clear the river it will be getting dark. Are you going to cross the lake tonight?"

"No," said Sailor Bill. "We'll anchor under Peach Island and get up sail in the morning. What about dinner?"

"I lit a fire in the galley," said Bob; "it's drawing nicely. For their first attempt, our Mates will have a spanking bed of coals and a red-hot oven."

"Well," said Captain Williams to Katy and Spinach, "it's up to you. I'll guarantee everybody's appetites. But remember, no tearoom menus. Sailor's whack—and plenty of it."

The Mates went below to the cabin. Together the girls explored for dishes, table linen and utensils. They looked into the icebox to make sure all the good things that they had loaded aboard that morning were still there. Then they got out a pencil and wrote up a bill of fare.

"Think that's enough?" said Spinach, after they had added soup to the roast and vegetables, and squinted into the icebox in the deck saloon to see how the frozen dessert was coming along.

"Coffee for the Skipper and Midshipman Bob," said

Katy; "I suppose Morgan will want it too. Cocoa for the rest of us."

Then they set to work in earnest. Water put on to boil. Potatoes to peel, and vegetables to clean and wash. A great roast of beef was popped into the oven. And the table to set. Great care was taken with the two places of honor. Before Captain Williams was placed the carving set—knife, fork and steel. Midshipman Bob was at the foot. His job was the vegetables.

"Don't Chief Engineers rate something special too?" asked Spinach.

"Not aboard this ship," said Katy. "Although we will put him along side the Skipper. Mates next and opposite. Then the Able-seamen—near Bob where he can stop any fights. Maybe we had better give him a belaying pin instead of a fork."

In the meanwhile the ship swept on up the river. Through the galley portholes the girls could see Belle Isle, the city's great island park. Its lagoons were covered with canoes, and here and there along the shore road family picnics were gathered about charcoal grills, cooking steaks and roasting hot dogs. Then some more open water with the freighter track swinging away from them, and then a bit of marshy land rising quickly to trees and solid ground. Overhead they heard some queer thumps and bumps, and some feet running to and fro. The engine stopped. The schooner lost way. Both girls listened.

"Let go," came the Skipper's command. "Splash," went the starboard anchor. The first leg was over.

THE *Gull-Flight* dropped back with the current and brought up with a jerk on her anchor chain. Before she could catch herself, Katy shot across the cabin and slammed hard against the engine-room bulkhead.

"Hang on," said Spinach, who had a death's grip on the back of Sailor Bill's bolted-down chair.

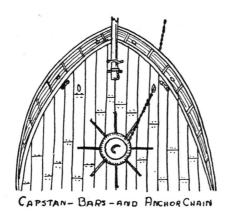

CAPSTAN- BARS -AND ANCHOR CHAIN

Both girls ran up the companion stairs and out on deck. Morgan stood by the capstan brake. The starboard anchor chain stretched taut across the deck and out through the hawsehole, angling off and quivering a little as it met the water.

Midshipman Bob hung over the bowsprit. "She's holding," he cried back.

Sailor Bill was eyeing the shore a little way to port. "Give her a few more feet," he called.

Morgan eased up on the brake. The capstan turned a few times and several links of chain rumbled out, and over the side. The *Gull-Flight* settled back a little and the anchor chain stopped quivering.

"Enough," said Sailor Bill. Morgan clamped down on the brake.

"She's secure," sang out Bob.

They were in quiet water, behind a little point, with the reach of Lake St. Clair stretched away up ahead, far and clear for tomorrow's sail. Twilight was gathering now and the crew went quickly about their work of making all snug for the night.

Midshipman Bob came forward with another anchor, a small one with several hundred feet of line attached.

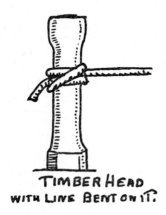

TIMBER HEAD WITH LINE BENT ON IT.

This he put in the stern-sheets of the dinghy. Morgan swung the davits outboard and Brick and Teddy slackened away on the falls, lowering the small boat into the water. Bob worked the dinghy a little way astern of the *Gull-Flight* and threw over the light anchor. Then he rowed back to the ship and passed the end of the line under the taffrail to Morgan who took a slight strain on it and made it fast around the timber head. Anchored fore and aft, the ship rode secure for the night.

Midshipman Bob came back on board and went below. He appeared back on deck in a minute or two carrying a white electric lantern, from the end of which dangled about a hundred feet of rubber insulated wiring. One end he plugged into a deck socket, fastened the other to the flag halyard, and hoisted both lamp and wiring high to the mainmast truck. Then he snapped on the connection, and far above their heads shone the white glow of the lantern, the *Gull-Flight's* riding light.

"There it is," said Sailor Bill. "Everyone will know we're here at anchor. So will the mosquitoes. Let's go below before their committee arrives. Mates! How about dinner? It's after seven o'clock."

"All ready," said Katy.

Captain Williams went to the head of the table. Midshipman Bob took his place at the foot. The Mates disappeared into the galley. Presently Katy stuck her head back into the cabin.

"Able-seamen, bear a hand," she said.

Soon they all came in each with a dish, Katy and Spinach carrying between them the great platter with its roast, brown and smoking hot. This was put in front of Sailor Bill. The Midshipman got the vegetables at his end.

The roast was carved and the dishes passed around. Everybody fell to. The sharp air, the work and excitement of the day had made them so hungry that in spite of all there was to talk about, for several minutes nothing could be heard but the scrape of knives and forks on plates and the request to pass this and that.

The Mates and the Able-seamen cleared up. Sailor Bill and the Midshipman smoked and talked. Morgan slipped away to coddle his beloved motor.

"Let's have a look at the chart for tomorrow's sail," said Captain Williams finally.

He and Bob climbed the companion stairs to the chart-house, followed shortly by Brick and Teddy, for most of the work below was out of the way. Morgan got a book and went up the saloon stairs to curl up under a reading light in the forward-deckhouse. This left the girls alone in the main cabin.

"Come on," said Katy to Spinach. "We'll make up the bunks. Real ocean liner service."

First they made up the cabin that belonged to the Able-seamen. There was lots to do in there. Clothes were flung about, and one of the sea bags had tipped over, spilling everything out on the stateroom floor. There were also two very dirty towels hung over their rack, and two spotless and absolutely unused washcloths. The Mates made up the bunks, and Katy, leaving Spinach to tidy up, went around to the Midshipman's and Morgan's cabin. In a few minutes she called to her.

"Come here," she said. "Look at this."

"Look at what?" asked Spinach, coming into the other stateroom.

"I can't make it out," said Katy. "Here's Morgan's sea bag and all his things, just like ours. Enough for all summer, aboard and in camp. But where's the Midshipman's gear? All I can find is a little zipper bag with his shaving things, and a spare suit of underwear. How can he go all summer with only that?"

"You mean he has no clothes other than the uniform he's wearing," said Spinach.

"Yes," said Katy. "And it looks very fishy to me."

"You've been suspicious all along," said Spinach. "And now I'm getting that way too. What's up, do you suppose?"

"Those Sealed Orders," said Katy. "I do wish we could open them."

CHAPTER V

CAPTAIN WILLIAMS had piped his crew down early that first night aboard. But it was nearly midnight before everyone was quiet and finally asleep. Brick and Teddy had to have a pillow fight and tore up their bunks, and raised a racket generally until Bob came in and promised to knock their heads together if he heard another sound. Before turning in Katy and Spinach talked about the success of their first dinner, and the ease with which they had prepared it.

"No trouble to cook on that galley range," said Katy.

"Wait until we're sailing," answered Bob. "When there's a sea making up, and we're running before the wind with the ship yawing all over her course. And the pots and pans dance around, and the water spills on the stove and threatens to put your fire out. And when the stack won't draw, and a puff of wind comes down and blows smoke in your eyes. That's why Navy cooks all drink lemon extract, and die off young."

"There's no lemon extract on board," said Spinach. "So I guess we're safe."

"I wasn't exactly suggesting it as a remedy," said Bob. "I just want to point out that you won't be able to laugh all the time."

Then there was that business of the Midshipman's lack of gear. Afterward when they were in bed, both Mates had to talk that over pretty thoroughly and try to figure out what this voyage was really all about, and why there was so much effort to make it look like a simple family cruise.

"And I know it's not," said Katy. "There's too much mystery about it. Who owns this boat? I haven't heard anything about that. And how was Sailor Bill able to get leave for a Navy Bosun and a Seaman! To say nothing of Midshipman Bob. There's something queer about this whole voyage."

"And families don't sail under Sealed Orders," said Spinach. "If you think your mother raised a fuss about your going, you ought to have heard mine. Sailor Bill talked himself blue in the face the night before we left. But anyway, here we are—and I'm having the time of my life."

But whether or not anybody thought sleep possible, it finally did come, and when they woke after what seemed only a few minutes, it was broad daylight, and feet were already stirring on deck overhead. No shower bath for the Mates this morning. There wasn't time enough. First they had to rouse out the Able-seamen, who weren't very keen about it. No worries about the "Port and Purpose" of the voyage bothered them. Each day's excitement and activity were enough in themselves. But they tumbled out and scrambled into their uniforms. Morgan's and the Midshipman's door was wide open and their cabin empty. They were already on deck.

The girls ran up the saloon stairs and into the forward-deckhouse. A big kettle was already boiling on the hot

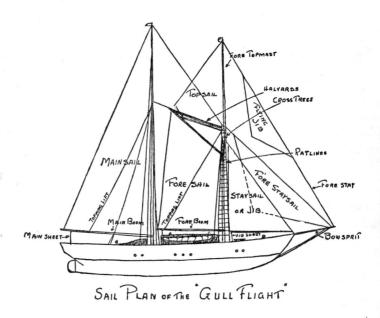

SAIL PLAN OF THE "GULL FLIGHT"

plate and someone had set the table in the breakfast nook. It didn't take long to make the coffee and cocoa and put out the cereal, and start a frying pan sizzling with bacon. Toast and eggs would complete the meal.

When they went out on deck to call the crew to breakfast both Mates looked interestedly around, for the ship seemed altogether different than she had the day before. The tan sail covers had disappeared, taken off and stowed away out of sight. Along the varnished booms the beautiful new canvas lay in creamy folds, held but lightly with a few lashings. Not long now before hoisting would change them into white clouds that would be the set sails of the *Gull-Flight*. Already the jib, in stops, had been run aloft up the forestay and a sheet bent on the foot, so that a sharp jerk would break out the furls and haul it taut into sailing position. A strain had been taken on the topping lifts and the deck lashings cleared so the booms could swing free and outboard. The dinghy was back in her davits. The stern anchor had been taken in, and the riding light down from the truck.

"Breakfast," said Katy loudly.

But in the confusion and bustle, and the running about on deck, nobody seemed to hear.

"Come and get it!" she called, this time at the top of her voice.

Bob was sitting on the foredeck, facing aft and straddling a mast with a leg on either side. He waved his hand, but kept right on with what he was doing. He was putting a seizing on the crotch of the boom, and Teddy held the ball of marlin, feeding it carefully out, while Brick stood handy by with a marlin spike and clasp knife. Morgan as usual, was down under the engine-room hatch, and Sailor Bill nowhere in sight, probably in the charthouse. Spinach joined hers to Katy's shrieks.

"Hi!" she called. "If you don't want it, we'll throw it over the side!"

But they did want it. For presently the Midshipman got up, and followed by the Able-seamen walked briskly enough back to where the smells of broiling bacon wafted through the saloon door. Morgan showed up in a minute with the usual smudge of grease under one eye, and pretty soon Captain Williams came in too.

The only ones who sat down in the breakfast nook were Brick and Teddy who began shoveling in cereal and sipping away cautiously at the hot edge of steaming mugs of cocoa. The rest of them stood around here and there with a bacon sandwich in one hand and a cup of coffee in the other. Every once in a while one of them would duck out on deck with his sandwich in his hand and duck back in again—minus the sandwich. Katy would have his coffee cup refilled and a fresh supply of bacon and toast.

And the weather was different too. There was the hard bright sunshine of a rather blustery summer's day, and more than a cap full of wind. Flying white clouds scudded along, driving sharp shadows across the blue

water in a patchwork of sullen gray. Out in the channel
a chop was making up, with a few whitecaps here and
there.

Sailor Bill left them and went into the charthouse, coming back a few minutes later.

"Barometer's all right," he said. "It's high enough to
show there's no storm gathering. But the wind's freshening, and from the northeast too—dead ahead for where
we want to go. That means a long tack—good thing
though. Trial trip for a new crew."

A little later they were all gathered in the after-deckhouse about the navigating table, where a chart of Lake
St. Clair was pinned down with thumb tacks.

"We're right here," said Sailor Bill, pointing to where
the *Gull-Flight* lay in a little sheltered bay behind Peach
Island. "We'll go out into the lake with the motor and
head up into the wind a few miles. That will give us
plenty of leeway off the Canadian shore. Then we'll get
up sail and bear away due east until we pick up the
Thames River range lights. Then we'll come about on
the starboard tack and head for the south end of the St.
Clair Flats Canal." *

Brick picked up his ears. "Thames River," he said. "I
thought that was in England."

"There's one in Canada too," said Sailor Bill. "And

---

* You ought to get this straight early in the voyage. Port is the left side
of the ship looking forward. Starboard's right. No ship can sail directly
against the wind, so you have to tack—go at it on an angle. A starboard
tack is when the wind's from the right. Port's the other way—the wind's
from the left.—KATY.

over there and back to the Flats Canal makes about a forty-mile sail. Enough for the first day with a green crew. There'll be some sore hands tonight. Morgan, start your engine."

Soon came the purr of the motor, and Morgan took his place at the clutch-control lever.

"Katy, take the wheel," said Captain Williams. "Spinach, stand by to help her. There's nothing to do with it for a minute though," he added.

Both Mates were rather glad of that, for the *Gull-Flight's* wheel was a much more terrifying instrument than the simple tiller on the *Bonny;* and they wanted some time to look it over and get used to it. You turned it the way you wanted the ship to go, and not in the opposite direction as you did the rudder stick on the little cutter. But there they were, alone, with only Morgan to help, and he looked as though he were going to be too busy with his own job to do much for them.

Everybody else was on the foredeck gathered about the capstan. Bob had some short wooden bars which he was fitting into the head, so they stuck out like spokes from the hub of a rimless wheel. Against each of these spokes, or capstan bars, leaned a member of the crew—Teddy, Brick, the Midshipman, and even Sailor Bill.

"Maybe you had better come up here too," called the Skipper to Spinach. "Katy can handle the wheel alone for a minute."

"Lean over the side," he added, when she had come forward. "Tell us when the anchor chain is straight up and down." Then, "All right, Morgan—kick her ahead."

Morgan threw in the clutch lever. The propeller turned and the ship moved up on her anchor chain.

"Enough," sang out Sailor Bill.

Morgan released the lever.

"Take up the slack," said the Skipper, straining against his capstan bar.

The capstan head turned and the slack chain came in through the hawsehole. The crew pushed around in a circle, winding it up on the capstan. Spinach was watching the angle of the chain where it met the water, and when the anchor was directly below her on the bottom, she straightened up and turned to the toiling crew.

"Up and down," she called.

"Break it out," said the Skipper.

Everyone flung himself against his capstan bar, and the anchor came up out of the mud. A few more turns and it was hard against the metal work of the hawsehole. The Midshipman hung over the side and caught the fluke of the anchor in a loop of line, and hauled it taut against the side of the ship. Then he gave the line a turn around one of

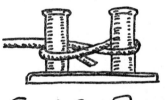

Two Little Bollards

the little bollards just inboard the hawsehole, and back out again around the fluke, so the heavy anchor was lashed tight and couldn't thrash around, no matter how much the *Gull-Flight* rolled in a sea-way.

"Half ahead," sang out Sailor Bill to Morgan. "Wheel hard a starboard," to Katy.

Katy spun the wheel to the right.

"Full ahead," to Morgan.

He threw in the lever, and came back to help Katy at the wheel. But she didn't need help. She was steering the ship herself, giving the spokes an experimental twist or two, just as though she were an old hand at it. Once out in mid-channel she put the wheel hard to port, and headed out•for the lake. Captain Williams watched her without saying anything and as the ship steadied away, nodded approvingly.

Katy felt pretty proud after that. For they were going to need all the help they had to get the sails up, and if she and Spinach could steer, and leave Sailor Bill, the Midshipman and Morgan to haul away on the halyards, why so much the better. And the Able-seamen would have all they could do, swigging away on the lines with them, and coiling them flat as the sails went up and the halyards came in.

There was some wind in the lake all right, but not too much. Just a spanking breeze.

"Keep her bow right in to it," said the Skipper to Katy, "and we'll get up the main. Jib's ready to break out now, and we'll haul away on our course with those two. The foresail and top can go up last."

Their big main had a Marconi rig, and while the spar

seemed very tall indeed to Teddy and Brick as they looked up at it, the canvas would go aloft more easily than the smaller foresail with its heavy gaff rig. Morgan and Bob grabbed the halyard and started hoisting away.

"Clear the lines behind them," said Sailor Bill to the Able-seamen. "I'll free the sheet so the sail won't fill." *

The sheet-blocks thrashed back and forth across the traveller on the after-deck, but Katy kept the ship's head

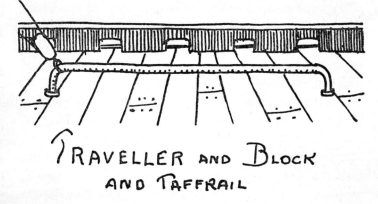

$\widehat{T}$RAVELLER ᴀɴᴅ $\underline{B}$ʟᴏᴄᴋ
ᴀɴᴅ $\widehat{T}$ᴀꜰꜰʀᴀɪʟ

well into the wind so the sail didn't fill, and only fluttered a little in the breeze. The creamy canvas went up and up, high over their heads, and at last the great steel ring at the very tip of the sail almost touched the block at the top of the mast. Bob jumped up in the air, grabbing as high a hold on the halyard as he could and hung there,

---

* On ship board, a sheet has nothing to do with a bed. It's the line you trim the sail with. It holds the boom where you want it. On our ship, only the foresail is gaff rigged. That means the sail has an upper boom. The mainsail has no gaff, just the big triangle of canvas. This is called a Marconi rig.—SPINACH.

pulling down with all his weight. Morgan swigged away
on the line hauling it down tight, and Brick and Teddy
helped all they could. Then he made it fast to a cleat at
the foot of the mast.

"There," he said, standing up and blowing on his
hands, "we won't need that line again till we lower sail.
Coil it up and hang it on the cleat."

Captain Williams came forward.

"Foresail next," he said, "as long as we're at it. That's
a tougher job—hardest there is on a schooner. With the
gaff, there'll be two halyards to handle. Morgan, you and
I will take the throat; that's the heavier. Bob, you and the
Able-seamen on the peak."

The Skipper and Morgan hauled away and the gaff
moved slowly up the mast, dragging the sail hoops behind it. The others hauled away on their halyard too,
but not so fast or so high as to bind the gooseneck at the
spar.

"Belay your peak," said Sailor Bill. "Everyone on the
throat halyard." *

They tugged and grunted, all together, until it was as
taut as a steel bar, and then made it fast. Up followed the
peak until little downward wrinkles began to appear in
the canvas, and then they made its halyard fast too.

By this time Peach Island had faded several miles astern
and Captain Williams took some bearings. Away off on
their port quarter was the Windmill Point Light, and a

---

* The throat is the end of the gaff nearest the mast. The peak's the other
end. A halyard is the rope with which you raise and lower the sails. Belay
means make fast.—KATY.

little nearer to them but in the same general direction was the Detroit River Rear Light. Soon, from where they were, both lights came into line.

"Closing the range," Sailor Bill called it.

And when it closed, he walked back to Katy at the wheel. "Head her due East," he said. "Morgan, kill your engine."

Then things began to happen, and happen fast. As the engine died, Katy spun the wheel and the ship began to come up on her course. Morgan hauled in on the jib sheet, giving it a sharp pull so that the stops broke loose, and the sail filled with a jerk. The fore and main sheet-blocks snapped over to the starboard end of the travellers. Midshipman Bob on the fore sheet, and Sailor Bill on the main, payed them out a little to ease off on the strain.

"Dead on," sang out Katy, as the East point on the compass card came even with the line at the back of the bowl.

Both men trimmed in on their sheets. The sails filled. The ship heeled to a decided starboard slant. Water gurgled along side and a bubbling wake stretched out behind them.

The *Gull-Flight* had spread her wings.

KATY had rather a bad few minutes at the wheel. When the wind first filled the sails, there was a strong pull, and the spokes almost tore themselves out of her hands.

"Help me hang on," she called a little wildly to Spinach.

And the two of them did hang on, grimly, and kept the

ship from falling off. But soon they got the feel of the thing and coaxed her along her course. The yawing back and forth stopped, and the wake behind them straightened out.

Why it was just like sailing the *Bonny,* only nicer and somehow more important. There they were, the whole crowd of them, and just a touch on the wheel could take them this way or that. It was almost as good as being in command of the Magic Carpet from Bagdad. You could go anywhere you wanted, provided you didn't try to sail on dry land.

The crew was busy on deck, hauling in on this line and easing off on that, and squinting aloft to see whether the sails were drawing their best. They set the fore staysail and the flying jib so that the *Gull-Flight* had all her canvas spread except the topsail, and there was a little too much wind for that. But there she was, just bowling along; heeled over and racing through the water.

Captain Williams came aft, bringing Brick and Teddy with him, and they all went into the charthouse. When they came out again a few minutes later, Teddy was carrying a coil of stout line. Brick brought up right behind him lugging two rather funny-looking instruments. One was made of brass and had a blunt nose with a little wire eyelet in it, and tapered off to a pair of fins at the tail. It looked something like a metallic fish, and acted as a spinner. The other was a dial, with markings from zero to ten, and a pointer resembling the second hand of a watch.

Brick led one end of the line through the eyelet in the nose of the spinner. Sailor Bill watched him do it.

"Can you tie a bowline?" he asked.

"Yes, sir," said Brick. "I've been working away on knots ever since those lessons at the seashore two years ago."

Captain Williams then took the other end of the line and fed it through the hole in the little turning shaft that stuck out at the bottom of the dial. Then with two other pieces of short line he made the whole thing fast to the deck, face up, and as far aft

A BOWLINE

as he could get. Around the stern of the *Gull-Flight* was a low rail, perhaps eight inches high. This was called the taffrail. Sailor Bill shoved the spinner under this rail and let it dangle.

"Pay it out," he said to Teddy. "And don't stop any twist you may feel in the line."

The metallic fish dropped astern, and as the spinner turned the log line, the little hand on the dial began to move around.

"What's that for?" asked Spinach.

"Sea speedometer," said the skipper. "In a few minutes it will be two bells—that's nine o'clock. Then we'll set the hand at zero. An hour later we'll read it, and whatever it points to—that's how far we will have gone."

Morgan came back and took the wheel.

"Good job of steering," he said, relieving the Mates. "Take it easy. There's nothing ahead for several hours but straight sailing."

Katy and Spinach sat down on the deck with their backs against the charthouse, pleasantly warm in the sun, and watched the Canadian shore as it unrolled like a moving-picture film, a few miles off to starboard. They had passed the ugly shacks of the summer colony above the Border Cities. Soon a more open country began to appear, with farmland stretching back from the lake, and comfortable houses and prosperous barns, and fat cattle browsing under great spreading trees that dotted the pasture lands. Here and there was a golf course with the bright of its greens patched vividly against the blue sky, and little groups of people moving about on its fairways. Then a stretch of yellow beach with a lawn reaching away to a quiet house, dignified and leisurely under the cool shade of its elms. Then Belle River, with the little stream meandering through the sprawled-out town, and a fishing dock or two with weather-beaten shacks at their shore end, and nets wound on great wheels or spread out on the grass to dry.

The morning wore on as the *Gull-Flight* sped along. They all had lunch, a casual sandwich or two, eaten in whatever part of the ship anyone fancied. Brick and Teddy had theirs as far up in the bows as they could get, hanging out over the blue water with the fresh lake breeze in their faces.

Gyp was fed, which helped soothe his ruffled feelings. The little dog had had an exciting and puzzling day. He hadn't known anything about "sea legs," and when the schooner first heeled over in the wind he slid down the slant of the deck, and brought up hard against the lee rail. Further than that he bumped his nose, and might have gone over the side altogether if Brick hadn't heard his sharp yelp, and grabbed him by the tail and hauled him back inboard. But soon he learned to stay on the high side, and finally picked out a place up in the sharp of the bows with solid rail on both sides of him. No room to slide very far there. And he would have been all right too, only for a little wave that came over suddenly and smacked him in the face, and gave him a bath he hadn't figured on at all. But he got used to it after a while and gnawed away on his bone, ready for anything that came next.

And Sailor Bill seemed to be up to something too, for all during the last hour he had been coming forward and looking through his spyglass toward the shore off to star-board. Finally he spied what he was searching for.

"There they are," he said, "Thames River ranges. We'll come about when we close them up."

Soon they were abreast of the black gas buoy with its flashing white light, and rows of red and black spars stretching away to the river mouth.

"Ready about," said Captain Williams.

Away went the peace and calm of the last few hours, replaced by the bustle and scurry of changing course.

The Midshipman and Morgan had the fore and main-sails and Brick and Teddy were put at handling the jibs. Sailor Bill went aft and stood by the wheel.

"Oh, please!" cried Katy and Spinach together. "Can't we bring her around?"

"Certainly," said the Skipper. "I'll just stand by in case you need help. Hard over to port with your wheel."

Down came the wheel and around came the bow of the ship, swinging across the bowl of the horizon. The sails spilled the wind and flapped idly for a second. Then the booms slammed over and the sails filled with a crack. Katy was watching the compass card and easing up on the wheel to check the schooner dead on her new course. And doing very well at it too. True, the lubber line showed a little past Northwest but the Mates soon remedied that, bringing the *Gull-Flight* back and holding her hard up.

"That's it," said Captain Williams. "Well done."

Their twenty-five mile eastward tack had carried them toward Mitchell's Bay into the corner of the lake, and rather lonely water. But now they were swinging back to the steamer lanes, and it looked as though they would meet other sailing craft too. Katy still had the trick at the wheel and was enjoying every minute of it. But after having had all the lake pretty much to one's self, this coming into traffic again—well, that was another business entirely—and maybe not such a pleasant business either. For off to the south was a big ketch, bearing down on their bows and spread with every inch of sail she could crack on—even to the cook's undershirt—it seemed to Katy.

What should she do? Give way and bear off? How did one do that? Or should she hold grimly to her course? Who had the right of way in this case—the ketch or the *Gull-Flight*?

Sailor Bill was looking at her and grinning.

"Here's some verse for you to remember," he said. "It was made to fit a case exactly like this:"

> *"Close hauled upon the starboard tack,*
> *No other ship can cross your track.*
> *If on the port tack you appear,*
> *Ships going free must all keep clear:*
> *While you must yield when going free,*
> *To ships close hauled or on your lee.*
> *And if you keep the wind right aft,*
> *Keep clear of every sailing craft."*

The first line, *Close hauled upon the starboard tack.** There's the rule, thought Katy. And that's us. Let the ketch look after herself.

And the ketch did. She ran almost up to them before changing course, falling off down wind and passing astern, and close enough so that Katy could see her name painted on the counter.

"*Petrel,*" she said to Sailor Bill. "Isn't that some kind of a gull too? Must be our sister-ship."

---

* Taken from Felix Reisenberg's *Under Sail,* by courtesy of Harcourt, Brace and Co.

"Well not exactly," he answered. "But I'd be glad to have her in the family. She looks like a sound craft."

The *Gull-Flight* sped along, drawing nearer to the red and black buoys that marked the south end of the Flats Canal. They had lots of company now. Other yachts, both sail and power, were making for the channel. Speedboats roared up and down, streaking past great freighters who ignored them in a dignified way, keeping calmly and serenely on their course.

"Time to take off sail," said Captain Williams. "It will have to be power all the way up the St. Clair River. Morgan, get your engine going."

With bare poles and her sails furled, the schooner chugged into the dredged and diked cut across the Flats. They passed the *Old Club,* with its gray buildings and gay dock, brave with colored umbrellas and bright bunting. Farther up, dilapidated landings and rotting spiles in front of forlorn hotels fallen out of repair, marked the once hospitable resorts that catered to the hunters of the great wild duck marshes of a half-century past.

It grew dark. The Mates went below to get dinner, and soon through the cheerful gleam of the cabin lights came the good smells of roasting and stewing, and of savory sauces. The hood had been put on the binnacle and the light hooked up. The compass card swam in its glow, and high over their heads the mast lantern rode in a misty halo. A splash of green to starboard and a triangle of red to port glimmered out over the water from their running lights. The shores were sketched in dim shadow, and the channel reached away before them, clearly marked by the gas buoys along its bank.

Only a part of the crew at a time could come down for the evening meal. Katy and Spinach fed them in batches, for someone always had to be at the wheel, with someone else standing by in case of emergencies. And another had to be forward on lookout.

"Sing out when you see anything," said Sailor Bill as he posted Brick for his trick up in the bows. "And report all lights."

The Able-seaman got along all right for a while. His eyes sharpened in the gloom and the black of the water became distinct from the gray of the land. The occasional faint gleam of light from farmhouse windows didn't bother him any more.

"But what was this!"

Around a bend of the river ahead, showed a red light with three white balls of fire above it, and then after a minute or two, a green light, on a level with the red, but with some distance in between.

"Look's like a drug store," said Brick to himself.

But he didn't say that to Sailor Bill, aft by the wheel.

"It's a freighter with two tows," explained the Captain. "You did well to mark it out. Hug the right bank of the channel," he added to the man at the wheel. "We don't want to run foul of her towline."

Shoved along by her powerful motor, the *Gull-Flight* made her way upstream. The miles of narrow swift river kicked astern. The glitter of towns along its bank brightened and faded as they drew up to them and passed them by. And the younger members of the crew grew sleepy, tired after the long day. Muscles, sore from straining at halyards and pulling in sheet lines, stiffened in the night air.

"Why don't you turn in?" said the Skipper finally. "You Mates have done enough for today—and as for the Able-seamen. Well, look at them."

Brick was sitting on the deck with his back against the charthouse, fast asleep. And Teddy, while still on his feet, looked as though he might fall over any minute. Katy marshalled them both below.

"Let's see your hands," she said, after they were in the cabin. "Hu-m-m. Just as I thought. Some rope burns and skinned knuckles."

Out came the first aid kit with its liniment and bandages, and the ship's surgeon got to work. "There," she said a little later. "You'll sleep better for that."

"I don't need that to make me sleep," said Brick.

"I'd like to stay up till we get to where we're going," said Teddy.

"We'll know where that is in the morning," said Spinach.

"And I think we'll know something else too," said Katy. "I've an idea we're going to get those orders unsealed at last."

CHAPTER VI

DOMINIQUE VERLAINE

KATY CAME awake for the second time since she had turned in the evening before. Only now it was gradually and easily, and she lay there comfortably, snuggling down under the covers and giving her toes an experimental wriggle before she even opened her eyes. Some time during the night she had waked with a start. Lying there in the dark, it had taken a minute or two before she realized what had caused it. It wasn't noise, she was sure of that. Rather it was lack of noise. For the engine had stopped and the *Gull-Flight* was no longer moving. Silence had replaced the musical whisper of water gurgling alongside, and the rhythm of the steady pulse and throb of the motor had ceased. She had heard some muffled thumps and bumps, and a squeak or two. Then there were some low voices. Feet had come carefully down the companion stairs and there was the gentle closing of a cabin door. Then everything was quiet, and she had dozed off again.

But here it was—light once more; although of a queer subdued kind. A sort of twilight, even though it were morning—and with a good deal of green in it. She stole, or rather slid down out of her bunk, and looked through the porthole. All she could see was a wall, made of planks, hard up against the side of the ship. It extended high over her head so she couldn't see over the top. Some moss clung to the planks, growing a foot or two above the water line; and it was the sun slanting off this, that gave the light its peculiar green tint. Katy went over and pinched the still sleeping Spinach.

"Wake up," she said. "We're here. Or at least we're somewhere, and tied to a dock again."

Both girls hurried through their shower and scurried out into the cabin. Nobody there! The other two staterooms were empty and there was no fire in the galley range. Probably all in the saloon having breakfast, thought Katy.

But there was nobody there either. Although someone had set out plates and cups and saucers for them, and cocoa was keeping warm on the hot plate with the burner under it turned down low. Without stopping to eat, the Mates went out on deck. Still no one in sight.

"For Heaven's sake, what time is it?" asked Spinach. "And where is everybody?"

"Ten o'clock," said Katy, looking through the charthouse windows where the ship's chronometers were. "And we've overslept. But I don't know the answer to your second question any more than you do."

The top of the dock was about even with the *Gull-Flight's* rail so they could see ashore. They were at the foot of a city street, or rather the main street of a little town. A town, however, that had nothing of the air of a sleepy village about it, for the bustle of the water front was on all sides of them. Huge vans were backed up to gaping warehouse doors. With her cargo booms rigged, a Great Lakes packet ship was unloading; and the squall of her winch shrieked in the morning air. Farther upstream another vessel was fueling, and the clouds of black dust arose as the coal roared down the chutes. Just below them was a ferry dock, with a railed-off inclosure in front of an office building that had an air of great importance about it.

Over its roof was flying a flag, not the Stars and Stripes of the United States, but the diagonal red and white bars on the blue field of the Union Jack. And below it a sign that read:

Sarnia, Ontario.

Canadian Customs.

"Well, we've gone abroad anyway," said Katy. "But what will we do now?"

"Have breakfast and wait," said Spinach. "They've probably gone up town to register the ship."

That's just what they had done. And pretty soon Midshipman Bob hove in sight, walking down the sidewalk with Teddy and Brick tagging along behind. Gyp was giving his legs a shore stretch too, and was exploring all doorways and sniffing under fruit stands in search of a stray cat.

"Who's late turning out now?" asked Brick as he came aboard.

"And who hauled you out?" said Katy. "You never got up early by yourself. But where have you been? And where's the Skipper? And what are we doing tied up here?"

"One question at a time," said Bob. "The Skipper's still ashore, up at the Government House; and I don't quite know just what we are doing here. Waiting for orders, maybe."

"Ah ha-a," interrupted Katy.

"But I do know that we'll be here for a couple of days," continued Bob. "So we'd better rig the deck awning, and have a good housecleaning so as to be ready for visitors. You Mates will have some supplies to take aboard, so get your lists ready."

Katy and Spinach worked away below. Mattresses, stateroom rugs, and all the pillows came up on the foredeck and were spread about to air. Table and bed linen, and their own soiled clothes went into a great bag and out on the dock to be called for by the town laundry. Galley pots and pans came in for their share of cleaning; and sweeping and dusting went on at a great rate. Then the mattresses, pillows and rugs went back down again, and the bunks were freshly made. Soon the cabin below was as spick-and-span as it had been the morning they left Grosse Ile.

A tan deck awning, brave with a blue fringe, was hung umbrella fashion from the main boom. A rug was laid out under it on the afterdeck, with easy chairs and cushions placed about in comfortable positions. A section of rail was taken up amidship, and a carpet stretched from gangway to deck awning.

And there was the *Gull-Flight,* with as trim, smart and shady a quarter-deck as ever graced a man-of-war in tropical waters.

Then the crew changed into clean whites and waited for Sailor Bill to come back, which he did, in the early afternoon. And he didn't look quite in the mood to put up with a lot of questions either, so Katy thought it wise to keep her curiosity bottled up a little longer. But she and Spinach exchanged a pair of pretty knowing glances.

"Anybody come aboard?" he asked the Midshipman.

"Not yet, sir," answered Bob.

"We won't have long to wait, I think. Unless I'm very much mistaken, here come our orders now."

"What orders?" asked Katy. "Where? What do you see?"

"Look over to port," said Sailor Bill. "Toward the American shore. See that black boat coming?"

Across the river from Port Huron, a powerful speed-boat with gray painted decks and a little forward cabin was cutting through the water and bearing down on them. At her stern flew the Stars and Stripes, and from her bow, a pennant with a circle of stars enclosing an anchor. In her cockpit were two men in the uniform of the Coast Guard Service, and in the cabin at the wheel could be seen another—evidently, a petty officer.

Soon the patrol boat swept alongside and the roar of her

motor died away, throttled down to an uneasy chug. One of the men in the cockpit ran forward with a boat hook in his hand. The other man in the stern also had a boat hook, and as the speedboat lost way both men hooked on to the schooner's rail. The man in the cabin left the wheel and came out into the cockpit with two rather business-like envelopes in his hand.

"Schooner *Gull-Flight?*" he asked, calling up to the crew lining the port rail.

"Yes," answered Sailor Bill.

"Is there a Captain Williams aboard? And a Midshipman by the same name?"

"I'm Captain Williams. This is my son—a Midshipman at Annapolis."

"Orders," said the man in the speedboat. "From Washington—relayed to us up here by wireless. Any answer?"

Sailor Bill opened his envelope and took out what seemed a rather lengthy message. He read it, and looked up at Bob who in the meantime had read his—just a few printed lines.

"Mine's sweet and to the point," said the Midshipman. "And the answer has to go by train."

"Then there's nothing to take back," said Sailor Bill to the man in the speedboat. "But I'm very much obliged for your trouble. A nice courtesy from one service to another.

"Not at all," was the reply. "It isn't often we get a chance to co-operate, up in these waters."

BOAT HOOK

"Shove off"—to the men on the end of the boat hooks. As the patrol boat drew clear, Sailor Bill looked at his son.

"Well?" he said.

"I'll read it," said Bob.

MIDSHIPMAN R. L. WILLIAMS
        ABOARD SCHOONER GULL-FLIGHT. SARNIA, ONTARIO.
    THRU COAST GUARD STATION. PORT HURON, MICH.
REPORT ACADEMY ANNAPOLIS IMMEDIATELY.
                SIGNED, ...
                REAR ADMIRAL, COMMANDING

"Old 'Storm Along,'" said Sailor Bill, reading the Admiral's signature out loud. "Mister, you better get under weigh. When he says 'immediately,' he means yesterday."

"Captain Williams," said Bob, "I've already gone. If you were to turn your head and look out to sea, by the time you got your eyes inboard again, your son would be in the smoking compartment of a southbound train."

Katy finally boiled over.

"What's all this about," she said. "I knew Midshipman Bob wasn't going to stay with us. He hasn't any clothes, other than the uniform he is wearing. Spinach and I found that out two days ago—the night we anchored under Peach Island. And now what are we going to do? You can't sail this schooner with only one grown-up aboard. I know that too. Four of us are only children, Mates or Able-seamen, or whatever you want to call us. And Morgan isn't much better. He's only sixteen, whether he's Chief Engineer aboard or not."

Sailor Bill laughed.

"Mate, cook, housekeeper, ship's surgeon, and Sherlock Holmes to boot," he said. "But it isn't fair to keep you jumping up and down any longer. I'll read you my orders. While that won't clear everything up, it may help. Listen to this":

CAPTAIN WILLIAMS

ABOARD SCHOONER GULL-FLIGHT, SARNIA, ONTARIO.
THRU COAST GUARD STATION. PORT HURON, MICH.

WAIT SARNIA FOR ONE DOMINIQUE VERLAINE WHO WILL REPORT ABOARD. STOP. CREATE IMPRESSION IN SHOPS AND ABOUT TOWN MIDSHIPMAN WILLIAMS LEFT UNEXPECTEDLY FOR OTHER THAN GOVERNMENT REASONS. STOP. YOURS IS OSTENSIBLY A FAMILY CRUISE AND YOU ARE NOW SHORT HANDED. STOP. VERLAINE WILL BE OTHER NECESSARY ADULT HAND. STOP. YOURS THE COMMAND BUT PORT AND PURPOSE THIS VOYAGE WILL BE AT HIS DIRECTION. STOP. VERLAINE HAS FULL AUTHORITY CANADIAN GOVERNMENT AND CONFIDENCE THIS OFFICE.

SIGNED, ...

CHIEF CLERK, INTELLIGENCE SERVICE.

(SECRET AND CONFIDENTIAL)

"Whe-e-w," said Katy and Brick and Spinach and Teddy, all together.

And then from Katy:

"What's it all mean? And who or what is Dominique Verlaine? And why is some government Chief Clerk mixed up in our vacation? And why is the Intelligence Service telling us where to go—or rather telling us to let this Dominique Verlaine order us about?"

"Katy," said Captain Williams, "I'm only a simple sailor man. And after nearly thirty years at sea, one of the things that I've found out is that 'Standing By' is a great virtue. You've asked more questions in the last five minutes than an Admiralty Court could answer if it sat for the next hundred years. Dominique Verlaine isn't going to order us about, as you call it. But I'll tell you a secret and I want you all to keep it. For three years I have been a member of the United States Secret Service. This isn't a vacation for me—it's duty—and I'm under orders here just as I am anywhere else. I am in command of this ship, but I take her where, and do with her, as I am directed from shore."

Katy felt a little snubbed—but also that she had it coming.

"Uncle Bill," she said, "I shipped aboard this schooner as Mate, and you're the Skipper. And I'll do exactly *what,* and go exactly *where* you decide. And I don't think any of the rest of us would have it any different. But I'm still little, and I guess curiosity is one of the things I've got to outgrow."

"Of course," said the Skipper. "And I knew I could count on you—on all of you. I watched you at the seashore two years ago, and I've watched you particularly since I came out here, and on the first two days of this voyage. And I want to say that I've never shipped a crew that showed so much promise, or that had so much spirit, or that was so willing to learn. And if I hadn't thought so we would not have been here, nor would the *Gull-Flight.* Nor would I have said what I did in Washington when the whole idea of this voyage began to shape itself. But perhaps I had better go back to the beginning."

Katy pulled a cushion over and squatted down on it. Brick and Teddy sat down too. Morgan draped himself around a deck chair. Midshipman Bob had gone below to gather up what few things he had, ready to go ashore.

Already his connection with the *Gull-Flight* must be described in the past tense.

"To begin with," said Sailor Bill, "there's a gang working somewhere up here, and they're operating across the lake. Or as a matter of fact, across any of the waters from Sault St. Marie to the Niagara River. Just how they do it we don't know, but we've a fair idea."

"Do what?" asked Katy. "And what have they to do with us? And why don't the police make them behave— whatever it is they're doing?"

"They're smugglers," said Sailor Bill. "Smugglers of men—Chinamen mostly—of opium or drugs, or anything else they can get a high price for in the States. And smugglers on the way back too, of tobacco or any other American product with a high Canadian duty. That's what makes it international, and not a matter for the local police of either country. And that's why the governments of both countries are interested and determined to break up the gang."

"I still don't see," began Katy.

But Sailor Bill interrupted.

"The Coast Guard and the other men stationed through here are handicapped. The gang is too well organized and has spies in most of the towns and cities along the border. They know all government craft, and most government men. But they don't know this boat, and they don't know me. That's why we are both up here, and why you are along, for the whole plan is to make this cruise look so much like a family one that the gang won't be suspicious—wherever we go, or whatever we do."

"Where does Dominique Verlaine come in?" asked Spinach.

"He's a Canadian. One of their undercover men, and for ten years he's been operating on the Atlantic Seaboard —something to do with the fishing trade. So they won't know him; nor do I, for I have never seen him. But he's been detailed to this job because of a boyhood knowledge of the country, and because he knows the Indian tribes of Georgian Bay. The gang has its base up there, and that's where we're going. The Indians are going to help us find their hide-outs."

"How," said Brick.

"I don't know yet," said Sailor Bill. "Dominique Verlaine has the plans, and we'll hear them when he comes aboard."

"I wish he'd get here," said Teddy.

"He will. But right now," he added, holding up the copy of the wireless, "it's up to us to obey these orders. That's where you can help."

"What can *we* do?" asked Katy.

"Talk," said the Skipper. "Say the right things in the right places. This is a small town and news will get about quickly. But small as it is—it is also the gateway to Lake Huron and the Georgian Bay region. Someone of the gang is bound to be here, keeping an eye on who passes through these waters. We want whoever that is to know all about us. Our idea of what he should know, that is."

"What idea would that be?" asked Spinach.

"The family cruise idea," said Sailor Bill, "and that it's broken up until we can ship another hand. But be careful how you refer to me. Always 'Sailor Bill,' or better still, 'Uncle Bill.' And the Midshipman as 'Cousin Bob.' And remember the reason for his leaving the ship is family sickness—sudden and serious. On no account mention the Coast Guard boat, or the relayed orders from Washington."

"Come on," said Katy to Spinach. "We've some supplies to get. We'll go to the store right now, and start the gossip spreading. When do you think Dominique Verlaine will show up?"

"I haven't any idea," said Sailor Bill, "either when he will arrive—or what he'll look like when he gets here."

"I'll walk up town with you," said Midshipman Bob, who had come back on deck with his little zipper bag in his hand, ready to say good-bye. "I ought to rate a feminine escort—at least to the railroad station."

"You don't," said the Skipper. "Get out of town—alone and quickly. And don't attract any more attention than you can help."

About a half hour later two girls, clad in a rather natty uniform of decided nautical pattern, walked into the general provision store on Sarnia's main street. Each of them

had a market basket on her arm, and one of them pro-
duced a list of needed supplies. The storekeeper came
forward to meet them eagerly—business was business, and
cruising yachts sometimes left big orders.

"Well, Mates," he said, his honorary title coming
closer to the truth than he knew. "What can I do for
you? Off the schooner docked at the foot of the street,
I suppose? What's her name? She's a tidy craft—and
where are you away for? And how big is your crew?"

Spinach nudged Katy.

Here was their Town Crier, made to order for them.
Now they wouldn't have to go out of their way to tell
their story. All they would have to do would be to
answer questions, and it was a safe bet the storekeeper
would do the rest. If he proved to be as good at dispens-
ing news as he was at gathering it, the whole town would
have the tale before noon.

"Our schooner's the *Gull-Flight,*" said Katy primly.
"And we'd like this list of supplies. We tied up to the
dock during the night. But how did you guess that we
two are her Mates?"

The grocer laughed. "Well, I'll have to admit it was
just a guess," he said. "But you certainly look the part.
Who else is aboard?"

"Our two younger brothers are the Able-seamen," said
Spinach, eager to spill her share of the news. "And we've
a cousin who's sixteen. He's Chief Engineer. That's all,
now that Cousin Bob has gone. Except of course Uncle
Bill. He's the Skipper."

"She's a pretty big ship, is yours," said the storekeeper, "for so young a crew to handle. Are you taking her out through the lake with only one grown-up aboard?"

"That's just the trouble," said Katy, looking as gloomy as she could.

"We *were* going up to Georgian Bay," said Spinach, horning right in, "and maybe on a family cruise to the North Channel, to be gone all summer. But our oldest cousin, Bob, got a wire this morning that his mother was sick, and he has to go home. He was the other grown-up aboard, and now I don't know what we *will* do. Uncle Bill says that unless we can find the proper kind of a hand, we'll have to go home and give up the cruise."

"Perhaps I can help you out," said the grocer. "There was a Blue Nose in here yesterday, and he talked as though he wanted to ship for a voyage around the lakes. Quiet, capable sort of chap he looked too. About forty, I should say."

"What's a Blue Nose?" said Katy. "It doesn't sound very attractive."

"It's a nickname," said the storekeeper, laughing a little at them, "for a Nova Scotia salt-water man. They're great seamen. Most of them are French-Canadian, or Irish and French mixed. Suppose I send him down to the dock so your uncle can talk to him."

Katy and Spinach shied off a little at his suggestion. That was going a little too fast. With Dominique Verlaine aboard, they wouldn't need anyone else. But it would never do to arouse suspicion by turning down such an obvious find as this—provided, of course, that the man was all the storekeeper said he was.

"Are the baskets ready?" said Katy, picking that out as the best way to wind up the conversation. "We'd better be getting along back."

And Sailor Bill wasn't any too sure about it either, when they told him about what had happened at the store.

"You did your best," he said. "It wasn't your fault that such a made-to-order sailor should happen along. But maybe he won't want to go—or can't go, right at this minute. Perhaps he won't even come down and let us look him over. At any rate you've spread the right rumors. We're a family cruise in the eyes of the town. And if any of this gang are about, they won't be suspicious of the *Gull-Flight* wherever they run across her."

"I do wish this Dominique or Dominick, whatever it is they call him, would show up," said Katy. "If he doesn't, things are going to get out of hand."

Brick and Teddy had been ashore too, carrying on the good work. Rumor certainly did spread itself fast in the little town. They had been to a movie, and when they came out, they had dropped into a drug store for a soda.

"What do you think?" said Teddy excitedly. "The man behind the soda counter knew all about us—and our ship too—and where we're going. And about Bob having to leave us and go back."

"And do you know what the man said when we came into the drug store?" said Brick.

"No," said Sailor Bill. "What did he say?"

"Hello, Able-seamen. That's what he said. Now how did he know about that? About Teddy and me, I mean —and our rating aboard this ship. And then something more about our troubles being over, and about a Blue Nose shipping aboard. What's a Blue Nose anyway?"

Katy and Spinach explained their conversation with the grocer.

Sailor Bill looked frankly worried.

But nothing happened that day, and after a night fraught with tossing about and curious dreams—morning finally came along.

"Do you know what?" said Katy to the Skipper at breakfast. "That Blue Nose business. I had the funniest dream last night. About all of us on a fishing smack over the Grand Banks. And there was a man in command who had an enormous blue nose. So big that he had to look sideways to see ahead. He had a gun strapped around his waist and he always seemed to be looking for somebody, and promising to shoot if he found him."

"See here," said Sailor Bill, "don't you be dreaming things like that. They might come true, and we've enough trouble now."

Afterward they all sat on deck in the morning sun. The Skipper was smoking away at his pipe, and spinning a few yarns for the benefit of Brick and Teddy. Katy and Spinach had a pencil and were working on their supply lists. Morgan wasn't doing anything. He was lying flat on his back, looking up at the blue sky.

Sailor Bill suddenly left off talking and grew quiet.

"Here it comes," he said, "I knew you shouldn't have had that dream."

The eyes of the whole crew turned toward the village street.

Down the sidewalk a man was coming. He was nearly a block off, so they all had a good chance to look him over before he got to the dock side. He had on a blue suit, the top of which was a reefer jacket. On his head was a peaked cap with a shiny visor, pulled down over one eye. But somehow this didn't give him a rowdy look at all, for in spite of his rough clothes there was a decidedly debon-air atmosphere about him. Maybe it was the gay flower that stuck jauntily from a button-hole that did it.

Across his right shoulder was slung a huge canvas bag, and on his left, was balanced a box about two feet square. Bending a little to the weight on his back, he bore down on them; and his seagoing gait as he rolled along, fairly shrieked Sailor Man to all who cared to notice.

"It's the Blue Nose all right," said the Skipper. "No landsman ever barged along like that. That's a salt-water swagger if I ever saw one. And he's got his gear slung over his back, ready to come aboard. We're going to have to decide this thing right now, whether we want to or not."

"What will we say to him?" asked Katy.

"I don't know," said Sailor Bill, "but maybe we're going to ship an extra hand.—I like his looks already."

The man with the sea bag marched straight on down the street and across the dock. A few feet off he stopped, lowered both bag and box to the ground, and stood up. With his hands on his hips he sized up the *Gull-Flight,* running his eyes over her from stem to stern.

"The nerve of him," said Sailor Bill, "picks out his ship. And if he doesn't like the looks of her, he won't sign on. But it's a good sailor man that can afford to be as choosey as that."

Apparently satisfied with the yacht's appearance the man picked up his bag and box and came on down the dock, bringing up at the rail.

"Schooner *Gull-Flight?*" he asked, coming to a dead stop.

"Yes, if you can read," said the Skipper. "Her name's there on the counter for anyone to see."

"Are you Captain Williams?" asked the man. "I hear you want another man aboard. Storekeeper tells me you're short handed."

Something in the man's calm assurance annoyed Sailor Bill. He seemed so sure of his berth.

"We are," said the Skipper. "I don't know whether you're the man or not. But come aboard and we'll talk it over. It isn't every pier-head jumper that'll fit on this cruise."

The man didn't bother to use the gangway. Dumping his bag and box to the schooner's deck, he jumped down after them. Then he turned to Captain Williams. A twinkle gleamed in his eye and his white teeth flashed into a smile. *"Mon captaine,"* he said. "I'll fit all right— I am Dominique Verlaine."

CHAPTER VII

FURTHER PLANS AND THE SCAR-FACED MAN

TO SAY that Captain Williams was astonished, would be putting it mildly. And to say that his crew was amazed—well—that would be an exceedingly mild statement indeed.

The Skipper had been annoyed from the very moment when Dominique Verlaine had first dropped his bag and box to the dock and stood there so calmly looking the *Gull-Flight* over. His feeling of annoyance had increased as the man swaggered down toward them, and his gorge continued to rise with every sentence that passed between them. He was about ready to squelch this brash sailor with a burst of quarter-deck vernacular that would wither him back to size like a dowse of boiling water on a head of lettuce.

But the man's introduction of himself had completely spilled the wind from the Skipper's sails of wrath. He gulped a few times, sparring a little for breath. And then:

"Welcome aboard, Mr. Verlaine. We've been expecting you since yesterday. Suppose you and I go below.

Each of us has papers, I think, that would interest the other."

"Well what do you know about that?" asked Morgan, as the two men disappeared down the companion stairs.

"That's having a plan and working it out," said Katy.

"He knew we'd stop here," said Brick. "At Sarnia I mean."

"He knew about those wireless messages too," said Teddy. "And that we'd wait here for him to come aboard, and put in some provisions while we were doing it."

"And where we'd probably go to get them," said Spinach. "And what kind of man that storekeeper is, and how he'd spread the news around."

"Of course," said Katy, "and that clears up the reason for that Blue Nose business. It's perfectly logical for him to ship as part of our crew. No one would be suspicious.

FRENCH FRIGATE

DOMINIQUE VERLAINE was the result of a queer mixture of parentage, difficult to understand possibly, but common enough in the history of Canada and the migration of its peoples.

Sometime during the past century and a half when the land was a French Province, a sailor of the same name deserted from the deck of one of Louis the Fifteenth's frigates. Instead of hanging about Quebec or becoming a habitant of one of the villages along the St. Lawrence, he had taken to the woods. Like many others, he had turned north at Sault St. Louis above Montreal, and wandered up the Ottawa River. Here that first winter, he nearly died from starvation and cold. Some friendly Algonquin tribes had taken him in, and from them he learned woodcraft, finally emerging a full-fledged coureur de bois. He married a Chippewa squaw and deserted her a few years later leaving a wigwam full of papooses. Back in Montreal he married again; had one son, and returned to sea. Nothing further was ever heard from him.

This one son was the grandfather of the present Dominique Verlaine. Nothing much was known about him either, except that he had married, and taken to the fishing trade off the coasts of Nova Scotia. He too was lost when his fishing smack foundered in a winter's gale, and went down with all hands.

His son, a Dominique too, had never known the sea, for his mother had moved back inland to prevent his ever going upon it. Later he had married an Irish girl, migrate from the hardships of a potato famine on her native bogs. The two had taken up some land near an Indian

reservation between Lake Nipissing and Georgian Bay, and almost, had they known it, within sight of the tepees of great-grandfather Verlaine's half-breed descendants.

Little Dominique grew up there. In the winter time he went to a cross-roads school. He and an Indian boy named Joe became fast friends. Joe wasn't the boy's real name, but he answered to it well enough, for Foot-in-the-Water, his Indian one, hardly seemed to suit in the school room. Later, the boys found out they were fourth or fifth cousins.

Afterward young Verlaine went to high school in Montreal, and then entered McGill University. But the call of the sea was strong in him too, and during vacations he formed the habit of enlisting for offshore voyages in Nova Scotia fishing smacks. Finally he stayed away a year, and when he got back, could pass for a typical Blue Nose. Some way or other he drifted into government service. Equally at home on deck or in the woods, and speaking English, French, and several Indian dialects, he became a valuable undercover agent.

The father and grandfathers Verlaine were all French, straight down the line of descent. But the present Dominique took after his mother. The *Mon Captaine,* with which he had greeted Commander Williams, was merely the habit of long usage in addressing the quarter-decks of French-Canadian schooners. True when he was excited, a few *Ou-la-la's,* crept into his speech. Everything else about him, and all his reactions were Irish—even to his name.

"Dominick will do," as he said later to Brick, who had stumbled a little over the pronunciation. "Although it's Dominique properly—or at least it was at the Christening. So Dominick it'll be, I guess, for the rest of the voyage."

This was the man who was to determine the detail of the cruise of the *Gull-Flight.* It promised to be an interesting summer.

A FEW minutes later a hail from below took all hands into the cabin. Sailor Bill and Dominick were seated at the table with papers and charts spread out before them.

"Let me introduce the crew," said the Skipper. "The two girls are the Mates—Katy and Spinach. Morgan here, is our Chief Engineer. And a good one too. He uses engine oil for salad dressing."

"Does he now?" said Dominick. "No iron filings in the salt shakers, I hope."

"No," said Sailor Bill. "The Mates are cooks. So you needn't worry. By the time we are flying our 'Homeward Bound' pennant, your belt will be out three notches."

"Trouble in the fo'c'sle never starts over good food," said Dominick. "And the boys here? Are they our Able-seamen?"

"I'm Brick," said one.

"I'm Teddy," said the other.

"And it's pleased to meet you both, I am. Is it just aboard ship that you're 'able'? Or would it be that you can handle a paddle in a canoe? Or follow over a portage if you had an Indian guide to break the trail? Is it a bunk you've got to be sleeping in always? Or can you cuddle up to the shadowy side of a hill and shoulder your pack again in the morning, fresh as a daisy at sunup?"

"I've been to summer camps, Mr. Verlaine," began Brick bravely.

"Dominick," interrupted the undercover agent. "Remember it's only a hand I am aboard this ship. And I'll stow in up forward. It would never do for me to be sleeping aft with the owners. With the Captain in the deckhouse, and Morgan at the foot of the companion stairs—

there's all three ways into the ship, guarded as best we can."

"Tell them what we're up to," said Sailor Bill. "Katy has been one continual itch since we left Grosse Ile. Not that she hasn't figured it out pretty well, and acted accordingly. It's chiefly on account of her, that you're aboard with nobody the wiser."

"Oh it's you, was it—that set the storekeeper off. Well that was a job well done. But there's more yet, before we ever start away at all."

"What would that be?" asked Spinach, a little nettled at the skimping of her share in the matter. "We acted together, you know. I'm the other Mate aboard."

"Two's better than one," said Dominick. "There's more wits at work. And you'll need them for this job. We haven't found out who the gang's got here in town. Maybe he's important, and maybe he isn't. We don't know about that either. But we may meet him later. And if we know what he looks like—it's better off we'll be."

"How will we go about that?" asked Katy.

"This time, by keeping your eyes open," said Dominick. "Your tongues have wagged enough. From now on let somebody else do the talking. But spread about in the town. You'll see someone, and he'll be the over curious kind. Not the storekeeper. This will be somebody that has no business sticking his nose in anywhere. Answer his questions, just like you did at the market. But it's marking his looks you'll be—all the time he's talking;

and describing the cut of his jib afterward to the Skipper and me."

"What did you mean by handling a canoe paddle?" asked Brick.

"And by following a trail?" put in Teddy.

"We're going up to the North Country," said Dominick, "back to where I was born. And it's glad I'll be to see Joe again, so I will."

"Joe?" said Brick. "Who's Joe? And what's he got to do with all this?"

"Joe College," said Dominick.

"Joe College?" repeated Katy. "That's a funny thing to be called."

"Joe Foot-in-the-Water then," said Dominick. "If you want his real name—the Indian one I mean. He's a sort of off-side relation of mine. He's Chief of his tribe up there. And a good Chief too. After I left to go to school in Montreal, he went away too. Some way he got into Carlisle—that's an Indian college in the States. There's the reason for his nickname. A good many of his braves are guides. They get all around up there. What they don't see themselves, the other guides tell them."

"Tell them what?" asked Spinach.

"Who's in the country and what's going on," said Dominick. "Our plan is to make a landing in a bay somewhere. Then we'll use the *Gull-Flight* as a base—a movable one—changing station as often as we have to, and working gradually north. We'll send out for a guide, and we'll see that we get Joe College. From then on, I don't know. It will be up to him. But we have the *Bonny,* and Joe will have his canoe."

"Will he take us out in it?" asked Teddy.

"Of course," said Dominick, "and it's grand trips you'll have. Back inland, up the streams to the Indian reservation. Two boys and a guide off a cruising yacht. It's a smart gang that will connect that up with the Intelligence Departments of two governments."

As the plans unfolded, the spirits of the Mates sank farther and farther. Being officers on a real schooner was all right, but it was beginning to look as though the Able-seamen were going to have all the fun, once they got up to the North Country. And in the meanwhile what were they to do? Stay aboard and cook? Housekeep and sweep? Tend ship and watch stores? With adventure on all sides, were they to be held fast to the deck?

Sailor Bill noticed their glum faces.

"Dominick," he said, "don't leave the story half told. We haven't brought the *Bonny* along for nothing. Pick your crew. You can't sail her alone."

"It's not alone, I expect to be. With two fine sailor lasses like Katy and Spinach. 'Tis I that know how to pick my company. Boys are all right, but it's girls that are a comfort in camp. With a bright fire on the beach and a rock ledge behind; and a fresh-caught fish broiling over the coals. And a moon maybe, with the stars overhead and a cool wind from the lake. And it's off we'll be of mornings; with never a cove or inlet able to hide their secrets from us."

"You mean Spinach and I are going to leave the *Gull-Flight* and go exploring in the *Bonny* with you!" said Katy.

"It's nothing else that I mean," said Dominick. "With the Indian and the boys inland and us working close inshore, and the schooner standing off and keeping an eye on the wide waters—it's a smart gang that will be able to hide out the whole summer long."

"Are you satisfied?" said Sailor Bill to the girls.

"Satisfied!" said Katy. "Uncle Bill, there never *will* be a more wonderful summer."

"And I don't think there ever *has* been," said Spinach.

So peace was restored and the battle of the sexes was over. Here was work and adventure for all—all except Morgan and Sailor Bill. They would have the dull times, shifting the *Gull-Flight* northward as track and trail led up and up. And with not even hands enough left aboard to raise sail.

But the Chief Engineer would like that. The crew had an annoying habit of referring to his engine as "the kicker." As though it were not entirely necessary—and sail was the thing. Who had gotten them through the swift St. Clair? And what had taken them to Peach Island that first night? But now here *was* something. The motor and Morgan. The Skipper and the wheel. Helm and engine room. Together they could go anywhere.

"WHAT's the best way to find out if the gang has a man

stationed here?" said Sailor Bill a little later. "What do you suggest, Dominick?"

"Nothing drastic at all. The last thing we want to do is to let the impression get around that we are looking for anything, or anyone. We'll stay here in port one day more. If the man doesn't give himself away by that time, we'll call it a bad job."

"How do we go about it?" asked Morgan.

"Organize a sight-seeing trip," said Dominick. "The whole five of you. Spend the afternoon ashore, and keep your eyes peeled. I don't know what you'll see—or what to tell you to look for. But it's grand detectives you are I'm thinking, after what happened with the storekeeper."

"And keep together," said Sailor Bill; "nothing can happen to you that way. But take in the town. Hang around the docks for a while. Buy yourselves a couple of sodas. A couple, I said, Mr. Able-seamen. There's souvenirs too—post cards to send home, and things like that. Katy, you've some towels to get. I heard you say yesterday we've nowhere near enough. You girls needn't bother about dinner tonight—we'll get it for once. Come back about six o'clock—all of you. It's a long time since I performed on a galley range, but with Dominick aboard, maybe we'll give you a surprise."

"It's a French twist the menu will have tonight," said the Blue Nose. *"Ragoût à la Gull-Flight."*

The docks were dusty and hot. And not very interesting

either to five young people. But the plans for the afternoon called for a thorough inspection, and they stuck to
them. Stevedores, sweating over hand trucks were glad
enough to knock off and talk; but their bosses weren't
quite so pleased. In fact the crew of the *Gull-Flight* was
invited to leave, several times—and in not a very polite
manner.

"Get out o' here," said one straw-boss, forcibly breaking
up a conversation between Brick and a roustabout. It was
the third time the same stevedore had been kicked off the
crate on which he chose to rest. "What do you think this
is—an information bureau? We can't talk the cargo out
of that ship."

The crew left.

"That was a very determined man," said Katy as they
were walking up the main street. "But did you notice
anything suspicious?"

"Not a thing," said Morgan. "Nothing but work and
orders."

"Work for the stevedores," said Brick. "Orders for us
—orders to get out."

"How about one of those sodas?" said Teddy.

"Good idea," said Spinach. "These Scotland Yard tac-
tics are a dry business."

"Well Mates!" said the man in the drug store. "What
will it be this time?"

This was the same man by the way, who had such a
complete understanding of their doings and conditions
when he interviewed Brick and Teddy the day before.

"Did your Blue Nose come aboard?" he went on, after filling their orders.

"Oh yes," said Spinach. "And we like him very much."

"Another able-seaman in the fo'c'sle," said the man behind the soda counter. "Well, you can't have too many. It's a full-rigged ship is yours."

All this while Katy wasn't saying anything. Let the others do the talking. She was busy keeping her eyes open. And already she had found something to fill them. On the way up town she had noticed a man lurking on a doorway near the dock side. Not a very nice-looking man either. When the cousins passed by, he came out of the doorway and followed them along the street. When they turned into the drug store, Katy watched through the windows to see whether he would go by.

He did—after a minute. That minute he spent spying on them inside. Then he disappeared from view.

She sucked away on her straw. She expected further developments. So when the man came in the door a few minutes later, she wasn't surprised. In fact she looked at her other cousins a little amazedly. With events taking this turn, how could they be so absorbed in chatter about this and that?

The man sat down at the counter and ordered something that fizzed up in the glass as the clerk mixed it before him. Then he drank it with a wry face. He didn't try to start a conversation, but his ear nearest the crew of the *Gull-Flight* was an obvious question mark. It was cocked definitely in their direction.

Katy had a good look at him in the five or ten minutes before they left.

She didn't say anything to the others. Maybe her suspicions were all wrong. Imagination played queer tricks sometimes. And if there were something worthy of notice, some of the other cousins would see it too. That would share the responsibility—blame possibly, if she *were* wrong.

At the toweling department of the general store she gave her order. The crash was cut under her direction into lengths best usable aboard ship. They stood around waiting for the rough hemming of its edges so that it wouldn't ravel out. Always there was the same curiosity about them, and knowledge of their plans and conditions seemed universal.

"How do you like your new hand?" asked the clerk.

"Very much," said Spinach again. "But his nose isn't blue, in spite of all reports."

"Maybe not," said the clerk. "But you'll find he knows a tops'l halyard from an anchor chain."

There was that man again! And his order to the clerk seemed so silly to Katy. Just an excuse to stand by and listen to what they were saying. What would a man like that want with washcloths? There hadn't been soap nor water near his ears since the summer before. Then it was likely he had fallen overboard, or someone had towed him astern.   Like the cook in Jack London's story of the *Sea Wolf*.   Men like him didn't waste time washing.

THE *Ragoût à la Gull-Flight* was all that Sailor Bill and Dominick promised.   And it was nice too, sitting down and enjoying someone else's cooking.   But the capacity of the new member of the crew amazed Katy a little, and alarmed her a bit more.   How would she ever fill him up?   Eating was a business with him, and silenced all his flow of talk.

The first helping of savory stew disappeared with a whiff and a flourish.   A slab of bread wiped up the remaining sauce.

"Mr. Verlaine's plate," said Sailor Bill.   "True hospitality would recognize a polish like that without comment.   It calls for a second filling."

Katy carried the trencher into the galley and heaped it high once more.   This was going to prove interesting.

"*Bon?*   Eh, *Mon Captaine*," said Dominick, falling to again.   French delight in good fare had overcome all Irish influence.

The usual sensitive curve in the lips of the undercover agent had straightened into the converging lines of a yawning trap.   Food sluiced past the opening.   Jaws seemed to be hinged on ears.   The mouth was but an entrance to a bottomless pit.   Compared to this, the youthful maws of Teddy and Brick were but shallow pools, quickly and easily filled up.   The ample and generous icebox of the *Gull-Flight* would be under severe strain before the end of the voyage. Finally the others laid down their own knives and forks, and sat by fascinated.

"Perhaps a spoonful of duff?" said Sailor Bill, when the gastronomic antics at the far end of the table showed signs of slowing down. "A proper finish to any sailor's meal."

Two helpings of plum duff satisfied him, and at last Dominick sat back and pushed his plate away from him. Then producing a villainous-looking purple package, he hauled out papers and tobacco and proceeded to roll a cigarette. The color of the wrapping was no more bilious than the smell of the tobacco. Wreaths of choking smoke dimmed the cabin air.

"Have some of mine," invited Sailor Bill, throwing over his own well-filled pouch.

"Thank you, no," said Dominick. "Mine's shag. No other seems to satisfy after you've smoked it a while. Ordinary tobacco doesn't bite in."

"I can understand that," said the Skipper, coughing a little.

"But what about this afternoon?" he went on, talking now to the five cousins. "Did you see anything suspicious?"

"Nothing at all," said Morgan—"that I noticed anyway."

"We hung around the docks," said Teddy, "until we got chased off."

"That foreman was awfully mad," said Brick.

"But we didn't see anything," said Spinach.

"I did," said Katy, tossing her bombshell into the meeting. "I kept my eyes open."

The jaws of the rest of the crew dropped, and their eyes popped open. What had she seen that the rest hadn't? They were together all afternoon.

"Now what would that be?" asked Dominick.

Katy told him. Where she had first seen the man and didn't like his looks. And how he followed the cousins wherever they went, stopping whenever they did, and trailing them around from store to store. And how transparent and ridiculous his errands really were.

"Good for you," said Sailor Bill.

"Can you describe him?" asked Dominick.

"Of course," said Katy.

"Before you do—let me ask a question. Would there be a bad scar on him? On the left side of his face, maybe? Running from his ear to his chin, likely?"

"Yes, there was," said Katy. "But how did you know that?"

"Now finish telling us what he looked like," said Dominick.

Katy never got a chance to finish her description. Not even to begin it. Gyp saw to that. He barked suddenly and loudly, and flung himself frantically against the locked screen door in the deckhouse over their heads. He had been shut up there, out of mischief while the crew was at dinner.

Dominick jumped to his feet.

"Follow me," he cried to Katy.

Together they ran up the companion stairs and out on deck. Just in time to make out a figure—stooped and running. Running through the gloom of the evening, away from the ship, and off up the dock. Before turning out of sight around the corner of a building, he passed under a swinging arc light.

"Boarders, I'm thinking," said Dominick. "Repelled at the rail by the ship's mascot. You wouldn't have recognized that fellow now—as he ran under the arc light?"

"Yes I would," said Katy. "I'd know him anywhere. It was Scar-Face."

"That's all I want to know," said the undercover agent. "We'll leave in the morning. The *Gull-Flight* is going to do some sailing."

CHAPTER VIII

ANCHORS AWEIGH

NATURALLY the rest of the crew was excited and tried to crowd out on deck behind Katy and Dominick. But the Blue Nose stopped them at the charthouse door.

"Stay below for a minute," he commanded. "We want to find out what he was up to—if we can. Too many feet tramping around on deck will destroy all clues."

In the meanwhile Gyp was keeping up his clamor behind the screen door of the forward house.

"Och-one," said Dominick, calling softly up to him, "make all the noise you want. It's a good job you've done this night."

The shadowy gloom of evening brought with it a heavy fall of dew. Rigging, rail and deck planking were covered with it. Every step that Katy and Dominick took left a print, clearly marked and easy to follow. The two moved cautiously along the rail, their eyes alert and looking around with every step they took. Soon they ran into other footprints, thwart-ship, and leading from the gangway toward a ventilator that opened into the main cabin below, where they had all been gathered around the table.

At the base of the ventilator was a blurred smudge in a confused half circle where feet had shuffled around. Then there was a separate track back to the gangway.

"It's here the dog scared him off," said Dominick. "But I wonder how much chance he had to listen. If we know more about his plans now, than he about ours—it's the ship's mascot we have to thank."

VENTILATOR

"Good old Gyp," said Katy. "Let's let him out."

When the screen door was flung back the little dog bounded through the opening. He ran up to the ventilator and sniffed around it a bit, whining eagerly. In a moment he found the tracks leading to the gangway. He sniffed again here and threw up his head, barking once, sharply. He wasn't a bloodhound but he knew a strange scent when he found one. So he followed the footprints out on the dock and ran off into the dark. Katy and Dominick waited for a minute and then whistled him back. He didn't come right away and they had to whistle again.

"What's he up to, do you suppose?" asked Katy.

"Let him alone," said the Blue Nose. "If Scar-Face is around, he'll find him."

But the coast must have been clear for presently Gyp

came back, wagging his tail and panting hard. Katy picked him up and held him tight in her arms. The dog licked her face and wriggled all over with excitement.

"It's a puppy bone, he should have," said Dominick. "He's earned it."

"He'll get it," said Katy, "once we're below."

And when they did go into the cabin, what a storm broke about their ears!

"Who was it?" asked Teddy and Brick together.

"What did he want?" said Spinach.

"Did he get away?" asked Sailor Bill.

"It was Scar-Face, one of the gang, trying to hear what we were saying by listening through the cabin ventilator. The dog scared him off, but it's time we were away before he has a chance to snoop around further. The next time I want him aboard will be up in Georgian Bay, at the end of a line. And there's two others I hope to have a look at—all three of them bound up tight."

GRANNY

KNOT

"I'll tie the knot," said Brick.

"Can you do it?" said Dominick. "A secure one? One an eel couldn't wriggle out of?"

"What's the matter with a square knot?" asked Brick.

"Nothing," said Dominick, "but it must be a proper one. A granny knot would never hold them. No thief's knot for a gang like that. Why it's away they'd be, before you ever had a chance to look up at all." *

"All right," said Sailor Bill, "granny or square knot. We'll tend to that when the time comes. We may even use a hangman's noose. But first we must catch our thief. What next?"

"Anchors aweigh," said Dominick. "The *Gull-Flight* looks a proper ship. We'll stick her nose into it and lam her."

BANG, bang. Bang, bang. Bang, bang. Bang, bang. Eight bells.

The four pairs of clangs died away and the echoes rolled back and forth between the buildings on the dock side, fading gradually away to silence.

"For Heaven's sake, what's that?" cried Spinach, waked out of a sound sleep. "It sounds as though we were at sea."

* A square knot is the most common of all sea knots—and the most useful. It won't slip. A granny knot looks much the same, only it won't hold. Sailors call it a lubber knot—a granny—and sneer at it for a duffer effort. See if you can tell the difference from the sketches.—BRICK.

Katy slid down out of her bunk and looked through the porthole. They were still at the dock, and the familiar planks rose high above her head, so there was nothing to see but the green moss at the water line.

"Hurry," she said to Spinach. "We shove off this morning, and it looks as though 'this morning' would be in a minute or two. Get dressed."

The Mates fought over who would be first in the shower. Finally they compromised and had it together. Then they tore into their clothes. Underwear, socks, jumper, and skirt went on in a jiffy; but right in the middle of Katy's struggle with a knotted shoelace, came the sudden roar of the motor.

Things in the stateroom began to vibrate. Toothbrushes rattled against the sides of their mugs, and water in a glass standing on a shelf over the washstand, began to jump up and down. The glass itself began to jiggle perilously toward the edge. Spinach jumped up and made it secure in the holder. The catch on their shower door rattled and shook until Katy made that fast too. Their faces in the dressing mirror blurred as the image wavered and shook to the vibration of the ship.

When they got up on deck, both the Able-seamen were there ahead of them. But in what shape! Neither had stopped to dress, and they were both still in pajamas. Nor wash either, by the looks of them, for across Brick's nose was the same dirty streak that had been there last night, and Teddy's hair stuck up every which way.

But they were busy, hauling away and stowing below

the things that had made the *Gull-Flight* so smart during her stay at the dock. The awning was down; the carpets had been taken below and out of sight. Chairs were taken inside; cushions and shore knickknacks or anything else that might wash overboard, were stowed safely away. The after-deck began to look less like a front porch, and more like the business end of a ship.

Only two of the shore lines were left fast to the spiles along the dock edge. The others had been taken in and coiled neatly on deck. Sailor Bill was ashore, standing in the shadow of a warehouse, talking to a man in the blue uniform of a Customs Inspector. Katy saw him give the Skipper some papers and take his signature in a little book. Clearance papers, she decided. Morgan was out of sight as usual, swacking away in the engine room. But Dominick was busy on the foredeck, working away on a tangle of sheet-line that some one had flung down carelessly instead of clewing it up properly on its cleat.

There was a very decided yacht-like appearance about him this morning. Nothing of the looks of an undercover agent. All Blue Nose, and Nova Scotia deep-water man. But very natty just the same. He knew the difference between a fishing smack and a pleasure schooner, and dressed accordingly.

He had on a pair of dark blue wide-bottom sailor pants, and a wool jersey with cross stripes of lighter blue and white. Someone had worked a script in red yarn across his chest, and the name *Gull-Flight,* proclaimed to the world that here was one of her hands—Dominick of the fo'c'sle—taking a postman's vacation on the deck of a ship, and laying by a tidy sum doing it. On his head was a white, upturned gob's hat, very much like their own, only again there was the ship's name; worked in black yarn this time. A true, thrifty, salt-water man.

"Where did you get those?" asked Katy, coming up and pointing to the hat and jersey. "They weren't on board when we left Grosse Ile."

"Whist," said Dominick, "wouldn't a smart sailing craft like this have clothes for her hands? Would you be wanting me to ship aboard in a derby hat and suspenders?"

"Like the man on the freighter deck," asked Spinach, coming up and joining the two. "You know—the one who took the mail from the rowboat."

"Well, maybe it wouldn't do for you to look like a tugboat hand," said Katy. "But who struck the bells for eight o'clock? I thought that was never done till a ship was at sea, with all watches set."

"We'll be at sea," said Dominick, "as quick as a wink. As soon as the Skipper comes back aboard. And as for setting the watches—that's his job too. Before we're ever out of sight of land, he'll have the ship's company divided square in two."

"Will we be in your watch?" asked Spinach. "You know you picked us for the crew of the *Bonny*, once we're in the North Country."

"That's for the Captain to say," answered Dominick. "But never you worry now. And once we're under way, run along and get us a bite o' breakfast. It's hollow I am, from the top o' my pate to the heels of my shoes."

The skipper had finished his powwow with the man on the dock and was coming down toward them. Brick and Teddy at the forward springline, and Dominick at the other, were waiting for him. Sailor Bill ran his eye over the *Gull-Flight,* from stem to stern and up aloft at the masts, taking in decks and running gear, sails and rigging. Everything was shipshape and trim. They were ready to start.

"Cast off," he said, stepping over the rail and going aft to the wheel. "Able-seamen first, and lively aboard. We don't want to leave any of the crew on the dock."

Brick and Teddy freed their line and flung it on deck, and then made a wild scramble to get over the rail themselves. And none too soon either, for the bow had already begun to swing away from the dock.

"All right, Dominick," said the Skipper. "You next." Then, "Half ahead, Mr. Chief Engineer."

The *Gull-Flight* headed out into the river—off for the North. Sailor Bill straightened her up and gave the wheel to Katy. "You can handle her alone for a bit," he said. "Stay in mid-stream. There'll be a bend to the northwest in a minute."

"Spinach! Start some coffee. Make a few pieces of toast, and fry some bacon. It's catch-as-catch-can, this morning."

Katy had the after-deck pretty much to herself. Everyone else was busy with this and that, moving about on

the foredeck and getting ready to make sail. Brick and
Teddy had been chased below to get dressed.

"What do you think this is?" said Sailor Bill. "A
pajama parade? Get some clothes on—warm ones too.
When that wind off the lake hits you, you'll think you're
at the North Pole."

There *was* a chill in the air this morning. Even though
it was bright and sunny. A few white clouds chased each
other along, sharp against the hard blue of the sky. The
water in the river looked cold and a bit sullen, in spite of
the sunlight that sparkled off the waves and whitecaps
that were beginning to make up. And the wind certainly
did have a sting in it. Occasional bursts of spray slapped
over the bow and flung all the way aft, pelting the Mate's
face with hard bullets that made her eyes smart and
water.

The *Gull-Flight's* engine began to pound, coughing
and grunting at the hard going, for they had entered the
Port Huron rapids. Water swirled past their sides, but
the shores stood almost still as they clawed up against
the current. With the wind dead ahead of them and the
ship hardly moving, now was a good time to get up sail.
Spinach came back to help with the wheel.

"Keep her where she is," said Sailor Bill to the girls.
"We'll have our hands full with the canvas. A reef will
have to go in both the fore and mainsails. And one jib
will be more than enough."

Everyone else bore a hand. Tying in reef points was a
new experience for the Able-seamen, but they stuck at it

and worked away willingly. Brick and Dominick had the foresail and the Skipper and Teddy the main. Finally after some skinned knuckles and broken fingernails, a furl of canvas lay lashed tightly along both booms, shortening down the sail area nearly a third.

Their big Marconi main went up first, flapping and banging in an alarming way.

"The wind's getting stiffer," said Katy, a little nervously.

"It certainly is," said Spinach, ducking her head to avoid a dowse of spray.

Even with the sheet hauled flat, the leech of the sail cracked and snapped in rifle-like reports. Behind them on the after-deck the blocks worried the travellers, slamming and hammering as the strain tightened and then suddenly eased off. The other sails added to the racket as they went up.

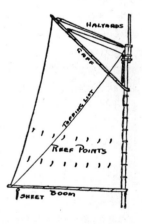

Katy noticed they were going a little faster. She could tell that by the increased pace with which the banks slipped by. But the water wasn't any smoother even though they had gotten over the rapids. And the thrum of the wind in the standing rigging, and the thrash of the sheets in their blocks, made a really terrifying noise. Sailor Bill cupped his hands and bawled back an order to her.

"Fort Gratiot Ranges," he yelled. "North by East, when you close them up."

The new course gave the wind some bearing on the sails so they filled and strained off to starboard, heeling the ship slightly. The thrashing and banging around stopped, and everything was steady again.

"You can even hear yourself think," said Katy to herself.

And though they were too close on the wind for real sailing, the engine helped them point up a little, and they bowled along well enough. Water sloshed past their lee rail and bubbled astern to a wake disturbed and uneasy, in the churn of the propeller.

They fairly shot past Point Edward, and suddenly they were in the lake, free and clear of the confining shores and narrows of the river. It was like coming into a wide sunny country from out of a choked city street. The great reach of water danced and sparkled before them—nearly three hundred miles of it—stretching away to the north. Land on both sides faded to thin edges in the distance, swallowed at last by sky and water on the horizon's rim. Giant freighters dwindled to specks and disappeared, leaving only smudges of smoke on the sky—hull down and lost to sight.

But this north wind—it worried Sailor Bill a little. There was too much of it for one thing, and it was always tricky at this time of year. Right now it was trying its best to kick up a sea. If it hauled a little to the east, they would have it dead ahead for their hundred-and-sixty mile course to Cove Island Passage. And too much of a haul either way—east or west—meant a real blow at this season.

And the crew, he thought to himself, well, possibly you might not call them exactly green, but you wouldn't say they were old hands either. However, there was Dominick. No kind of lake gale should bother him.

Dominick didn't seem to be bothered by anything either, as he moved to and fro on the foredeck. He was giving Brick and Teddy some orders about some odds and ends of straightening up, and herding them around and seeing to it that the Able-seamen carried them out.

Sailor Bill called him aft. "Rig the log," he said. "We'll bear away on our course when we come abreast of the Lake Huron Lightship. That should be about ten o'clock."

LIGHTSHIP

With the wind almost dead ahead and the engine full on, the *Gull-Flight* crept up on the lightship. There was some buck and pitch and more than a bit of spray flying, but the ship had almost no heel and very little pull to the wheel. The trick at steering under these conditions didn't take much doing so Katy and Spinach had plenty of chance to look around. Both were interested in the lightship for neither had seen one at close quarters before.

There was a short stumpy mast with a beacon at the top, something like an old-fashioned street light on the end of a pole. And the pole was doing queer things, swinging and swaying as though trying to cut figure eights across the sky. The light in the beacon flashed off and on in a regular pattern; bright for one second and eclipsed for two—bright for one more second, then eclipsed for six. Much like a mirror would flash in the sun, blinding in the eyes for an instant and then away again.

A young man was leaning over the rail of the lightship watching the schooner coming up astern.

He waved his hand. Sailor Bill waved back.

"Where away?" asked the young man.

"Cove Island Passage," answered Sailor Bill.

The young man didn't say anything for a minute. He looked as though he wanted to offer some advice, and then thought better of it. Probably he had been snubbed before by dog-barking* skippers who had resented any suggestions. But Captain Williams was too good a sailor to ignore advice from anyone familiar with local waters and weather conditions.

---

* *A Dog-barking Skipper.*—A scornful term used by blue-water men for captains of coastwise vessels. The idea being, that they won't go far enough from land to lose the sound of farmers' dogs barking on the shore.—KATY.

"Think the wind'll hold steady?" he called across the stretch of water separating the two vessels.

"I doubt it," said the lightship tender. "It's more apt to haul to the east. That'll be bad for your course to Cove Island. And I'd use the glasses, if I were you. I wouldn't be surprised to see the storm-warning signals go up any minute."

"Thank you," said Sailor Bill. "I'll keep my eye peeled."

"You've a tight little ship there," said the man. "She *should* be able to weather almost anything."

Before long Katy and Spinach began to have trouble with the wheel. They weren't able to hold the ship up on her course. She kept falling away to the east. Sailor Bill had one eye on the compass and the other on the set of the sails. When they were on their true course the sails no longer filled, and the luffs in both fore and mainsail began to slacken and flutter. The Skipper and Dominick trimmed the sheets a bit flatter. That helped some, but not for long. Soon the spilling of the wind began again. During the next hour they only made three miles, trying to buck the head wind and sailing too close in their effort to hold the true course.

"Wind's hauling," said the Skipper. "Ease her off a little."

The Mates gave on the wheel a bit, and the compass card swung toward the east.

"Hold her there for a minute," said Sailor Bill. "What's your course?"

"Northeast, by North," said Katy.

The Skipper eyed the sails, squinted at the compass, and sniffed the wind.

"Let her fall away some more," he said after a minute. "There's plenty of room out here. Try Northeast. She'll be easier that way. My watch is about to go on, and it will be the Able-seamen's first trick at the wheel. We don't want to make it too hard for them."

The wind kept freshening, but it didn't steady. It moved constantly around toward the east. Once more in the few minutes left in their watch, Dominick and Morgan had to trim in on the sails. Katy and Spinach had their hands full, and Brick and Teddy spent all their time aft watching them at the wheel and sizing up their every move. They were studying the knack of easy give and take to the puffs of wind that grew stronger every minute. By the time they were due to go on watch, they thought they had it all figured out.

"Twelve o'clock, noon," sang out Dominick suddenly. "Relieve the watch. Strike the bells. Read the glass and log."

Brick stepped to the wheel.

"What's the course?" he asked as he took over.

"Northeast," said Katy.

"Northeast it is," said Brick.

But it wasn't quite so easy as it looked. Inside a few minutes their wake looked like a corkscrew, yawing in crazy streaks behind them. Sailor Bill didn't say anything, but he stood close by to lend a hand if necessary.

After a bit the Able-seamen caught the knack of it, and their wake straightened out.

"Nothing to it," he said to Katy.

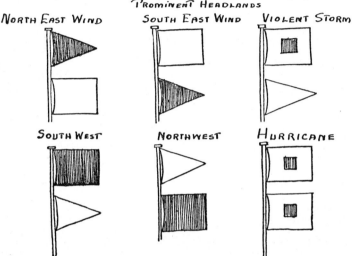

STORM WARNINGS

THESE SIGNALS ARE DISPLAYED AT ALL COASTAL TOWNS AND PROMINENT HEADLANDS

NORTH EAST WIND   SOUTH EAST WIND   VIOLENT STORM

SOUTH WEST   NORTHWEST   HURRICANE

But if he had known what was going to happen during the next four hours, he wouldn't have been half so sure of himself.

CHAPTER IX

STORM OFF KETTLE SHOALS

THE STARBOARD watch didn't go below. There was too much to do for that. "Everybody stay on deck," commanded Sailor Bill. "I don't know what's coming, but we'd better get ready for it. Batten down for a storm."

Dominick took the Mates and the Chief Engineer forward. The anchors got their attention first, and were secured more tightly still with an extra turn of heavy line. The cover to the fore hatch was clamped fast and a stout piece of canvas lashed over the combing. The saloon windows were locked and all the catches tried to see there was no chance of their blowing open. Gyp ran around excitedly, until they dumped him below without ceremony.

"Poor little dog," said Katy. "He doesn't know what it's all about."

"He's better curious than washed overboard," said Dominick.

Spinach was sent down into the cabin to shut all the portholes. "Don't leave a one open," said Dominick. "It may make things a little stuffy, but that's better than having a sea come in and lie down in your bunk."

The saloon door was shuttered tight, the deck lights closed and fastened, and all the ventilators trimmed aft. Katy and the Blue Nose worked away on the falls of the boat davits, pulling the seizings taut and securing them with an extra bit of marline. The canvas covers on the *Bonny* and the dinghy were looked to, and their lashings checked. At the top of the companion stairs was a pair of watertight swing doors, with patent fastenings. These were swung to, so that even if the navigating quarters were swamped and the charthouse flooded, no seas could get below into the cabin.

"You'd better take a look at your engine," said Sailor Bill to Morgan. "We may have to use it without a minute's warning, and we want to be sure it won't stall."

"It won't," said Morgan. "There's a motor you can depend on."

But he went below to have a look at it all the same. Katy didn't envy him going into that hot smelly engine room, with its stinks of gasoline and oil—away from the fresh air and the clean smell of the wind and the sting and brace of flying spray. She had heard about people being seasick, and had always thought it a rather silly business; one that a true Mate with salt behind her ears didn't give way to. Now she wasn't so sure. She felt a little squeamish and green around the gills, even out here on deck in the sunshine and cool of the wind. Her mouth watered unpleasantly, and she swallowed hard.

Brick and Teddy were having a hard time of it at the wheel. The wind was getting around ahead of them again, and though the sails had been trimmed flat as they would go, they were at their old trick of spilling the wind. Time had slipped quickly by, and soon it would be two o'clock. Only two hours since they had been forced to change course and now it looked as though they couldn't even hold what they had. Sailor Bill gave the Able-seamen an order and they eased off on the wheel, falling away down wind. The Skipper and Dominick payed out the sheet lines, and the *Gull-Flight* heeled over and gathered speed to the new pull on the sails. Katy went up to the compass to have a look.

"Due East," she said to herself. "Wind's hauled quarter way 'round. We'll never get to Cove Island if this keeps up."

There wasn't much of a sea as yet, but their new course put them pretty much in its trough. The ship took on a slithering weaving motion. With a rail buried, they would slide down the slope of one roller; only to shudder up the side of another, burying the opposite rail. The horizon swayed and rocked in a dizzy crazy manner.

Morgan suddenly appeared on deck. His face had a particularly unhealthy look—a grayish dirty green, and his eyes were glassy. Katy started to say something to him and then thought better of it. He wasn't looking at her—rather through her—as though not quite able to focus on the exact spot where she stood, and staring vacantly out to sea. Spinach burst through the charthouse doors right behind him. She too had a faraway look, and put out her hand uncertainly, groping for something to hang onto.

Then the stricken Mate and the Chief Engineer caught sight of each other. They could focus now all right, and it was too much for them. Both made a rush for the lee side and leaned over the rail.

Binocular

"Don't look," said the Skipper to Katy. "Come up here instead—but first get the binoculars from the charthouse rack."

Tucking the powerful spyglass under her arm, Katy went forward. Sailor Bill was looking off to port, up the lake, over its miles of uneasy water that were beginning to be troubled into an angry sea. She hurried past the seasick members of the crew with an averted head, her own stomach acting in a very uncertain manner.

Soon Morgan straightened up. He threw back his head and closed his eyes, gulping the fresh air in great sobs. The color flooded back to his cheeks, and in a minute more he was all right. Then he went aft down the deck; a little wavery about the knees and shaky on his pins, but on his feet nevertheless, and ready for whatever came next.

Not so with Spinach. Collapsed over the rail, one convulsive heave followed another in wretched succession. She turned a miserable tear-stained face toward her sister Mate.

"I'm sorry," called Katy. "But I daren't stay and talk. I'm all right—yet. But I don't know for how long."

The day was still bright and sunny, and so far, there hadn't been many clouds. But the wind was getting stronger all the time, and blowing from the northeast. A mounting bank of clouds was climbing the horizon and coming down toward them over the great north reach of the lake. The top was fleecy, and shot with silver; the sun's rays streaking through it. Below the shining tip of the bank were masses of clouds, sullen and ominous. A bright line of whitecaps drove before the teeth of the squall.

"Look through your glass at that freighter," said Sailor Bill. "That's what we're going to get before long."

About halfway between the cloud bank and the *Gull-Flight,* a freighter was making her way south—perhaps twelve or fifteen miles off. Katy fiddled with the focus on the telescope until the vessel, blurred and dim to the naked eye, leaped into sharp outline through the powerful lenses. Spray flung high over her pilothouse, and waves raced along the great length of her deck. The smoke from her stack streaked away to starboard, rolling out in a greasy black smudge and hugging the water closely.

"Uncle Bill," said Katy, a little frightened. "That's a terrible storm. Won't that freighter get into trouble?"

"No," said the Skipper; "she's all right. And there isn't more wind than we can take either. But you've missed the point. It's the direction of the wind that worries me. It's swung around due east."

"What does that mean?" asked Katy. "That we have to change course again? We've done that before—twice in the last two hours."

"That's just it," said Sailor Bill. "We can't change course again. Except to come about and head straight up the lake—come over here."

They went across the plunging deck and looked off to starboard.

"Now use your glass," said the Skipper—"over there." He pointed forward a little, toward a distant shore line.

Again Katy fussed and fretted with the focus on the binocular. About ten miles off, a point ran out into the lake. Waves were breaking around it, and toward them two or three miles out, was a seething and a surging, and a tossing about of the swells that were rolling toward the beach. Occasional bursts of spray flung high, and glittered in the sunshine.

"What is it?" asked Katy anxiously.

"Kettle Shoals," said Sailor Bill. "And with what's coming—too close on our lee for comfort."

"What shall we do?" asked Katy. "We can't keep on falling off down wind. That's just being chased around in a circle."

"A circle that would fetch us up on dry land," said the Skipper, "or crack us up rather, on those shoals."

Katy didn't answer. There wasn't anything to say.

She looked through the glass again at the boiling and sucking turmoil over the bar off Kettle Point. It was nearer now—a menace of angry sea and shelving sand. A graveyard for the stoutest ship, and disaster for her crew.

"In the meantime shall we keep on as we are?" asked Katy.

"Yes," said the Skipper. "And there's plenty to do to get ready."

Everything on the *Gull-Flight* had been battened down and made secure as possible. But even with a reef in both sails, the ship was still carrying too much canvas. The Able-seamen luffed up a little, and the foresail came down with a run. Its furls were made tight, and extra lashings were passed around the boom to keep it from thrashing or slamming about.

Under one jib and the reefed mainsail the schooner made along uneasily. There was a terrific pull and drag on the wheel. As she climbed a roller her stern almost kicked free of the water; and then as she slid down the other side, green seas tried to come aboard over the stern. The four arms of Brick and Teddy were no more than enough to keep her from yawing, or even from broaching to.

There was nothing to do now but wait—an anxious crew on a troubled ship. Oilskins were served out to all hands. Katy questioned the order with an inquiring glance toward Sailor Bill.

"Raise an umbrella in the sunshine?"

"You'll need 'em," said the Skipper. "What with shipped seas and half a cloudburst—and maybe a whack of hail."

The bank of clouds that Katy had first noticed to the northward, had swung around and was almost dead ahead of them. It was bearing down only a little off their port bow, and was terribly near. A low slate-colored ceiling like the roof of a cave swept toward them, blotting out the bright of the day. There was a green streak, clear and sharp between the gray of the sky and the leaden floor of the water. It was tearing down on them, and driving a crest of whitecaps before it in a long line.

The wind increased, but held steady.

She looked over toward the shore on their lee. A great stretch of sandy beach smoked and curled as the dunes whipped and fled before the gale. Gnarled and tortured pines curved and bowed as their branches twisted and writhed in the wind.

The fangs of Kettle Shoals were bared now. Waves seethed and dashed over them, breaking into clouds of flying spray and swirling wash that tossed and swayed to the great rollers that roared by on either side. A flock of gulls streamed past, screaming down wind.

Then suddenly the wind stopped.

Katy took a long breath and let it out again. Would the rest of the crew hear her beating heart?

In the stillness of the calm, the turmoil on all sides seemed separate and detached from their life aboard ship.

As though it had nothing to do with them—nor would have any effect. The sturdy rock that was the *Gull-Flight,* and the protecting arm of the splendid seamanship of her command would carry them safely through.

The crest of whitecaps with their tossing manes came galloping down on them.

Sailor Bill jumped for the wheel, knocking the two boys away.

"Hang on, everybody," he called.

For a second the sails flapped idly. Captain Williams twirled the spokes, throwing the wheel hard to port; and the bow came slowly around. Then the squall hit them. The jib and mainsail slammed over together and filled with a loud report. The schooner heeled, and buried her lee rail. Water sloshed along the sides of her deckhouses.

Then with a great bound, and under the full force of the blast, the ship dashed off on her new course.

A pother of water hurtled aboard—half rain, half sea. The sun and sky were blotted out in a sulphurous twilight, with low clouds driving across the mastheads in a haze of mist. Brick and Teddy crouched under the lee of the charthouse—a huddle of frightened boys and drenching spray. Sailor Bill at the wheel gripped the spokes savagely, throwing his weight against them and fighting the storm. With legs apart, and braced against the slant of the deck and drag of the ship, he stood there— a very Viking in the midst of the hiss and smother of flying spray. Foam and spume streamed off his oilskins and spread out down wind in runnels of flying water.

The schooner righted herself and tore along, spurning the seas behind her in a tossing wake. A volley of bullet-like hail spattered off the sails and pelted the deckhouses.

A loud crack made the boys look up. In coming about, the wind had caught under the canvas cover of the dinghy. It ballooned up, tugging and pulling at its lashings, and trying to tear the boat clear of the davits and carry it away. Suddenly it split down the middle and the severed halves stood out straight, thrashing and snapping in the wind. Dominick and Morgan made their way along the high side of the deck toward it, a pair of dripping clawing figures; prevailing somehow against the sea and wind, and helping each other with an outstretched hand and a grip on whatever was handy.

"Cut it loose!" bawled Sailor Bill. "And pass another line around the dinghy."

The two slashed and cut with their sheath knives and soon the torn cover whipped clear, sailing away over the ship in a tangled kite of slit canvas and snarled rope ends. With the new line in his teeth the Blue Nose climbed the rail; hanging on with both hands,—clothes flapping and slapping against the dinghy and almost tearing from his body. The end of the line was passed over the small boat to Morgan inboard, and then back and around again, and finally turned about the stand of the davits and made fast.

The first fury of the storm was over and the *Gull-Flight* had come through it with no damage but the split boat cover. In its veer to the east, the wind had lashed the lake into a wicked cross chop. The tops of the rollers came to an undeveloped crest and never had a chance to break. The gale picked them up bodily and flung them in horizontal streams of water that stung and burned when they hit. But things began to steady, even if on a slant; and Brick and Teddy crept back to the wheel. The Skipper gave it over to them, and stood by watching their brave struggles with the spokes. He laid a comforting hand on each of their shoulders.

"Stay with it," he said. "True salt-water men. There's nothing to it now. Keep her on her course. You've the whole lake out ahead of you."

But what of the Mates?

With the qualms in her own stomach not quite under control, Katy wasn't sure enough of herself to stop and comfort the seasick Spinach. Nevertheless she kept an eye on her, and when the crest of the squall was about down on them, she clawed back along the rail and grabbed her by the arm. When the lull came, and in the minute when Sailor Bill jumped for the wheel to put the *Gull-Flight* about, she half dragged—half prodded her sister Mate aft to the charthouse doors.

Spinach protested feebly.

"Let me alone! Let me alone!" she cried wretchedly. Her knees bent and her head wobbled from side to side.

"We've got to get below," said Katy. "Out of the way. Now. While there's a chance."

Supporting her cousin under the arms, Katy backed through the watertight doors at the top of the companion stairs. In some way or other she managed to fasten the doors behind her and lugged the limp Spinach into the cabin below. There she laid her on the day bed at the end of the table, where she collapsed utterly.

The silence in the cabin was a distinct shock. As the doors closed behind her, the scream of the wind and the thrum of the rigging were instantly cut off. They became remote and far away. It was a relief to escape. But gradually she became aware of the internal noises of the ship. There were muffled crackings, groans, squeaks, the swish of water along the keel, the gurgle and choke of the bilge, and the bubble and rush of water in the storage tanks. Confused as the noise was, there was a rhythm to it. A repetition and a stop—a continuing and a further pause. It went on—the unpredictable pulse of a driving ship.

The floor tilted down to where she sat. Then it was away again, slanting in the other direction. The curtains over the closed portholes on the opposite side of the cabin swayed away from the windows and stood straight out. The next minute they were nuzzled by the ship's wall. A towel on one of the racks in the galley was behaving queerly, as though it had a will of its own and could disobey the laws of gravity. It pointed out of the porthole over the range, and refused to hang limply toward the floor as it should. Katy had a detached lonely feeling, as though these things could go on about her, but be connected with her in no definite way. She held her cousin's hand and mopped her forehead with a cool moist cloth. The seasick Spinach was her only hold on reality, and her care became a grateful grasp on sanity in an otherwise detached and dimly unreal world.

She got up and went to freshen the damp towel with cold water, and was surprised to find that her legs wobbled at the knees and were strangely weak. She was dizzy but not sick, that is, not sick in the sense that Spinach was. She was able to continue, going through the motions of being nurse.

Time wore on. The straining and creaking lessened, and on the new course the cabin floor became a gentler hill, and walking to and fro across it less like trying to scale an upright wall. The faraway wail of the wind became faint. But gradually there came a steady roll into the drive of the ship. There was a twisting and turning action now—a writhe in the timbers—and her stomach indignantly rebelled. She stumbled to her stateroom and was violently sick. She clung desperately to the handrail, her eyes watering and tears streaming down her cheeks. After a few minutes she felt better.

A sharp spear of light pierced the gloom of the cabin as the companion doors were flung open, and Dominick came down the stairs. She heard him speak softly to Spinach, urging her to go out on deck. There were some feeble squeaks of protest and then the shuffling of feet going back up the stairs. The doors slammed to again and the gloom of the cabin darkened about her once more, in a comfortable sympathetic pall.

She was glad of that. For she was sick again, and ashamed of it. She who had been so dependable, so alert—a backbone of moral support for the rest of the crew. And now to be helpless like this.

The cabin brightened again as Dominick came back down. He went to her, where she was hanging desperately to the handrail.

"There," he said, putting his arm around her. "You'll be better in a minute. And it's a brave girl you are—looking after your cousin, and staying on your feet, and getting the both of you below and out of the way. But wouldn't it be the right thing now, to come up above and let the sun and wind blow all the sick away?"

"What time is it?" asked Katy a little tearfully.

"There's a half hour before you go on watch," said Dominick. "The storm's over and we've the foresail back up, and there's a fine breeze, with maybe a dowse of spray now and again to freshen you up."

"It's silly to be so useless at a time like this," said Katy.

"Come now," said Dominick, "it's anything but useless you've been. And before it comes four o'clock, there's plenty of time to stomp around the deck and get your sea legs again."

"But I'm so ashamed," said Katy.

"It's many a year I've been to sea," said Dominick. "And it's many a tar too, that I've seen hit the bunk the minute we cleared the harbor. You've nothing to be ashamed of. Would you like to be hearing a secret?"

"What kind of a secret?" asked Katy.

"When we were coming about on the new course," said Dominick, "and the *Gull-Flight* slithered away in the trough of the sea, it's a quick look I had around. When I found no one was looking—well over the rail . . ."

"You mean you were sick too?" said Katy, brightening up a little.

If a real salt-water man like Dominick couldn't stand it either, why maybe she wasn't such a landlubber after all.

"Yes," said the Blue Nose. "I was. But come on now. Up topside with you."

THE storm had passed them by—blown away to the southwest. The bank of clouds, so black, so solid, so ominous an hour before, was rent and split into jagged patterns, torn and harried to the horizon's edge by the same wind that had flung it down on them. Blue sky gleamed through its ragged patches, and a perfect rainbow arched its promise of fair days and pleasant weather to come. The lake seemed joyous at its own relief, and danced and sparkled in the afternoon sun. There was a lift and swing to the billows of its now mild and easy seas, and the *Gull-Flight* flew along over them, dipping and prancing, and tossing them behind her in a smooth untroubled wake. There was a good stiff breeze, steady and strong from the northeast. It hummed and sang in the rigging— a chant of contentment at the freedom of the open lake reaching on and on ahead of them.

When eight bells were struck, the starboard watch was on its feet, able and eager once more. Both Mates had recovered and their hour of trouble and despair seemed but an evil dream. They took the wheel. The reefs were shaken out of the fore and mainsails and the full expanse of canvas bellied in white clouds, high above their heads. The main jib was bent on its halyard and sheeted home. It filled with a crack, and the *Gull-Flight* answered the added draw and pull by burying her lee rail and taking a bone in her teeth. Her bow wave curled and foamed, and swished past her sides, bubbling and gurgling around the rudder post in a merry chuckle—the sweet song of a ship sailing her best.

Everyone stayed on deck enjoying the fine of the afternoon but keeping busy nevertheless. The dinghy was half full of water—rain and shipped seas—and had to be bailed out. Then a new canvas cover was cut, fitted, and lashed down tight. Ventilators were trimmed forward and the deck-light covers propped up again. Dominick went down to open the ports in the cabin, and the Able-seamen let him do it without offering to help. Neither wanted to risk going below after what had happened to the Mates and the Chief Engineer. The clean breeze blew through, airing out the dank corners and stodge between decks, and sweetening the living quarters to the fresh varnishy smell that is the right of every sailing ship.

Katy and Spinach relieved each other every hour. A trick at the wheel—a spell of lounging idly by. Bells were struck regularly again, and the glass and log read and the proper notations made on the chart. They were doing swimmingly—piling the knots behind them hour after hour in a great northerly tack. The joy and thrill of being at sea was theirs again.

Just before seven o'clock Dominick went below and started the fire for the making of their supper.

"Fit the fiddles!" called Sailor Bill after him. "I don't want the soup in my lap."

"Here," he added to Spinach and Katy, "you Mates are cooks again. The whole ship's about starved out."

The fire in the galley range sang and roared and glowed to a white heat. The ship had a cant to port, and the cabin table tipped like a toboggan slide. No dish would set safely on it. But there was a way to remedy that. Damp towels were laid across the boards so they were anything but slippery. Then the fiddles were clamped down over them.

Fiddles at sea have nothing to do with musical instruments. They are detachable wooden frames, in a sort of lattice-work pattern, that divide up a table into small sections, so that when a dish slides as the ship rolls, it can't slide far.

"Baby trays," said Brick when he first saw them. "One for each of us."

The port watch was fed first and Brick and Teddy tucked it in, keeping a fearful eye on the clock and afraid that eight bells would strike before they were full up. For at that time they would have to take over the wheel and be on steering trick until midnight. But they finished their meal all right and followed Sailor Bill up the companion stairs. Katy and Spinach cleared the table and set it again, and after a few minutes, Dominick and Morgan came down. The starboard watch had their meal together and Dominick wound up even with the boards, eating enough to make two complete dinners. So the one he fed the fish could hardly be called a loss.

"And how do you like life at sea?" he asked the girls a little later.

"Wonderful," said Spinach. "Except for that seasick business."

"Now, now," said Dominick, "you mustn't mind that. It's the way we make a true salt-water man."

"A fresh-water storm did enough to us," said Katy.

It was getting dark and the cabin lights were turned on. The galley range glowed away cheerfully, pleasantly warm in the sharp chill of the evening. Dishes were washed and stowed away in the china lockeer. A pot of coffee was put at Dominick's elbow, and a bowl of raisins, dates and nuts placed on the table. The Blue Nose lit his pipe and all three of them sat around—peacefully quiet and comfortably relaxed after the trouble and work of the day. The *Gull-Flight* drove along in great easy swings, with only a slight roll, but with considerable heel to port. Overhead was the creak of the rigging, and the stretch and groan of boom and halyard answering the pull of the wind in the sails. A wash of water gurgled and slipped by the sides in a musical drone. A stronger puff than usual tilted the cabin floor to a slant, and the fruit bowl slid down the table and was only grabbed in time to save it from falling.

"I'd better fit the berth rails in the starboard state-rooms," said Dominick. "It's a bad fall you could take, when you're sound asleep."

Katy got up to help, and soon hers and Teddy's bunks were railed in, safe to any roll of the ship. It was a long ways from the top berth to the cabin floor.

"To bed with you now," said Dominick.

"Already?" asked Katy. "It's only nine o'clock."

"You're on watch at midnight," said Dominick, "and three hours snooze won't hurt you any. Skip along now. A true sailor never misses a chance to get some sleep."

"Will you call us?" asked Spinach. "We'd hate to be late for our first night watch at sea."

"Never a fear," said Dominick. "I can't sail her alone in the pitch dark."

CHAPTER X

THE SWARM of bees zoomed and buzzed to the attack. If she could only get over that board fence, Katy was sure she could escape. But something was the matter with one of her legs. It ached and burned and she knew she couldn't run on it, even though she might be able to climb the fence. The bees came nearer and the buzzing grew fearfully louder. Terrified, she broke into a cold sweat and tried to scream. Then she woke up.

The swarming of the bees was the buzz of an alarm clock that Spinach had hidden under her pillow, and the board fence was the storm railing Dominick had fitted to the berth the night before. The tilt of the bunk to the driving ship had rolled her against its sharp edge, putting a welt down one arm and cutting off the circulation in her leg so that it tingled and hurt. She snapped on the light over her head and yelled at Spinach. It was twenty minutes before midnight.

"Wake up," she called. "And turn off that alarm clock. They'll think we're both dead in here."

"Why! What's the matter?" said Spinach coming to

163

suddenly, and reaching under her pillow to still the clamor of the clock.

"It's time we were up," said Katy. "Hurry and dress. We have to go on watch at twelve."

For once their clothes were laid out where they could find them without having to hunt around for a missing shoe or sock. In a jiffy they were dressed and out in the cabin. Dominick was already there, with a cup of coffee in one hand and a huge sandwich in the other. He nodded approvingly.

"Good for you," he said. "That's turning out for your watch. I was just going to call you."

Spinach didn't say anything about the alarm clock having failed to arouse her, and Katy didn't give her away. Both girls looked curiously around, for the familiar cabin looked altogether different than it had even a few hours ago. It seemed a sort of dark and gloomy cavern with the floor on a slant. Most of the lights were turned out, and the few that were lit struggled feebly to shine through towels draped around them. The curtains were drawn over the portholes, so that no cabin light could escape to blind the helmsman's eyes in the dark of the night. The three of them standing there cast weird and wavery shadows that fled and swung to the rise and fall of the ship.

But in the galley was the red and comfortable glow of the range, and the cheerful song of the kettle boiling away on its top.

"There's cold meat set out," said Dominick. "Suppose you slice some bread and make a pot of cocoa. Have it ready for the watch that's coming off. Stay below and have something to eat with them. I'll take the wheel till you're on deck."

The eight bells for midnight rang out and the Blue Nose disappeared up the companion stairs. In a few minutes Morgan and the Able-seamen came down. They made a dive for the sandwiches and cocoa, not even stopping to take off their peacoats. For a while all were too busy to talk—and then . . .

"We steered nearly all our watch," said Teddy with a rush. His voice was somewhat muffled, trying to escape from a mouth stuffed with sandwich.

"It's scary at first—in the dark," said Brick over the edge of his cocoa mug.

"It makes you sort of dizzy," said Teddy. "Staring into the binnacle—and sleepy too."

"But after a while you learn to pick out a star and steer by that," said Brick. "Mine was the Pole Star, and I kept it just over the crosstrees on our foremast."

The doors at the top of the companion way flung open and Sailor Bill came down the stairs. He threw off his greatcoat and looked eagerly at the remains of the midnight lunch on the table. Finally he picked out a slice of beef and placed it carefully between two slabs of bread. Katy went into the galley to get him a cup of hot coffee.

"You two had enough?" he asked the boys. "If so, to bed with you. It's only four hours before you have to stand the next watch. Skip along now."

The Able-seamen crammed down another sandwich and departed for their bunks.

"What's the weather like?" said Katy, coming back with the hot coffee.

"Blowy," said the Skipper. "But still from the northeast."

"We've been making knots," said Morgan. "She's a flyer, is the *Gull-Flight*—even without the engine."

"You and your engine," said Spinach.

"Well, you'll have to admit it was handy at times," said Sailor Bill. "But up topside with you now. You mustn't make Dominick stand his watch alone."

It was dark on deck—black as the inside of a hat. But as their eyes grew accustomed to the night, the Mates began to make out the familiar outlines of deck and rigging. First the masthead light in a luminous ceiling of faint glow, reflecting the sails in sheets of silvery canvas against the dark water. Then the red and green triangles from their port and starboard running lights; the tops of the waves spilling and tumbling through them in colored froth as they fled astern. The deckhouses were but masses of shadowy bulk, and a stab of yellow shone off into the night through an open chartroom port. Aft at the wheel was the glow of Dominick's pipe, a red spark in front of a face that hung detached from its body, and swam without visible support in the wan glow of the binnacle light. In the dark behind them, their wake spread away in faint luminous specks.

Katy took the wheel.

"Don't let the night bother you," said Dominick. "Once you get the feel of the wheel, it's just like daytime steering. The course is North by West."

"North by West it is," said Katy in a confident voice.

But she wasn't so sure when she got the spokes in her grasp. She missed the familiar sweep of sky and water against the rim of the horizon. And the compass wouldn't behave either. The line at the back of the bowl showed North —now Northwest—and then North again as the ship yawed back and forth. The sails spilled the wind and their leeches flapped. Dominick helped her out.

"See that rag hanging from the mainmast stay," he said. "Keep it blowing inboard. When it points over your left shoulder, you've got the wind and course about right."

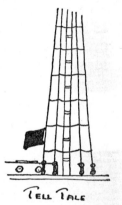

Tell Tale

Katy looked up.

About ten feet above the deck someone had tied a white handkerchief to the starboard afterstay of the mainmast. It was in such a position that the light from the charthouse window picked it out sharply against the black of the night. There it fluttered bravely, a telltale for the direction of the wind. Katy moved the wheel a little until it pointed about over her left shoulder. Then she glanced down at the compass. They were on their true course and the sails were nicely filled. That much accomplished, she looked around for Brick's star. There it was, a little off the starboard bow; a shining spot twinkling over the foremast truck.

"Guide on me," it seemed to say. "Many's the mariner I've showed to a safe harbor."

Two bells were struck—one o'clock. Spinach relieved her Sister Mate at the wheel and Katy and Dominick read the log. Then they went into the charthouse. The sailor did some figuring and finally made a pencil point on the chart. This he connected up to a long black line that crept ever on from the shoals of Kettle Point, far behind. The long black line represented eighty miles of course worked astern.

"Where are we now?" asked Katy.

"Off Saginaw Bay," said Dominick.

There was a wide stretch of open water at this point, nearly two hundred miles of it, and the northeast wind had a good sweep. It piled the waves down in great rollers that swept hissing by to lose themselves far away in the shoals and marshes of the bay. The *Gull-Flight* swung along, tossing spray high in red and green mists, the reflection of their running lights. They were doing about ten knots an hour.

But Dominick seemed to be disturbed about something, and was pacing the deck uneasily. His figure would be lost in the gloom as he went forward, and then outlined sharply as he came aft to squint at the compass. He spent a good deal of time searching off to the northeast, his eyes boring over the dark water. After a bit he hauled in on the sheet lines, trimming the sails flatter. The breeze was stiff but getting somewhat puffy.

"What's the matter?" asked Katy. Dominick's fidgets were giving her the jumps too.

"Wind's hauling again," said the Blue Nose.

"Oh, dear," said Katy. "Another session like the one off Kettle Shoals?"

"No. The wind's only swinging back to the northwest. That's where it should be this time of year. I'm glad it's held steady this long. We've come a long ways up the lake. But would you like to be hearing another secret?"

"What sort this time? Don't tell me you've been sick again?"

The sailor laughed. "No," he said; "this is a real one— just between you and me. The Skipper doesn't know it yet."

Katy wasn't sure that it would be exactly right to have anything between her and another member of the crew and keep it from Sailor Bill. She said so to Dominick.

"Oh, he'll know it quick enough. The minute he comes on for the next watch."

"What is it then?" asked Katy, relieved now, and eager to hear the news.

"The morning we left Sarnia," said Dominick, "I was sure the wind would do just what it did. Only I didn't expect such a squall. And I knew we could never lay a course direct to Cove Island Passage and sail it on through. And I knew too that as the wind swung back to the north-east it would take us far up the lake. And I hoped that it would haul farther—to the north—sometime in the night."

"Well?" said Katy.

"That's just what it's doing," said Dominick. "And we're only about forty miles from Thunder Bay. In a few minutes we are going to change course and put in there."

"Without the Skipper knowing it," said Katy.

"He won't blame us when he does," said Dominick.

"But what's the secret?"

"There's a Coast Guard station there," said the undercover agent. "And I wired Joe College to let me know where we can meet him. We don't want to be barging all over the North Country asking for him. That would be giving us away entirely."

"You're full of plots," said Katy. "But most of them seem to work out."

"It's the better it will be, if we can meet Joe with nobody the wiser. What do you say? Shall we bear in and see if there's a message?"

"All right," said Katy. "But we must tell the Skipper the minute he comes on deck."

"Northwest by West," said Dominick to Spinach, giving her the new course.

The wheel was put over to port. "Dead on," said Spinach a few seconds later.

Dominick and Katy went forward to trim in on the sheets, starting with the jibs and working back to foresail and main. It was the first time she had helped handle canvas at night and Katy was a little worried about it. Suppose she let go the wrong halyard or line in the dark, and dropped the sails on her head. But nothing happened and by the time four bells rang out everything was in proper trim and she went aft to relieve her sister Mate at the wheel.

"Where are we headed for now?" began Spinach who had rather an idea that something was going on she didn't know about.

Katy didn't answer for a second. She was trying to figure out just how much to tell her. But Dominick settled that by calling Spinach to where he was, somewhere forward in the dark.

"Come here a minute," he said. "Bring the binoculars with you."

"Take a look," he added, when she had found him at the port rail. "Can you see a white flash off there on our beam?"

"Yes," said Spinach after searching awhile.

"Call the flashes while I time them. 'On,' when you see them. 'Off,' when they go out." Then he took out his stop watch.

Spinach's spoken Off's and On's, worked out as a white flash for one second—eclipsed for five.

"Sturgeon Point Light," said Dominick. "Just where it should be. We're about fifteen miles off shore. Now come over here," he added, leading her across to the starboard side. "Look away. Forward a little, and not quite so far. See anything?"

"Yes," said Spinach with her eye to the glass. "More flashes."

"Call 'em off."

This light was bright for four seconds—eclipsed for twenty-six.

"Thunder Bay Island," said Dominick. "We're about half way between the two—and headed right."

Finding one's way over the dark waters wasn't so difficult, if you knew how. Log and compass, lighthouse and buoy—each speaking its language, and marking the direction of all the avenues of the sea—a safe guide for all its traffic.

"We'd better call the watch," said Dominick. "It's nearly four o'clock."

The Able-seamen tumbled up first, shivering a little in the chill morning air. Peacoats were not more than enough in the sharpness that comes just before dawning, and both snuggled deep into the collars. Captain Williams followed them on deck, rubbing the sleep from his eyes and looking around generally. He stepped to the wheel and glanced down at the compass.

"Northwest by West?" he said sharply. "Why are we on that course?"

Dominick immediately 'fessed up.

"It's the wind mostly," he said. "It's hauled around to the north. But that's only one reason—and not the main one."

"Well?" said the Skipper.

Dominick explained what he had told Katy a few hours

before. "And tomorrow it's a definite landfall we should be making for," he said. "That's provided of course, that the right word comes from Joe."

"But how did you know we would be anywhere near Thunder Bay?" asked Sailor Bill. "And have just the right slant of wind at the end of the day to carry you in?"

"Mon Captaine," said the Blue Nose. "For twenty years as a young man, I watched the winds on Lake Huron. The habits of weather do not change."

By noon the next day the *Gull-Flight* had up her anchor and was under weigh, eastbound for Cove Island Passage. With a following wind they soon cleared the islands and shoals that marked the mouth of Thunder Bay. Lighthouse and buoys dwindled to dots that lost themselves in a shore line that dimmed and faded behind them as they headed out across the lake. The day was fair with a blue sky, and little waves skipped and danced, and fled along with them in friendly company, flashing and sparkling in the sun. All the canvas was spread—foretop, two mains, and three jibs. The log was streamed and the line spun merrily, chasing the little black pointer round and round the dial, and counting out the miles as they flowed astern.

Katy and Spinach were seated on the fore hatch talking over the events of the morning. They had been interesting enough, and exciting too.

Shortly after breakfast Dominick lowered the dinghy over the side. Then he and Morgan fitted the outboard motor to the stern. After some preliminary pops and snorts the small boat shot away, and the steady put-put-put of the motor grew fainter as they rounded a wooded point toward the Coast Guard station on Thunder Bay Island. Only the Skipper and Katy knew their errand.

Afterward the girls did their housekeeping and Sailor Bill and the Able-seamen swabbed down, overhauled lines, and made everything shipshape. Then they all went swimming.

By the time they were dried and dressed again, they heard the noise of the outboard clattering around the point, and soon Dominick and Morgan drew along side. The dinghy was hoisted back aboard and the falls to the davits made secure. Then the Blue Nose handed the Skipper a piece of paper. He read it and gave it to Katy.

"Do you know where it is?" he asked Dominick.

"That I do," was the reply.

Katy looked down at the paper in her hand. It was addressed to Dominique Verlaine through the Coast Guard Station, and bore but two words, *Nis-ta-ba Wik-wed*. There was no signature.

"It's an Indian name," said the undercover agent, "for a deep hidden bay, or sound rather. Joe College and I fished and hunted there when we were boys. No one else knew where it was in those days, and we discovered it—or at least we thought we did. But I suppose it's charted now. At any rate we named it. Translated, it means 'Drowned Man's Cove.'"

"What a name!" said Katy. "There must be a story to that."

"There is," said Dominick. "It happened the second winter we fished and hunted there. We had our lines through a hole in the ice. Joe caught something—only it wasn't a fish. It was a dead man, a sailor, by the looks of him—drowned off a ship I suppose in the fall gales before the close of navigation. We never knew who he was. We were scared, and buried him in the frozen shore that night. And a hard time we had too—building fires to thaw out the ground, then scraping away the ashes to scoop out a little earth. Then piling back the fire, and scooping again till we had a hole big enough to cover him."

"What a horrible experience," said Katy.

"Well, that's the way the cove got its name," said Dominick. "And that's where we're to meet Joe."

"But if it's charted now," asked Katy, "won't everyone know where it is?"

"Not by that name," said Dominick. "So even if they read Joe's wire, they won't be able to spy on our meeting."

"It looks to me as though they were going to do their spying in other ways," said Morgan, breaking suddenly in. "Do you hear what I do? If I'm right, you'll see it in a minute."

Everyone immediately stopped talking and looked wildly around, staring at all four points of the compass. Morgan shook his head.

"Look up in the air," he said.

Morgan's ears were tuned to the sound of any motor, and he heard this one before any of the others. Silently the rest looked up and listened. Presently came a faint drone and high over their heads, and coming from the Canadian side of the lake, was a silvery speck in the sky. The speck grew rapidly, changing to a winged insect, and the drone swelled to a roar. As it neared Thunder Bay, the airplane lost altitude and swooped down on them like a great bird.

Flying only a few feet above them, it circled the *Gull-Flight* twice. Two goggled and helmeted heads peered down over the side of its open cockpit and looked them carefully over. Then the plane flew away—headed back across the lake.

"What do you suppose they wanted?" said Brick.

"Sightseers," said Teddy.

"I wonder," said Sailor Bill. "There's a lot of water between here and the Canadian shore—just for sight seeing."

"I'm not wondering," said Dominick, "I know. We'd better get out of here. The quicker we meet Joe College, the sooner we'll find Scar-Face."

"So that's why we put into Thunder Bay," said Spinach after Katy had told her about the Coast Guard wire, and what the plans were for finding Joe College. "I thought something was up when we changed course last night, and you two were so mysterious about it."

"He's mysterious about everything," said Katy. "That's part of being an undercover agent I suppose. But his plans always seem to work out."

"I do wish we'd hurry up and get there," said Spinach.

"We won't," said Dominick, startling them both by coming up behind, "not today, anyway. The wind's dying down."

Katy and Spinach looked quickly around. Both had been so interested in talking over what had happened during the morning, that neither had noticed they were running into a calm.

The lake no longer danced and sparkled. It was smooth, with slow lazy swells that seemed too tired to break, and moved with an oily creep that died away to nothing in a feeble effort to lift the schooner over them. The sheet lines on both fore and mainsail drooped in discouraged arcs, and dragged dispiritedly in the water. An occasional cat's-paw of breeze rippled down on them, dispending itself fitfully in a half-hearted effort to fill the sails.

The rest of the day the crew fussed and fretted. It grew hot and the wind dropped to a dead flat calm. The water stilled to a mill-pond surface—lifeless and without motion. A fierce glare burned the eyes and the afternoon sun hung in a suspended ball of fire, and by its very example discouraged all movement. Supper was of cold meat, colder drinks and ices, and served from the box in the saloon. The bare thought of a galley fire below was horrible. The stifle and choke of the cabin drove everybody on deck, and as evening came on, mattresses and pillows were spread about on top. The stars began to come out and a faint whisper of breeze annoyed sail and rigging into a protesting whine, but failed to cause even a ripple under the bows. The log line hung straight down, and the dial pointer seemed frozen on a constant number.

From his place up in the bow, Gyp panted and whined and got up occasionally to go to his water pan. The sound of his eager lapping was followed by the pad-pad of his feet and the plump of his body as he dropped down on the foredeck again. The helmsman dozed over the wheel and the curl of smoke from his pipe rose in a quiet spiral, lit at its vortex by the glow of the binnacle light, and losing itself in the thin air and dark of the night. Cove Island Passage was a dim unreality over a horizon far beyond the rim of an endless starry bowl.

Katy fell asleep at last, lying there on the deck on her mattress with Spinach beside her. Before dawn she woke up shivering to find a fresh morning breeze, cool and clean, and blowing from the north. The whisper and run of water washing along side came sweetly to her ears, and she knew the *Gull-Flight* was moving again.

The Skipper was at the wheel and hailed her cheerily as she came back to where he was.

"We're sailing again," he said. "Suppose you and Spinach start some coffee boiling. Then go into the charthouse and get the binoculars. There'll be something for you to see."

When the Mates came back on deck, there was a faint rosy gleam to the east ahead of them. They looked through the glass. A low dim shore line stretched down from the north and lost itself, dipping into the open water of a strait. Southward they caught the beam from a lighthouse, and could make out a wooded shore of dark pines.

"The Passage!" they cried.

"Dead ahead," said Sailor Bill. "The open door to our adventure."

CHAPTER XI

DROWNED MAN'S COVE

HOW LONG will it be before we enter the passage?"
asked Katy, after a long look through the glasses.

"Sometime around ten o'clock," answered Sailor Bill.
"We're only doing about six or seven miles with this
breeze."

"Oh, dear," said Spinach, who was also eyeing the far-
off shore line. "It seems as though we never would get
there."

"We'll get there all right," said the Skipper. "And we
couldn't ask for a better wind. We don't want a gale
when we're maneuvering through the strait. Too many
sunken reefs and rocks—'Sleepers,' they call 'em up here.
But you two skip along. Call all hands. This schooner's
a mess. Clean up the cabin and make the Able-seamen
look after their own staterooms. Send Dominick and
Morgan up here. We look like an Erie Canal barge."

The Mates ran below and started in. Their own cabin
was bad enough. Mattresses off both bunks had been
dragged up on deck in the heat of the evening before, and

bed covers were strewn around the floor or flung about helter-skelter. Uniforms had been much too warm and lay on the floor where they had been shucked off in favor of pajamas. Now there was all this to clean up, to say nothing of the cabin. And neither Brick nor Teddy was very anxious to get up. They had been bothered by the heat too, and in the cool of the morning both had sunk off to a deep sleep.

"Lem'me 'lone," said Brick sleepily when Katy shook him. And Teddy wasn't any better.

"What's the idea?" he asked. "I've only been off watch two hours."

But their protests didn't do them any good and they rolled out, and with not too bad grace, met the news that they were to tidy up their own cabin.

"What next?" asked Brick a little later as they came out of the stateroom.

"Swab down," said Katy. "Sailor Bill says the *Gull-Flight* looks like a coal scow. Morgan and Dominick are up top now—suppose you bear a hand. Spinach and I will finish up below."

Once on deck, the Able-seamen could see Dominick, bare-footed and with his pants rolled to his knees, bending a line around the handle of each of two buckets. A swab and a squeegee lay in the lee scuppers.

"Douse your shoes and socks," he said as Brick and Teddy went forward to help. "One of you take a bucket and fill it from over the side. Then sluice it down the deck—here, like this!"

A Squeegee

The Blue Nose picked up one of the buckets and with a firm grip on the end of the line, flung it out and forward. There was just the right flip to his wrist so that the bucket hit the water dipper fashion, filled and immediately sank. As the schooner rode up to it Dominick gave a heave, pulled it up brimming, and sloshed it along the deck.

Brick tried it next.

The first time he got very little water and somewhat disgusted he tried it again. This time he got the bucket full all right, but let it sweep past him, and when he tried to pull it up the drag nearly yanked him over the rail. But for Dominick's quick grab on the line he might have lost the bucket over the side. But finally he caught the knack of forward swing—dip and upward heave—and was able to keep ahead of Teddy and Dominick with their swab and squeegee.

And so the *Gull-Flight* got her morning bath.

By nine o'clock the flash of the outer gas buoy was in plain sight, six miles out in the lake from the passage. As they bore down on it its vertical black and white stripes came into bold relief, and the melancholy Wh-o-o-sh of its whistle sounded clear above the slap of the waves under the schooner's bows and the gurgle and wash of water alongside.

They left it to port and headed directly between the lighthouse on Gig Point at the north tip of Cove Island, and the red and black buoy on O'Brien's Patch.

A GAS BUOY

"We'll go through the main channel," said Sailor Bill. "The East and West Sisters are no relations of mine, and it's well to keep away from Bad Neighbors."

The Mates looked at the chart. They knew the Skipper was talking about the shoals and hidden rocks to the north of the channel, and not about people, relatives or otherwise.

"It's many a year since I was last through the passage," said Dominick. "But it doesn't change much. There's Tobermory. Been a yacht anchorage ever since I knew it. And there's Bear's Rump and the Flowerpot, with the steamer track marching to Owen Sound and the east ports in between. Our course will be North, Northeast—a half East, Mr. Helmsman. We've twenty-five miles or more to the Lonely Isles. What do you say Mates? Here's great fishing grounds. Shall we try for a trout?"

"How can we do that?" said Katy. "I never heard of anybody fishing from a ship moving as fast as we are."

"Many's the time I've trolled from the old lumber schooners," said Dominick, "and six or seven miles an hour's not too fast. We used to catch them up to twenty or thirty pounds. It was lake trout we had, morning, noon and night—till even a navy bean was a treat. Come with me, and we'll rig the line."

The *Gull-Flight's* fishing gear was stowed in a locker at the forward end of the saloon. There were rods and reels, hooks and leads of all sizes; spinners and trolls, flies and artificial bait, but nothing quite up to the job at hand. But Dominick finally found a great reel of braided copper wire. In its side he fitted a crank handle so that it resembled a windlass on the top of an old-fashioned farm well, only of course it was considerably smaller. Then he looked around for a weight.

"Nothing heavy enough," he said after a few minutes' search. "But we'll fix that. Get me a marline spike— one that weighs something over three pounds."

After Katy had brought it to him he drilled a hole a few inches from the point, led the braided wire through the hole, and tied a knot, securing the marline spike about four feet from the end of the line. There was his weight, and a heavy one—one that would carry the line down, well into the deep.

"Now for a spinner," he said. "We'll have to make one. Where's the can opener?"

"Can opener?" said Spinach. "How are you going to fish with a can opener?"

"I'm not going to fish with it," said Dominick. "I want it to cut the top out of a sardine can. We'll make a homemade spinner out of that, and fasten some gang hooks to its end."

When he got through, the whole contraption looked something like this.

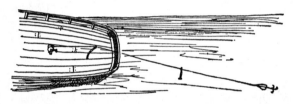

REEL   UMBRELLA RIB   MARLIN SPIKE   SPINNER

Then he fastened the reel to the after-deck with a pair of thumb screws and let out about three hundred feet of wire. Between the reel and the taffrail he stuck an umbrella rib into a crack in the deck planking and took a turn around it with the copper wire so that it bore the whole strain of the dragging weight and line. The umbrella rib bowed into an arch under the pull.

"Watch it," said Dominick. "If a trout gets on, he'll bend the rib into a half circle."

With a following wind the *Gull-Flight* bore along in easy comfortable swings. Brick and Teddy had the wheel. To the right of them stretched the reach of Georgian Bay, its hundred miles of cold blue water dancing and sparkling under the bright northern sky. Their course took them across its upper and westerly end and for a while Fitzwilliam's Land marched with them, a dim and distant shore with a low line of cliffs showing under a dense pine forest.

"Is it anything like you imagined?" asked Spinach of Katy.

"Not quite. I must have gotten my idea from reading about Norway. I had a picture of frozen fiords half covered with ice and snow, and gloomy bays under black and rocky headlands."

"You're here at the wrong season," said Dominick who was sitting on the after-deck with them and keeping an eye on his umbrella rib. "In the winter there's ice all right, and blinding snowstorms and gales too. I remember once Joe College and I came across here with a sledge and dog team. We fought a westerly blowing up through the passage, and the wind was so strong it opened up the ice in great cracks under our very feet."

"Do you mean the sledge and team dropped through into the water?" asked Katy.

"Oh, no," said Dominick; "the cracks weren't wide enough for that, but the water drove up on top and froze as it ran along. Our dogs' feet kept getting wet and ice formed between their toes. Every little while they would stop and lie down, and wave their four paws in the air. Then Joe and I would have to bite the ice out from between their toes. Finally we cut up a deerhide that we were using for a pack cover and made each dog four little moccasins."

"How cold was it?" asked Spinach.

"Oh, it would drop to twenty or thirty degrees below during a Norther," said Dominick. "And as for deep sounds and bays—wait till we make our anchorage tonight."

"In Drowned Man's Cove?" said Katy excitedly.

"No other place," said Dominick. "But you watch the Skipper, and you'll see these are no easy waters even in the summer."

With an eye on the compass and a constant checking of the log, Sailor Bill moved continually between charthouse and deck. He counted the tiny islands and partly submerged reefs as a hen would her chickens, conning the ship carefully along. Shingles and shoals leapt up from forty-fathom depths to within a few feet from the surface. Half-hidden rocks lay awash and were marked on the chart as spots of blue. The chart was also marked with dotted lines in circles and odd shapes with queer names printed over them. There was Three Fathom Patch, Watson's Ground, Two Finger Ledge, and Sailorman's Woe. All these needed watching and the Able-seamen were kept to it. No talking to the members of the off watch.

"Keep your eye on the wheel," said Sailor Bill to Teddy,

who had looked up in answer to something Spinach was saying. "If we go to yawing about in here, we could easily pile up on a rock."

"That's right," said Dominick. "And it's your eye, Spinach, that should be on the umbrella rib. It's a fine pair of fishermen you are. By the looks of that rib, it's a whale maybe that's on the end of your line."

The umbrella rib was bent in a sharp half circle. It quivered and strained to the pull of some great fish, tugging and jerking at the end of the three hundred feet of copper wire. The Mates jumped to their feet and ran excitedly to the reel. Dominick fitted in the little crank handle. Then with a firm grip on the line he eased the strain on the umbrella rib, freeing it from the loop in the wire.

"Wind in slowly," he said, "and keep an even strain on the line. I'll go for the gaff."

Soon he came back carrying a short pole to the end of which was fixed a curved, murderous steel hook—a sort of half open circle, pointed, but not barbed. This was the gaff.

Then he went aft and leaned over the taffrail, seizing the line outboard and leading it around to the side of the ship. Hand over hand he hauled in the wire, and in a minute and about twenty feet astern was a sudden swirl and rush, the death struggles of a great lake trout. The fish pulled and tugged and tried to dive, but tired out from his long struggle with the heavy copper wire, he was

finally hauled along toward his unwilling destiny of frying pan and soup kettle.

Dominick handed the line to Katy.

"Keep him in close to the ship," he said.

Then he leaned over the rail and gave a slashing, downward lunge with the gaff, ending up his stroke with a
strong inward and upward pull. The sharp point at the
end of the steel half circle hooked the trout through the
gills, and the force of the blow stunned it. Dominick
hove it over the rail with a mighty heave and tug, and
there it lay, flapping and gasping feebly—a great twenty-
pound beauty, dark green with a scarlet edge to the fins
and gill covers.

"Nay-ma-cush," said Dominick in great satisfaction, giving the fish its Indian name. "The salmon trout. It's
many a one Joe and I have caught. And it's grand steaks
we'll have for tonight, and fish-head chowder for the
morning."

During the early afternoon they had been sailing past the
high headlands of a cape covered with a pine bluff, and
slashed through here and there with lumber clearings.
Now they came to an open passage that reached to the
east and set their course through it.

"It's your helm, Mister," said Sailor Bill. "From here
on it's a pilot's job, or rather one for a guide."

"Trim in on the sails," answered Dominick. "We've a
close haul for the next five miles and I'd like Teddy and
Brick aloft—into the crosstrees to keep an eye open for

rocks and shoals. The higher up you are the better you can see them."

"What about it," asked Sailor Bill, "can you climb those rope ladders to the top without fear of a fall? There's no sea running and but little wind. The ship's steady enough."

"We'll try it anyway," said Brick.

"I've done plenty of climbing at home," said Teddy.

"Up you go then," said Sailor Bill. "Keep your eyes peeled when you get there—and don't look down till you do."

The Able-seamen each ran to a rail and jumped for the rope ladders. With heads thrown back and eyes on the little platform at the top of the mast they went up hand over hand. Then Brick made the mistake of looking down to see how far he had climbed.

Instantly he froze, dizzy, rigid, and unable to move. The deck seemed so far below, so hard, and the streaks between the planks had such a horrid fascination. He clung to the ratlines with a death grip, unable to tear his eyes from the deck and powerless to lift a leg further.

"What did I tell you!" roared Sailor Bill. "Look back at that masthead and start climbing."

The sharp command in the familiar voice broke the spell. Brick flung up his head, and eyes on the crosstrees started climbing again. The fear—the dizziness—and the inability to move were suddenly gone. Quickly he reached the top.

"Hook your arm through the ratline," called Sailor Bill, this time in a calm steady voice. "There, that's it. Now look off over the water, away from the ship."

Brick did, and somehow that wasn't terrifying at all. He grew confident and felt perfectly secure, just as though he were up in the old apple tree at home. And they had a wonderful view. The schooner was sailing across an open and rather shallow bay, and both could see bottom easily provided they didn't try to look too far ahead. Quick rising shoals and jutting rocks would be easy to spot from up here.

They were headed toward a high rocky cliff, and still some miles away, it seemed to form a barrier without an opening. It was guarded by a pair of high hills, sentinels towering nearly a thousand feet above the steel-blue water at their base. In the fading afternoon fingered shadows of purple and violet crept out from the granite wall ahead, and the twin peaks mirrored themselves in reversed images in the still water. The shore line at the base of the cliff took on a gloomy forbidding look.

Sailor Bill grew nervous.

Was the Blue Nose going to wreck the *Gull-Flight* against that impassable granite wall?

The boys could see the two of them talking earnestly together and Dominick was describing something, using his hands as well as his voice for complete expression. Finally Sailor Bill left off talking and called to the Able-seamen on the masthead.

"Do you see anything?" he asked.

"Nothing between us and the cliff," shouted Brick. "There seems to be deep water right up to the shore."

"Come down," called the Skipper after a minute. "We're going to need you on deck."

By the time the boys had climbed down the ratlines Sailor Bill and Dominick had their course of action all figured out and the crew was on the jump carrying out orders. First the jibs and topsail were lowered, then the foresail and main came down with a run. Morgan went below and soon the roar of the motor broke the peace of the afternoon.

With her engine at half speed the *Gull-Flight* bore on down toward the rock cliff. Everyone had the fidgets. The granite wall ahead looked as impassable as ever. But Dominick wasn't concerned. He knew what he was do-

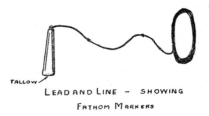

TALLOW

LEAD AND LINE - SHOWING
FATHOM MARKERS

ing, and when the shore was about a mile off he ordered the engine slowed still further.

"Just keep her turning," he said to Morgan. "And, Captain Williams, will you go forward to take soundings?"

Sailor Bill got the lead and line from the charthouse and

went up into the bow. He also took with him an old can full of mutton tallow. Then he called to Brick.

"Come up here," he said. "Stand by close enough to be able to hear what I say and then sing it back to Dominick at the wheel."

Brick took his stand by the foremast stay about ten feet aft of Sailor Bill, and where the sweep of the bows put him in plain sight of Dominick. They all watched the Skipper swing the lead easily back and forth a few times, and then with a final whirl let it fly forward well ahead of the ship where it dropped into the water with a splash.

"By the mark ten," he said, taking in the slack and marking with his fingers a certain little leather stop fastened to the line.

"Mark ten," called Brick in a loud voice.

Sailor Bill hauled in the line and coiled it carefully on the deck ready for his next cast. Then with his thumb he pushed some tallow into the claw at the bottom of the lead. His movements were as calm and deliberate as though he were loading his old pipe.

The *Gull-Flight* slipped on. The blank face of the granite wall drew nearer. Again the lead whirled, dropping out and forward with a splash.

"By the deep eight," called Sailor Bill, noting the depth by a bit of colored stuff tied a little farther toward the end of the line—"and sand."

"Eight and sand," repeated Brick.

"Mark five," sang out Sailor Bill a minute later—"and sand."

Nobody else said anything. The cliff came nearer and nearer.

"Three—and sand."

Again the line flung forward. Everyone held his breath. Would they go aground to add to the complications?

"Ten feet," said Sailor Bill sharply, furiously coiling his line for the next cast.

"Full stop," said Dominick to Morgan.

The clutch lever was thrown out and the *Gull-Flight* drifted, almost without way. Once again the lead spun forward. This time the line ran out freely till checked by Sailor Bill.

"Plenty of water," he called back in a relieved voice.

"We're over the bar," said Dominick. "Look to starboard everybody. Kick her ahead, Mr. Chief Engineer."

Startled, all hands looked around. Everyone had been so anxious about the rapidly shoaling depths that all eyes were glued to the Skipper and his lead line. They had completely forgotten the bold shore line ahead.

There was not one rock cliff, but two, almost parallel. The inner one which they had seen over the ship's bows stretched for miles to either side in an unbroken line. The outer one rose abruptly from the bay to the same height as its fellow and marched with it to the east. Between the two was a deep narrow sound, slashing back as far as the eye could see. In the sheen of its calm water were pictured mountain and forest, rock ledge and cliff; the

rugged confines of its boundary. This was Drowned
Man's Cove.

But there was no time to look or admire. Dominick's
orders cut short their exploring gaze.

"All hands man the port rail," he called. "We're heading in. Walk her along the cliff. I'll keep the rudder
against you a little."

The Blue Nose swung the *Gull-Flight's* bow toward the
cove. The natural leeway of the turn brought her broad-
side to the frowning rock wall. They drifted down on it
much the same as a ship would warp to a dock. The few
feet of water between the ship and the cliff narrowed to
a ribbon and then squeezed out to nothing. By leaning
over the rail you could touch the granite bluff.

"Keep her off!" said Dominick sharply. "And work
her ahead. All right, Morgan—just a kick forward."

It was touch and go between the sand spit and the cliff.
Both tried to clutch the *Gull-Flight.* But the lake tides
and the rush of spring water from the sound had scoured
out a passage, narrow but deep, and there was room to
edge the schooner through. The fender of human hands
held her off the rock wall while the engine shoved her
along. Over the starboard rail one could see the swirl of
sand at the outer edge of the bar as the current rippled
and swayed, disturbing the patterned rifles on the bottom.

But they got through.

Inside, they moved about three miles from the entrance to where a table rock formed a natural wharf.

There was no anchorage as the ledge dropped off sheer to shadowy blue depths. Bow and stern lines were carried ashore and made fast to pine trees. Then they decided to cut shore props to hold the ship away from the rock.

"Break out an axe," said Sailor Bill to Brick and Teddy. "Cut down a pair of young firs and trim off the branches. Bring the trunks here."

The Able-seamen picked out two small trees about six inches thick. They swung the axe and down they came. When trimmed, each was about twelve feet long. Back from the water's edge two rock cairns were piled over their stumps and the small ends lashed inboard. With the shore lines holding her in, and the props keeping her off, a protecting strip of water lay between the ship and the ledge. The *Gull-Flight* lay secure for the night.

"What about dinner?" asked Katy. "That trout, you know. We've the steaks broiling now."

"Lead the way," said Dominick. "It's famished, I am."

"We could eat a horse," said the Able-seamen.

"You won't have to," said Morgan. "These are fish cutlets."

"I think we deserve them," said Sailor Bill.

CHAPTER XII

CHIEF ABA-KA-MAS

VERY EARLY the next morning Katy heard a scrabbling and scratching outside of her cabin door. Then a faint scared whine, and she knew it was Gyp. At night the dog always had the run of the ship—the 'tween decks part, that is. They kept the screen doors leading to the deck locked, but the little dog looked on the cabins as his own and roamed pretty much all over. Sometimes he slept in the forecastle with Dominick, but usually he picked out the rug at the foot of the companion stairs where he could keep an eye on everything. And there was never a stir that he didn't investigate. In the week since leaving Grosse Ile the crew had learned to take this self-appointed guardianship pretty much as a matter of course, but it was a serious business for the dog. And after the first night he could never be lured into a stateroom.

"No sleeping behind closed doors for me," his air plainly said. "I'll stay out in the cabin where a watchdog belongs."

But immediately after dinner last night he had begun

acting strangely. He made one trip ashore, disappearing into the fringe of forest that came down to the edge of the rock landing. In a minute he came back, bounding out on the ledge with his tail between his legs and a puzzled frightened look about him. When he saw his friends, who were working away on the shore props, he stopped and started back, sniffing along the edge of the woods. Once he growled, the ruff on his neck rising and bristling. Then he went back aboard and nothing could get him ashore again.

"Spoor, I suppose," said Dominick. "There's bear and deer about in here, and maybe even a wolf. Yours is a house dog. He can't figure out just what to make of so many strange scents."

But whatever it was, Gyp hung close all evening and was right under everybody's heels. Now here he was again, timid and afraid, whining to get in the stateroom, and anything but his usual cocksure self.

Katy shinned carefully down from her bunk so as not to wake Spinach and slipped into her clothes. She had wanted to be early on deck, before anyone else, this first Northland morning. The night odors from the pine forest were clean and sweet, and had blown through her open port in a tantalizing tang. She had been strangely alert to them and it had been difficult to get to sleep. There were queer noises and calls; the distant squall of a tree-cat, the mournful wail of a loon—a crashing in the underbrush, the far-off howl of a wolf, the grunt and snort of a bear, disturbed and lumbering away through the bushes—all the sounds of wild folk about their nocturnal business.

And now to see it all in its morning freshness. So she opened the door of her stateroom and went quietly out. The minute she got into the cabin Gyp darted for the companion stairs, stopping at their foot to see if Katy was coming along. Strangely enough he didn't bark and his eager whines were almost clucks of instruction.

"You go first," he seemed to say.

"Why, what's the matter?" asked Katy. "There's nothing going to hurt you."

But suddenly her heart leapt into her mouth. There was something, or somebody, out there on deck, in the cockpit. She heard a rustle and a clicking as though someone had rattled an old-fashioned beaded screen hanging. Then everything was still—so still that she could hear her heart pound.

"This will never do," she said to herself. "There's nothing to be afraid of."

And then loudly, careless whether she waked anyone else or not, she called, "Come on Gyp. We'll see what it is."

She ran up the stairs and flung open the screen doors, and went out on deck. She half expected to find something as big as an elephant—a deer, a bear, or any other wild animal. But for a minute she saw nothing and looked wildly around. Then she spied the intruder.

It was an animal all right, but a small one, and the funniest she had ever seen.

Huddled in front of the steering wheel was a living pin-cushion, with all the pins sticking out. It stared at the girl and the dog with an unwavering glare, impudent and un-afraid. It was a porcupine, the most curious of all wild things, come aboard over the shore props to investigate this strange invasion of his Northland home; and he didn't propose to be hurried about it by any mate or ship's mascot.

Katy laughed and took a step forward. The dog seeing his mistress was not frightened wagged his tail, and then as though ashamed at his own scare, grew indignant, and gave a sharp bark to show that he was boss of the situation after all.

But the porcupine could move fast if he wanted to. In the flick of an eye he whirled completely around and curled up into a tight ball, his prickly spiney tail pointed directly at them. Gyp danced up, stiff legged and with a very truculent manner. But he got his nose too near that dagger-spiked tail. There was a swish and a slap, fol-lowed by a sharp yelp from the dog.

"Ki-yi! Ki-yi!" he yapped, dashing frantically down the deck, and clawing at the quills sticking from his snout.

Sailor Bill heard the racket and appeared at the saloon door in his pajamas. He saw the dog, then Katy, and finally the porcupine. Then he started to laugh.

"The first North-country casualty," he said. "Let him alone. He'll waddle ashore in a minute." Then, "Come here, Gyp. Let's see what we can do for that nose."

But the little dog had a very injured air even after they had all done their best for him. The quills were pulled out and Katy's first-aid kit called into play. The healing salve she plastered over his muzzle might have helped soothe the pain if he hadn't licked it all off the minute they let him go. But a whacking good breakfast fixed him up and made him forget his troubles. They let him come in around the table, which was much more sociable than his usual pan on the foredeck.

"Well, we're here," said Katy after their meal was over. "What next?"

"I don't see any smugglers," said Spinach.

"Nor any Scar-face," said Teddy.

"Nor even any Joe College," said Brick.

"He'll be here," said Dominick. "Joe, I mean. And as for the smugglers, maybe you won't be so anxious to see them, when we finally do catch up with them."

"Can't we go ashore?" said Teddy. "I'd like to climb that mountainside."

"I was just going to suggest it," said Dominick, "to you and Brick—the three of us. You need some woods practice. And it's with Joe College you're going, I'd hate for him to think you're not as good on the trail as you are on a deck. We'll make a camp and cook lunch. It's a long time since I've had a steak broiled over a wood fire."

"I'll be cook," said Teddy.

"Let's shove off," said Brick.

"Don't let them cut their heads off with the axe," said Sailor Bill.

A few minutes later the little shore party went down the gangplank and crossed the rock landing. Immediately they plunged into a wilderness. In every direction the trees, their feathered tops forming an arched canopy under the sky, darkened the bright of the day into the half gloom of a cavern. Sometimes there were pine groves—vast, solemn, grand. Then a jungle of birch, cedar and spruce; now a tangle of berry bushes, sumach and fern. And always the way led up and up.

The going was hard and rough and the cool lake breeze cut off by forest and thicket. They were traveling light and both boys knew it. So, hot as they became almost immediately, and tired as they grew before the end of the first half hour, neither would admit it. If they couldn't carry a frying pan, a small axe, and the few things they intended to cook for lunch, how would they be able to swing a full pack on miles of wilderness trail behind a tireless Indian? This was but a simple test for the endurance that would be needed on the track of the smugglers.

So they scrambled and slid over the rocks, clawed their way through the brush, bent grimly to the steep places, breathed deeply and gratefully on the smooth level ones—and kept up.

Suddenly Dominick stopped, froze where he stood almost, and pointed with his finger to a little clearing a few yards to their left.

"Look," he whispered.

Sitting up on his haunches in the clearing near a clump of blueberry bushes was a little bear cub. He wasn't much

bigger than Gyp.   But he was in a fine hot rage over being disturbed at his meal.   Purple drops of blueberry juice
dripped off his snout, as he grunted and snorted and let
out little growls of baby fury.

"Let's catch him," said Brick.

"And take him back to the ship," said Teddy, starting
toward the clearing.

"No!   No!" said Dominick sharply.   "His mother's
about here somewhere, and we don't want to spend the
rest of the day up a tree.   We'd better get out of here now
—in a hurry, before she hears his complaints."

They left—as quickly and quietly as possible—slipping
around the glade and off through the timber.

The forest closed in again and the way grew steeper
and steeper—also hotter and hotter.   The boys panted and
groaned and would have been glad of a halt.   But Dominick kept on, his long strides eating up the trail and forcing the Able-seamen almost into a run.   The trees finally
became fewer, thinning out to jack pines and scrub oaks.
Suddenly they came out on a flat rock ledge, jutting high
over the treetops, and the forest dropped away entirely.
Pines and spruce dwindled and dwarfed down the sheer
of the mountainside, and far below was the blue water of
the cove, a shining strip reaching away in the distance.   A
toy schooner lay almost directly under them with little
dolls moving about on her decks—the *Gull-Flight* and her
crew.

Brick and Teddy threw themselves down on the rock
ledge, not even troubling to look for a soft spot.   Both

were puffing hard. Dominick looked at them, a twinkle in his eye and an Irish grin on the face of him.

"It's not bad on the up-trail, you are," he said. "But if we hadn't stopped for the bear, would you have been dropping behind now?"

"No," said Brick, "I'd have dropped dead first."

"You went pretty fast," said Teddy, "and it was kind of a tough climb. But here we are."

"We'll rest for a few minutes," said Dominick. "You've earned it. Afterward we'll have lunch—here's as good a place as any. We'll see what you can do over an open fire."

And it was a good place, for lunch or dinner or any other kind of meal. The ledge was flat, about a hundred yards across, and protected in its landward side by a sheltering cliff. Ages of winter frosts and spring thaws had rent and split its floor into crevices and cracks, some only a few inches and others several feet deep. Rock mosses grew in these—springing up green and thick, only to wither and die in the summer heat—and the bright sun had dried them to tinder. Fall gales had stripped great branches from the trees and flung them down on the rock ledge. The bark had shriveled and peeled and the wood had dried and hardened. In sheltered corners fir cones had piled up in little windows, and over all this lay a blanket of crisp dry pine needles. Here was material for a hundred campfires.

Dominick spied a crack in the rock floor just under the cliff. It was about a foot deep at its inner end and maybe twice as wide. Its bottom was almost level, excepting that it inclined upward toward its outer end, scaling gradually to nothing as it met the surface of the ledge. Here was a shallow bowl, a perfect fire pot, with a natural flue from the down-draught off the cliff.

"The very spot," said Dominick. "If you were to design a fireplace yourselves, you couldn't do better."

Then he looked around and finally found a square chunk of rock, split off from the face of the ledge. It was about ten inches across the top and perhaps a foot thick. This he placed in the middle of the fire crevice.

"There's our hot plate," he said. "It's not electric, but it's even better to cook on."

Around the chunk of rock he laid a layer of dry moss, and over that, about two dozen tinder-like fir cones. Small twigs, brittle and crackling with dryness, came next. Then from a waterproof box he drew a match, struck it and lit the fire. Instantly the whole pile caught, and some thicker pieces of branches were placed on the blaze.

"Now for some real wood," said Dominick. "Get busy with your axe. They're plenty of fallen limbs about."

For a half an hour they piled on fuel, let it burn brightly and die down. Finally a deep bed of red coals flickered and glowed, and the square chunk of rock at their center grew sizzling hot. Out came the frying pan and into it went a gob of bacon grease. Then several handfuls of thinly sliced raw potatoes. The fat sputtered and spit and the browning potatoes gave off a delicious smell. Before their golden centers began to crisp at the edges, Dominick skewered a fine thick steak with a forked stick and hung it over the fire. Every few minutes he turned the stick a little and the steak dropped spatters of hot fat which struck the coals in blazing plops.

"Break out the plates," said Dominick after a bit. "Both the steak and potatoes are about ready."

"Plates?" asked Brick. "We didn't bring any plates. I thought this meal was to be 'woods' style.'"

"It is," said Dominick. "And the woods are full of plates, birch-bark ones, I mean."

With their knives, the boys cut three slabs of white clean bark from a huge birch that grew a short distance from the ledge, and laid them on the rock a little way from the fire. A generous helping of steak and potatoes was put on each. Coffee and cocoa from the thermos bottles completed the meal. Sheath knives and fingers were all the table utensils they needed and they soon fell to. The climb, the sharp air, and the tantalizing smells of the cooking meal had made them ravenous, and for a minute nobody said anything.

Suddenly Brick looked up. What made him do it, he never quite knew, but in some way he felt the nearness of a strange presence. The next moment his hair stood on end and his heart skipped a beat. His mouth fell open and his eyes nearly popped out of his head.

For at the edge of their rock, and under the shadow of the cliff, was an Indian. His arms were folded across his chest as he stood there motionless and silent, regarding them all with the steady unwinking gaze of his race. Neither the boy nor the Indian spoke a word—Brick because he couldn't, and the Indian because he wouldn't.

How long had he been standing there? Where did he come from? Who was he? And how did he get there without their hearing him?

All these thoughts raced through Brick's head. The boy and the man stared silently at each other.

"How!" said the Indian suddenly, the word ringing out in the silence like a shot.

Dominick's hand leaped toward his hip pocket. He turned in a flash, jumping up and whirling to face the voice. Then his face lit in recognition, and his hand fell away from his hip pocket. He straightened up from his half crouch.

"Aba-ka-mas," he said simply. "Nin a-we-ma. My brother."

"I have come," said the Indian, stepping toward the fire. "Is there no offer of food after the long trail?"

Dominick broke into a torrent of talk, half French, half Indian, scraping off his bark plate the while, and turning it over fresh side up. Then wiping his knife on a bit of moss he speared the remaining piece of steak, and along with what was left of the potatoes, put it on the clean side of the bark. This he carried to the Indian who had squatted crosslegged a little apart from where the boys sat, and laid it before him on the rock.

"Aba-ka-mas. Chief Foot-in-the-Water. Joe College," said Dominick affectionately, laying his hand on the Indian's shoulder. "Eat, my brother—we make talk afterward."

Without a word the Indian fell to. In the silence that followed Brick and Teddy eyed him with great interest. It was the first time they had ever seen one close up, and his silent coming had lived up to all the legends and preconceived ideas with which reading had filled their heads. Here was Leatherstocking come to life—Hiawatha to join their band—Deerslayer to lead them on the chase.

But he looked altogether different than they had imagined him. Of course he wore neither blanket, skin shirt, nor fringed leggings. Nor was there feather headdress, or tomahawk in his belt. And as yet he hadn't uttered a war whoop, which was probably just as well, for he would have scared them to death if he had. The manner in which he had made his appearance was startling enough.

But he was Indian all right, from his head down or his feet up, either way you wanted to figure. He wore leather moccasins—a sort of shoe pac—beaded on top, and high enough to extend half way up the calves of his legs and enclose the bottoms of a worn pair of corduroy trousers. Here they wrapped around, and were tied in an intricate knot by soft buckskin thongs, the ends dangling. His blue flannel shirt was tucked under a braided belt worked over with colored beads in a tribal pattern. The collar was open at the throat and around his neck was a gaudy bandana fastened in a loose knot something like a sailor's neckerchief. His skin was swarthy, the sun and wind having almost obliterated its copper tinge. His cheekbones were high, and on either side of a hooked nose, a pair of glittering black eyes regarded the world in a level unblinking stare. But there was nothing blank about this stare. It was comprehending, understanding, and intelligent. He wore no hat, and his blue-black straight hair was parted in the middle. He was about six feet tall, erect and broad shouldered, slim and lithe—a splendid specimen of the Red Race.

Later they found he was taciturn but articulate enough when he wanted to be. Due to his Carlisle training, he was in no way confined to the "Ughs" and guttural grunts of the average reservation Indian. His speech was direct and to the point. He neither wasted words nor had to grope for the ones he wanted to use.

When the Indian finished his meal Dominick filled his own pipe, lit it, took a few puffs, and passed it gravely over. The Chief accepted it in a dignified manner and smoked away with evident enjoyment. Finally he laid it down.

"The pipe of peace," he said, "or of war? In either case, may my brother find good hunting." He paused. "We hunt now, I think."

"Aye," said Dominick, "and rare game."

"Talk," said the Indian.

And Dominick did. First he introduced the boys, and the Chief nodded gravely without speaking. Then he told of the co-operation between the two governments in the effort to track down the gang of smugglers. Of Sailor

Bill and the *Gull-Flight,* and her disguise as an innocent summer cruiser. And of her crew, and even of the Midshipman whose place he took at Sarnia. The eyes of the undercover agent twinkled as he described his own coming aboard, and something that could pass as a smile flickered over the face of the Indian.

Then of Scar-face, and how he would have heard their plans had Gyp not scared him off. And maybe how he did anyway, at least part of them. And of the airplane over Thunder Bay. And of the scheme for the Indian and the boys to go back inland on an apparent camping trip—really to enlist the Chief's braves in the search. And how he, Dominick, would take the Mates in the *Bonny* and work the shore line. And how they would all meet the schooner at Little Current . . .

"Say in four days' time," he finished up.

The fire in the rock crevice had burned down and died to gray ash before the tale was done. Chief Aba-ka-mas smoked gravely on without saying anything. His face was impassive, expressionless, and whether or not he approved of the plans, no one could say. The silence grew uncomfortable, but the boys didn't dare fidget. At last the Indian got to his feet, knocked the ashes from the pipe and handed it to Dominick.

"The plan is good," he said. "We go. This Scar-face is known to my people. Let the boys be ready in the morning. By canoe to the village—by trail after that."

Then Brick sprang a question he had been itching to ask for the last hour, and hadn't quite dared.

"How did you know where to find us, Mr. Foot-in-the-Water? On this ledge, I mean."

This time the Indian really smiled.

"My brother," he said, looking at Dominick, "has been too long away from the woods. He has forgotten how to hide his trail."

"You mean you saw the smoke from our campfire?" asked Teddy.

"No, I stood at the edge of the cliff and watched you make it. It is a good fire. There was no smoke. Come, I will show you."

They back-tracked down the mountainside, the Indian leading, pausing every now and then to point out signs that gave away their up-trail. For eyes that could see, the signs were many. A broken twig with its bark peeled and hanging, the fresh raw stump showing white against the dark of the other branches. Scratches on rocks they had scrambled over. Footprints in damp patches of earth. A woods' plant bent over, with the stem snapped off close to the ground. And farther on a circle of trampled grass, and moss bruised by heavy shoes. Here the Chief stopped, sweeping his hand around the telltale marks and pointing to a little glade a short distance from the trail.

"Here you stood and watched Nakons, the cub bear. It was well that you left quickly. Nojek, his mother, was not far away. But you see," he added, "a child could follow."

Dominick's face grew slightly red, but he accepted the rebuke in good part.

"The lore of the woods is hard to learn, and easy to forget," he said.

THE next half hour's descent carried them well down the mountainside. They were strung out along the trail single file with the Indian leading, Dominick bringing up the rear. Much impressed by the Chief's lesson in woodcraft Brick and Teddy watched his every move, trying to copy his noiseless, effortless glide through the brush. He went in a straight line but touched nothing. Bush, overhanging bough, and thicket seemed to shrink aside to let him pass without sound or rustle. His progress was swift but absolutely silent.

When almost within sight of Drowned Man's Cove he stopped again and waited for his little party to bunch around him.

"I go now," he said. "Be ready in the morning, early."

"Oh, come on down and see the ship," said Brick, who would have given his eyetooth for the chance to show him off to Katy and Spinach.

"I have seen the ship," said the Chief.

"You have!" said Teddy. "When?"

"Last night. I stood at the edge of the woods while you landed. Many schooners come here now. I would be sure the *Gull-Flight* was yours. . . . The little dog did not like my being there."

Brick turned to Teddy.

"So that's what was the matter with Gyp. I didn't think he would be afraid of animals."

He turned back to say something to Chief Aba-ka-mas.
His jaw dropped. . . . The Indian was gone.
And Dominick was grinning.
"How did you like Joe College?" he said.
"Boy!" cried Brick and Teddy together.

CHAPTER XIII

THE RESERVATION

"UP WITH you now," said a voice. "Ten more minutes in the bunk and you'll be burning daylight. What will Joe College think of that?"

The voice was Dominick's, and there was a hand with it—a rude hand that jerked the covers from their bunks and left the Able-seamen shivering in the half dawn of a chill Northland morning.

"We haven't started to burn any daylight yet," said Brick, snapping awake and shinning down out of his bunk, "because there isn't any. It's still dark."

"Is the Chief here?" asked Teddy. "And what's his canoe like?"

"Not yet," said Dominick, "but he will be by sunup, And you'll know all about his canoe before tonight. There's a twenty-mile paddle to the portage, and you don't want to do that in the dark. That's why you mustn't waste any daylight."

This morning they didn't dress from their sea bags, for it wasn't ship's clothes they would wear from now on, but a shore outfit, designed for the woods and trail. Each boy put on a pair of thick knee-length socks and heavy shoes, then wool shorts and a flannel shirt, both olive drab. There was a web belt, with loops for a hand axe and sheath knife, and finally a wide-brimmed felt hat.

When they got into the cabin, they found everything they were to take with them laid out and ready. There was a waterproof shelter-half, so that by buttoning the two halves together, the boys could make a pup tent. On this was spread a double blanket, two changes of socks and underwear, a spare shirt and a toothbrush. There was also a hank of stout line and about ten feet of soft malleable iron wire. This formed their bedding roll, and with the shelter-half on the outside, would be slung over the right shoulder, around the body, and under the left armpit.

It was half of their equipment. The rest was contained in a canvas pack-carrier, something like a haversack or musette bag, and fixed to shoulder straps leading to a waist-high belt. When slung, the carrier rested just above the small of the back and under the blanket roll. In it was a mess tin with spoon, fork and cover—regular Marine Corps issue—plus a collapsible drinking cup. There were two special condiment cans, divided into compartments so that salt, sugar, soda and baking powder could be carried without running into each other. A pair of flat tins with tight covers held bacon and salt pork—about thirty strips of one, and a pound and a half of the other—cut into slices a quarter of an inch thick. Under the pack straps, Brick would lash a frying pan, and Teddy, a short-handled shovel. Each boy had a waterproof box full of matches.

Everything else would go into the canoe, and there was plenty of it. Two great canvas bags of provisions, pots and pans, spices and canned goods—all the *Gull-Flight's* gesture of hospitality to Chief Aba-ka-mas' tribe. Out of this, the boys could take what they needed for the trail. The balance would be left on the reservation.

"Where is this Chief of yours?" asked Katy, coming out of the galley. "Spinach and I got up early to give the three of you a good breakfast before you start out."

"Yes," said Sailor Bill, "and I'd like to have a look at him. It's my Able-seamen he's taking with him, you know."

"You will," said Dominick. "He's out there now, I'm thinking. Look at Gyp."

The little dog's lips were writhed back in a snarl over bared fangs, and the ruff on his neck raised and bristled. Aba-ka-mas' second arrival was as silent as yesterday's appearance on the rock ledge. Gyp was the only member of the crew who knew he had come.

"Why does he act that way?" said Spinach. "He's usually such a friendly little pup."

"Smell," said Sailor Bill. "Even an educated Indian is very close to wild things."

But Brick was delighted that Chief Foot-in-the-Water had come, smell or no smell. "Come on," he shouted excitedly, jumping for the companion stairs.

Teddy and the two Mates followed him on deck and

over to the seaward rail. The Indian was standing in a little canoe, fastening a bow thong to one of the *Gull-Flight's* belaying cleats. In a second he was over the rail, catlike and sure in every movement. His leap to the deck was a vault and a spring that hardly even rocked his little craft.

"Oh," said Katy, not even waiting to be introduced, "I thought yours would be a birch-bark canoe."

"And it's cedar," said Spinach, disappointedly, looking down over the rail.

"Why, Mates," said Dominick, who had followed them out of the companion-way, "is that how you welcome a guest aboard?"

Recalled, both girls minded their manners.

"How do you do, Mr. Foot-in-the-Water," said Spinach. "Our Able-seamen told us all about you last night. We think it was wonderful—the way you found them."

"We feel as though we know you already," said Katy. "What with everything Dominick has said."

"Come here, Gyp! Aren't you ashamed?"

The wirehair was backed against the charthouse, bristling and stiff legged. The muscles along his throat tightened and rippled in a half snarl, half growl. The Indian stood stock still. Then he held out one hand, palm up. "Osh-ka-sim—little dog," he said. A series of soothing and encouraging noises followed, a guttural invitation of friendliness. The Chief was talking to Gyp—and in a language the dog understood—for his ruff lowered and he took a tentative step forward. Then the stump of his tail started to wag, and his nose wrinkled. Finally he wriggled all over, and frisking up to Aba-ka-mas, he licked the outstretched hand. From then on, they were fast friends.

"Captain Williams," said Dominick, introducing the Skipper.

"From the Government at Washington, greetings," said the Skipper, extending his hand, "I bring two gifts. May you find them useful."

The gifts were a beautiful jointed fishing rod, with flies and leads, all in a waterproof metal case, and a modern bolt-action hunting rifle. Useful anywhere, and valuable beyond price to an Indian hunter, trapper and guide.

"The Great White Father is generous," said Aba-ka-mas. "My braves are at your command. My Brother," turning to Dominick, "has told me of the plans. They are good. We go now."

The business of loading took only a few minutes. The two canvas provision bags and the other supplies went squarely amidships, and the blanket rolls and carrier kits stowed just forward and aft of the pile. Over them all was tucked a rubber sheet.

Perhaps it was just as well that the canoe was not made of birch bark. It was light and skittish enough as it was, really a one man affair, and entirely the work of Aba-ka-mas during long winter evenings. The ribs and frame-work were of finest ash, slender and delicate, and cured to an agate hardness and rawhide toughness by endless turnings over the smoke of an open fire. Each was rubbed and sanded, oiled and polished, and fitted with careful joinery to the sharp but graceful oval that formed the gunwale. Over this framework, and fastened with copper rivets, was a thin skin of split cedar, cut in squares about ten inches across. A long strip of oak formed a shallow keel, starting at the tip of the prow and curving and bending to the stern. The canoe was less than fourteen feet long, about three across, and when loaded had only about six inches freeboard. On a portage, one man could swing it easily over his shoulders, for it weighed only seventy pounds.

Hardly stopping to say farewell, Joe College dropped over the *Gull-Flight's* rail into the stern of the canoe, kneeling and steadying the craft with nice balance. The Able-seamen lowered themselves carefully into the bow, Brick forward of Teddy.

"Sit down," commanded Sailor Bill from the deck of the schooner. "You don't want to tip over before you even start."

Their progress up the twenty-odd miles of Drowned Man's Cove was swift and silent. The Indian did not speak, and the powerful dip and swing of his paddle was absolutely noiseless and without a splash. For a while, neither of the boys dared turn his head, so tippy was the canoe, and so anxious was each of them to become used to the swaying rhythm of the steady paddle strokes. By the end of the first hour Brick was cramped and stiff, and decided to risk a turn-around to see how far they had come. He made it without accident, but what he saw upset him about as much as though he had dumped the canoe.

The *Gull-Flight,* far behind them now, had cut loose from her moorings at the rock landing and was heading for the entrance to the lake. Her graceful hull nodded a good-bye, and the twinkle of her brass fittings in the morning sun winked a friendly farewell. In a few min-

utes she would be gone—floating home and gallant crew —and they would be truly alone in the wilderness. With the realization came a gone feeling in the pit of the Able-seaman's stomach, and it was hard for a while to keep back the tears.

He was brought to by the steady level gaze of the Indian.

"Kneel in the bow," said Aba-ka-mas. "Paddle for an hour."

The change in position was a relief, and Brick worked away, trying to be as silent as the Indian. Of course he wasn't, but the splashes weren't too many and he really helped. The canoe flew along, and before long his arms began to ache and a sharp pain stabbed him between the shoulder blades. But his paddle dipped and swung with the Chief's, and they ate up the miles toward the head of the cove.

They made three landings, an hour apart, hauling the canoe up on bits of sandy beach, stretching their legs and running up and down to ease cramped muscles. Each time they started the boys changed places, one resting, the other taking the bow paddle. The cove was not so wide now, and finally narrowed to a gorge between low rocky cliffs covered with scrub pine. The roar of a waterfall could be heard in the distance, faint at first, but deepening constantly to the thunderous roll of rushing water. Rounding a bend in the gorge, the canoe came suddenly on it—the pouring of a river over a cliff—the headwaters of Drowned Man's Cove.

A sand spit jutted out from the shore just below the left base of the fall and led to a rough trail that angled off through the scrub, climbing the bank and disappearing over the top. With a strong sweep of his paddle, Joe drove the canoe onto the spit.

"Jump out," he ordered. "We unload here and rest. Then we make the portage."

Brick scrambled over the bow, followed by Teddy. The Indian stepped into the water and calmly waded ashore. Then they hauled the little craft farther up, unloaded, and turned it over to dry in the sun. From the provision sacks they made a lunch of fresh bread and cheese, washed down with drinks of cold water from the pool under the fall. For an hour afterward they lay flat on their backs, resting for the hard work ahead. It was peaceful and quiet and Brick could have lain there all afternoon, snoozing in the sun. But the Indian had other ideas.

"We start now," he said. "Put on your blanket roll and pack carrier. Each of you take a provision sack. I'll handle the rest."

The reason for the lightness and smallness of the canoe was now apparent. Joe turned it bottom side up and lifted one end. First slinging his own blanket roll, he crouched and ducked under it, the forward thwart making a sort of chest band. The prow projected over his head like a high hood and the weight, softened by the blanket roll, fell across his shoulders, balancing there without being held. When he stood up the stern was clear of the ground. Picking up his rifle with one hand, and some remaining pots and pans which he had strung together with wire in the other, he strode off up the trail without a word. From behind, you couldn't see the Indian for the canoe, so it was a sort of animated water craft that the boys followed as trail leader.

The going was hard and the way was steep. Leaves and branches slashed them across the face, and thorns tore at their clothes and the canvas sacks they were carrying. They slipped and slithered over rocks, and slid and lost footing in moist greasy patches of earth. They tripped over roots and the sweat ran into their eyes, blinding the trail. Their blanket rolls half choked them and the carrier packs bored holes between their shoulders. The cords on the provision sacks which they were using for handles cut into their hands, and broke the blisters raised by miles of paddling. A portage is the hardest kind of wilderness work. A canoe is traveling in luxury.

"Whe-e-w!" said Brick. "How do you like this?"

Teddy didn't answer. He had no breath to waste.

The top of the trail came out suddenly on an open plateau, only sparsely covered with berry bushes. Here it led directly away from the river that tumbled over the fall at the head of Drowned Man's Cove. A half mile farther on it climbed a low ridge and then fell steeply to a tangled thicket of spruce and fern. For an hour they fought a wilderness of dense underbrush and winding overgrown trail. Then the path dropped away abruptly and ran under a cliff, ending in a few yards at the shore of a little pool fed by a clear cold spring that welled and bubbled from under a rock ledge and ran off gurgling in a tiny stream. This was one of the head waters of a maze of rivers that formed the great north watershed, draining finally into Hudson's Bay.

Here they stopped, dropped their loads, drank, and rested for a while.

"How much more of this?" asked Brick. "I can't go on much farther."

"Neither can I," said Teddy. "I bet they loaded this sack with bricks."

"Pretty soon we take to the canoe again," said the Indian briefly.

The rest of the portage was easier, down hill to begin with, and much smoother going. The trail followed the stream which grew and grew with the constant welling of springs every few hundred yards. Its gentle and musical murmur swelled by the addition of other rivulets that joined it, and soon the tinkle of a small fall could be heard ahead. The path wound down and around this and led to the bank of another stream which combined with the one they had been following. The two made a sizable river, deep enough to float the canoe.

The portage was over.

Joe lowered his canoe and shoved it into the water. The boys dropped their provision sacks and took off the blanket rolls and carrier packs. Then they all stretched and eased their shoulders, wriggling and twisting to get free of sweaty shirts.

"We load," said Aba-ka-mas. "Take your places in the bow."

The hourly shift of paddle and rest between Brick and Teddy began again. But their progress was much faster, sped on by the rush of the river. Other streams joined it by tumbling down over falls or cutting sharply into it from the woods on either side. The current grew less rapid, and the rock gorges and ravines grew shallower as they wound into a more open country. Finally the river rounded a bend and emptied through a reedy lake with stretches of sandy beach, and groves of birch, pine and spruce.

"Look," said Teddy excitedly.

"My village," said Joe proudly.

Between the stands of trees were glimpses of farmland and pasture for sheep, and fields of corn ending in sunny meadows. Sometimes in the grasslands, but oftener near the shore of the lake or under the shade of a beech or pine woodland, were houses. A few of these were of boarding, painted white, but the majority were of peeled logs. This was the reservation, the home of Aba-ka-mas' tribe.

"Oh," said Brick, disappointedly, "I thought Indians lived in wigwams."

"Not any more," said Joe. "That was when we followed the game migrations. Now we farm and act as guides. The hunting and trapping grounds are gone."

But this colony was as superior to the squalid collection of shacks and huts that make up the usual reservation as Joe himself was to the average Indian. There was an air of prosperity about it, and of permanence. It was clean and tidy. The houses and farmlands were well kept and carefully tended. Fish nets and farm implements were mended and put away, and not flung down to rot or rust. Rowboats and canoes were pulled up on the bank and duck punts were turned over on wooden horses. Even now some were being painted and caulked against the coming fall season. There were neat gravel paths with whitewashed stone markers, and a sizable community dock.

Except for one thing, anybody coming suddenly on the settlement the way the boys had would take it for a summer camp or woods club, with separate cabins for its members. That one thing, or rather many times that one thing, were dogs—packs of them—gangs of them. They were of all ages, sizes and breeds—from puppies to gray muzzled oldsters, curs to full blooded sled huskies.

And what a fuss they made.

One dog had either seen, heard, smelled, or some instinct had warned him of the coming of the canoe. Instantly his alternate snoozes and flea hunts had given way to a wild rush for the dock, and his yaps and shrieks had summoned the pack. Dogs came from everywhere—from cabin steps, from naps on the warm sand of the beach; from the woods and rabbit trails, and from sheep pasture and farm patch. And every one of them was making all the racket he could. Yelps and barks, snarls and growls, howls and bays—all helped swell the din.

Brick looked nervously at Teddy.

Teddy looked nervously at the Chief.

Aba-ka-mas didn't look at anything. He kept right on paddling, drawing nearer to the landing, dogs or no dogs.

The clamor on the dock finally got the attention of the village braves. Two of them came to their cabin doors and looked out. Others, working on boats or nets along the shore, raised their heads to see what the rumpus was

about. Then they all started on a run for the pier, stoop-
ing on the way to pick up some sort of club.

Four of them reached the dock edge at the same time.
The hubbub of the dogs immediately swelled to bedlam.
The howls and barks of the pack changed to yelps and
snarls of pain as the braves laid about them in a calm
stoical manner. There was a strict impartiality about the
whole proceeding. There were no favorites. The Indians
thumped their own dogs just as stoutly as they whacked
those of their neighbors.

The dogs left, some streaking along the dock between
the legs of their attackers and others by the water route,
jumping in and swimming frantically off. The canoe had
a free landing.

"Well, that's that," said Brick from the bow.

"I won't miss those dogs," said Teddy in a relieved
voice.

"We stop here," said Aba-ka-mas briefly, swinging
alongside the dock.

Teddy and Brick clambered out. The Chief pitched up
the provision bags, packs and blanket rolls. His new
rifle and fishing rod, he handed to a waiting brave who
folded it tenderly in his arms like a mother would her
child. Then he followed the boys onto the pier. Another
of the tribe got into the empty canoe and paddled it off
toward the beach where he hauled it up on the sand, and
with a bit of seaweed and moss, proceeded to give it a
thorough scrub and rub down. Later, when it was dry,
it would be oiled and polished.

Aba-ka-mas strode up the dock, followed by his gun bearer. The other braves lined up parallel to the dock edge, and the boys passed in front of them in the track of the Chief and his bearer. There had been no introductions, no greetings. The whole landing had been performed in complete silence, and the boys didn't try to talk nor scrape up an acquaintance with the other Indians. There had been something noble about the Chief's reception—a dignity that did not permit of questioning nor of familiarity. There would be an explanation in due time—the Chief's time—and when that would be was entirely his own business.

The house of Aba-ka-mas was built of peeled logs and set squarely in the middle of the village. It faced the lake and had its own bit of beach with a garden patch behind. In front were carefully tended flower beds and a splendid white birch with a single totem cut in its bark. This was a rude picture of a boy bathing his feet in a stream—the legend or childhood happening from which the Chief drew his name.

Inside was a great room with a huge stone fireplace at its end, and a flagged hearth. An iron kettle simmered on the hob and other pots and pans were stacked neatly under the arch of the fireplace. On the mantel was a line of gourds, hollowed and dried for use as drinking horns, or for the storage of herbs and spices. The rafters groaned under the weight of strings of smoked meat, haunches of venison and bear, and slabs of bacon and fat hams. There were festoons of corn, peppers, squash, and pumpkin. Rude benches covered with bright-colored Indian blankets lined the walls, and a plain deal table was drawn up to one side of the fireplace.

Behind the living room were two bedrooms. Into one of these the Chief led the boys.

"A bunk for each of you," he said. "Spread your own blankets. You can wash up at the pump outside."

The bunks were really shelves, or rather shallow boxes with homespun linen sacks filled with corn husks for mattresses. The Able-seamen dropped their packs and laid out their blankets. Then they went out to wash. There was a tin basin on a bench beside the pump, some coarse yellow soap, and a harsh towel. The well water was icy and the soap didn't lather very well but they made out all right, stripping to the waist and scrubbing each other, and then rubbing themselves into a glow with the towel.

"Let's look around," said Brick. "I wonder what this village is like."

"How about those dogs?" said Teddy. "I don't feel much like running into them.'

"We'll get a club apiece," said Brick, "and we don't have to go far from the house to see all there is. I'm hungry anyway."

Brick was right, there wasn't much to see. The dock— they had seen a thousand of those. The beach—just like every other stretch of sand. Nor were there many Indians in sight, and those few didn't pay them any attention. When the boys said "Hello," they merely grinned and got out of the way.

Finally they spied a boy about their own age, and thinking they might have better luck, tried to scrape up an acquaintance.

"Hi there," said Brick.

"What's your name?" said Teddy.

The Indian boy stared at them for a full minute, looking them over from head to toe.

"Pete," he said briefly. "Where you come from?"

"Grosse Ile," said Brick.

"Ugh," said the Indian boy. Then he turned on his heel and walked away, going through a nearby cabin door.

"Talkative," said Brick, "and curious—I don't think."

"I could hardly get a word in edgewise," said Teddy. "Let's see if Joe has supper ready."

"We'll tell him what a swell welcome we got," said Brick.

Inside the Chief's cabin everything was cheerful and warm in the glow of lamp and fire-light. The table had been drawn up close to the hearth and three places laid on it. Some perch were sizzling away in a pan and some corncakes browning in another. A bowl of blueberries sat beside a pitcher of cream, and there was a loaf of maple sugar with a small hammer to break it up with. In a few minutes everything was ready and Joe set it before them.

"Eat," he said. "We talk about tomorrow afterward."

Conversation wouldn't have amounted to much anyway until they had knocked the edge off their appetites, so they tucked in the food in silence, and stuffed themselves until they could hardly wiggle. Joe seemed to have a joke all of his own, and smiled occasionally to himself.

"You didn't get much of a welcome," he said, when they had finished.

"Well, it wasn't exactly Old Home Week," said Teddy.

"I've heard nearly five words since we landed," said Brick. "What have we done, Mr. Foot-in-the-Water? They act like they were mad at us."

"No," said the Chief. "That is the custom. An Indian wouldn't think it polite to ask questions before you have eaten and rested. In the morning there will be a council, and you will have to be present. Coming here this way with me, their Chief, you are the messengers to my tribe from the Government at Washington. In front of my braves you must make the presentation of the rifle and rod which your Captain Williams gave me. In the name of your ship, you must also give the provisions in the two sacks. You must talk directly to me and to no one else, and when you have finished you must sit down."

"You mean I have to make a speech!" said Brick wildly.

"Yes—and I will repeat what you say in Chippewa. Then I and my braves will discuss the plans and decide what we will do. All this time you must keep silent. At the end of the council I too will make a speech. In it I will tell you what our course of action will be. Then you must say, 'It is well.' Then you must turn, and without a word, come into this house. Now we will go to bed."

"I feel kind of scared," said Brick to Teddy after they had turned in. "Did you ever do anything like that?"

"I should say not," said Teddy. "I'm glad you have to do the talking. I'd fall all over myself."

"I hope I don't gum it up," said Brick.

CHAPTER XIV

COUNCIL FIRE AND THE STICK MAP

NO INDIAN ever held any kind of ceremony without a fire. This has been true of many savage races since the dawn of mankind. It is the symbol of victory over wilderness and cold—the element that has made civilization possible. Without it there could be no cookery, and for food man would be forced to tear his flesh raw from living animals, and grub in the woods for roots and herbs. Nor would there be either hearth or home. Shelter would be reduced to the level of the dens and lairs of wild beasts. And so the Altar Fire became a part of every religious rite, and the Council Fire the seat of every decision and the center of every ceremony.

And Joe's tribe wasn't any different.

Soon after breakfast the next morning the squaws began to gather on the beach in front of the Chief's house. There wasn't a brave in sight, and Brick and Teddy itched to go out and scatter among them. Maybe from the women of the tribe, they would get a more friendly welcome than the cold shoulder of the night before.

But Joe wouldn't allow it.

"Stay here," he said. "When the council meets, two braves will come to the house and get us."

So the boys watched the proceedings through the cabin windows. First the women gathered a number of smooth round stones and laid them in a circle, perhaps a few yards across. In the center of the circle they dug a shallow pit and began to lay a fire. Next they piled on brush and made a bright blaze. Then·they added chips and driftwood until they had a glowing center, and the pit was filled with live coals. Then came the logs. These were of dried birch with the bark on, about three feet long and six inches thick.

There was a definite pattern to the way they laid on the logs. They all pointed inward toward a common burning center like the spokes of a wheel. The circle of stones formed a sort of broken rim, and when the tribe assembled they sat, or rather squatted, on the outside of the stones. Each brave had charge of one of the burning brands, and when he arose to speak he withdrew his log from the blazing fire center. When he finished his speech, he shoved it back in again and sat down. This was in the interest of brevity—a sort of amateur night gong—else the council would go on forever. It was considered a disgrace if a brave didn't finish what he had to say before the end of his brand went out.

The fire made, the squaws began to clean up. With some rude brooms made of fir branches and cones, they swept down the beach. Neither leaves, seaweed, nor any other beach rubbish was allowed to remain, and the sand was slicked to a hard even surface. Blankets were spread on the outside of the circle of stones for the braves to sit on, and after a final look around the squaws left. A lonely council fire blinked on a forsaken beach.

"What next?" asked Brick.

"Watch," said Joe.

The boys eyed the path along the lake front. The houses facing it stared vacantly out over the water. Suddenly through the door of the farthest cabin came a solitary brave. He marched down the path toward the meeting place. As he drew abreast of the other dwellings the door of each in turn was flung open and an Indian came out, until there was a procession of about twenty. They circled the fire and squatted on the blankets on the outside of the stones. Then a large carved pipe was hauled out, filled with tobacco, lit, and passed round. Each brave took a puff and handed it to the man next to him. Finally two of the tribe got up, turned away from the fire, and stamped gravely toward the house. One was the gun bearer of the day before, the other a total stranger, although there was an air of considerable importance about him.

"Here they come," said Teddy.

"Don't I know it," said Brick. "I wish you had to make that speech."

The two Indians entered. One of them picked up the provision bags which were stacked by the door, and to the other, the Chief handed his new rifle and rod. Then without a word, Aba-ka-mas stalked through the open door, followed by his gun bearer. Brick came next, and then Teddy. The Indian with the provision sacks brought up the rear.

Single file, they marched down toward the council fire. When they reached the circle of stones surrounded by its ring of braves, Chief Aba-ka-mas stepped to the center. His gun bearer stood behind him on the outside of the stones, stolid, expressionless. The other Indian dropped the provision bags to the ground and squatted beside them. Brick and Teddy didn't know quite what to do. So unconsciously they did the right thing. They stood there—silent, grave—waiting for what came next.

The Chief began to talk in Chippewa. Neither of the boys could understand a word, but both knew there were many references to them, to the ship, and to its crew. The name *Gull-Flight* was used several times—Captain Williams once or twice—and many gestures in their direction told how much they were a part of the explanation.

Finally Aba-ka-mas finished his speech. For a minute his glance searched the ring of braves. Then he turned and walked over to Brick and placed a hand on his shoulder.

"Speak," he said, in English. "Tell my brothers why we are here."

Brick gulped and stepped into the ring. Teddy eyed his cousin a little enviously, but glad underneath that his part called for silence.

"Chief Foot-in-the-Water," began the redheaded Able-seaman, "from the Government at Washington to you, as head of this tribe, greetings. And from my uncle, Captain Williams, two gifts."

He walked over to the gun bearer and took from him the rifle and rod. He handed them to Aba-ka-mas, and then turned back to face the tribe.

"These," he continued, motioning toward the provision sacks, "are from all of us—your good friends—the crew of the *Gull-Flight.*"

"Ugh," said the braves.

"Good boy," whispered Teddy.

"There is a band of smugglers," Brick went on, "that has its base somewhere in this country. They are committing crimes against your government and mine. We have come a long ways to catch them, but it is only with your help that we can track them down. Your Chief tells me that Scar-face, their leader, is known to you. This council is met to talk over ways to capture him and break up his band. On whatever plan you decide, it is my uncle's order that we follow it. . . . I have finished."

Brick stepped out of the circle, and over to Teddy's side. Then they too searched the faces of the ring of braves for some sign of approval of what Brick had just said. But there was none—nor of disapproval either. The braves stared straight in front of them—stolidly, blankly—in that complete silence that was always so disconcerting to the boys in all their dealings with the tribe so far.

Finally the Indian who had come to the house with the gun bearer, got to his feet and stalked a short way from the circle. Before, neither of the boys had paid much attention to him. Now, they looked him over carefully. He was short, broad shouldered, almost squat of body, and powerful, and his face was frightfully scarred. Not only the scars, but his name, came from the same source—the result of a slashing blow from a grizzly's claws. Later, they learned that he was one of the tribe's most fearless hunters, and best guide. His name was Bear Hunter.

After searching a while on the beach the Indian found a short stick, and taking out his knife, whittled the end into a blunt point. Then with the stick, he began to make some marks in the sand. No one paid any attention to him, at least outwardly. But Brick and Teddy fairly itched to know what he was up to.

The Indian scratched away busily for several minutes. Then he let out a series of grunts. Apparently the grunts had some meaning in Chippewa, for the rest of the braves got up and walked over to where he was working. Aba-ka-mas turned to the boys.

"Go and look," he said. "But don't talk."

The Able-seamen crowded round, watching what Bear Hunter was doing. Or rather at what he had already half done. For with his stick he was making a picture map in the sand, much in the same fashion as beach artists carve their relief drawings in front of the boardwalks of every seaside resort.

First, he had drawn a line about four yards long. For about six feet from its west end, the line ran fairly

straight. Then it crooked sharply, jutting out to form a
ragged peninsula. For a few feet farther the line was
straight again, and then looped to form another peninsula. After that it twisted and turned, curving almost
back on itself to shape the slashes and bends of deep bays
and fiords. On the south of this irregular line, Bear
Hunter had smoothed the sand to look like the level surface of a lake. The line itself represented a portion of the
shore of Georgian Bay and the North Channel.

Roughly parallel to the line and a little to the north of
it, the Indian had pushed up a ridge of sand into a minia-
ture mountain chain that followed the coast. On the
map, the chain was about a foot from the shore. Actually
the distance was several miles. Inland from the mountain chain was another long line, but lightly scratched in
the sand and crossed by a series of marks. The line represented a railroad track and the cross marks, the ties.

Brick nudged Teddy with his elbow.

"What do you suppose it is?" he whispered.

"Sh-sh," said Teddy. "I don't know any more than you
do."

For as yet the relief map looked like nothing at all. But
the Indian continued rapidly and silently at his work,
and the sculptured ridges or mountain chains pushed
down and along. At the lower end of the map, the high
cliffs that formed Drowned Man's Cove began to take
shape; then the plateau, the scene of yesterday's difficult
portage. Another twisted scratch marked the river down
which they had paddled, and finally an oval loop traced

the shores of Reservation Lake. Some little dots represented the Indians' houses.

Bear Hunter stood up, looked at his work carefully, and grunted. Then as a finishing effort, he made two crosses in the sand. The first was on the shore of Georgian Bay, not far from the entrance to Drowned Man's Cove. The other was way up near the end of his beach line on the edge of the North Channel.

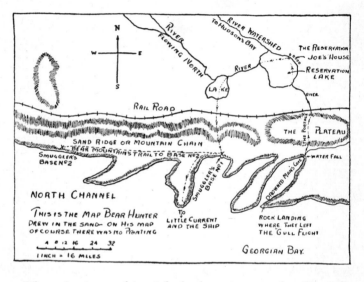

Throwing away his stick, he began to speak. His talk was a mixture of Chippewa and English. But as he got really under way, he began to gesture with his hands, using more and more English all the time. So by watching the sand map and listening closely, the boys understood most of what he was explaining. The two crosses were the camps or forwarding bases of the smugglers. The railroad was their means of supply. Working always with a confederate on the train, the contrabrand would be dumped off in the wilderness and taken to one of the bases. Later a boat would call, usually a lumber schooner or fishing tug, but sometimes a fast speedboat would do the work. To actually catch the smugglers, it was necessary to pick the base in use. The other would be deserted, bare, an uninhabited camp or a desolate shore.

The guttural sounds of Bear Hunter's half-Indian, half-English talk ended. He crossed his arms as a signal that his speech was done. Brick and Teddy looked at each other.

"Watch Joe," said Brick.

Chief Aba-ka-mas had drawn a hunting knife from his sheath at his belt. He was leaning over the stick map in the sand, looking at it carefully. With the point of his knife he began to trace a line leading across Reservation Lake. The line then followed the course of a stream and on through another little lake.

Then he stood up.

"Bear Hunter and I," he said, "will each take a canoe and one brave. The redhaired boy will go with me. His cousin will be in the other canoe. Tonight we will camp on the shore of the lake where I have drawn the circle. Tomorrow the braves will bring back the canoes."

He turned back to the map.

The knife point made another scratch, this time south, crossing the railroad track and mountain chain, and stopping where Bear Hunter had made his first cross, at Smuggler Base Number One, on the shore of Georgian Bay.

Once again the Chief addressed his council.

"In the morning we will take the trail to the first camp of the smugglers. If we find them there, the boys and I will go quickly to Little Current and join the ship. Bear Hunter will stay and watch. With the ship, we will come back. The capture will be made from the water side. Bear Hunter and I will prevent their escape by land."

"Ugh," grunted the braves, whether in disapproval or not, neither of the boys could say.

"If Base One is deserted," the Chief went on, "Bear Hunter will go immediately on foot to Base Two. His trail will follow the shore and he should be there by the third day. He will scout the camp and watch for the *Gull-Flight.* As in the other plan, the boys and I will go to Little Current and board the ship. We will drop anchor off the Smuggler Base and put off small boats as though we were on a fishing trip. Bear Hunter will watch his chance and swim out and join us. We will then make final plans for the capture of Scar-face."

When Aba-ka-mas finished the outline of his plan, he folded his arms and waited for a minute to give his braves a chance to think over what he said.

"Do my brothers agree?" he asked at last.

Bear Hunter spoke for the tribe. "The plan is good," he said.

Brick remembered his instructions of the night before.

"It is well," he said.

"It's more than that," whispered Teddy, "it's swell!"

PERHAPS the council had been slow and deliberate in reaching its decision. But once arrived at, immediate and rapid action quickly followed. There was neither haste nor waste motion. The preparations for departure were as efficient as those of a veteran army breaking camp. Bear Hunter went directly to his cabin, and Brick and Teddy followed Aba-ka-mas to his.

"Make up your blanket rolls," said the Chief. "Bring your pack-carriers here into the living room."

In a jiffy the Able-seamen made up their rolls and slung them over their shoulders. On the table near the fireplace Joe had ready some slices of bacon and salt pork. Gourds containing salt, pepper, sugar and other condiments were set out and waiting for them to take what they needed. The Indian had a small sack of flour, a still smaller bag of cornmeal, and a few handfuls of coffee tied up in a clean rag. These he put into a tin pail with a cover to it. Then he handed Brick a frying pan and Teddy the short-handled shovel, and helped them sling their packs. Picking up his own duffel, together with his rifle and rod, he turned toward the door.

"We go now," he said briefly.

By the time they got down to the dock it was the middle of the afternoon. As usual their departure was in complete silence. And no one came down to see them off. Apparently the other Indians were completely indifferent, and as Brick looked back at the tight little village and the comfortable cabin they had just left, he had a gone feeling in his midriff. What was ahead he didn't know, but events were rapidly shaping to a climax, and he wished Sailor Bill and Dominick were near.

"I wonder what they're all doing," he said to himself. "And where the ship is?"

The canoes swung down Reservation Lake, a matter of some eight or nine miles. With an Indian at both bow and stern paddles, their progress was very rapid. Inside an hour they entered a small stream that ambled away, generally to the south and west. For a while there was quiet water, but this soon gave way to some easy rapids, and the canoes fairly tore along. Another hour took them its full twelve-mile course. Then they came to a second lake, perhaps seven miles across. Joe and Bear Hunter drove their canoes through this lake and up on the beach at its south end. The canoe part of the trip was over, and the braves in charge would take them back in the morning. Joe, Bear Hunter, and the boys would make the rest of the journey on foot.

Then they made camp for the night. And there wasn't any lost motion about this either, for the Indians knew just what to do. One fished for their supper and brought in a couple of dozen good-sized perch; another dug a pit a short way up the beach and made a fire. Bear Hunter was the cook. He gathered their tin pail full of blueberries and using the cover for a pan, made a pie. He mixed up some salt, corn meal and bacon grease, and made a pone. Then he fried the fish and served the meal on clean birch-bark plates.

Joe set about making a shelter for the boys to sleep in. First he picked out a slim standing birch sapling about ten feet high, and trimmed off all the branches. Then he bent it over to a bowed right angle and held it down with a short piece of line secured to a peg driven in the ground. This formed the ridge pole for the tent. Under it he laid four logs in a hollow square, and filled in the space with a mat of freshly cut fir and spruce boughs, soft and springy. Next came the shelter-halves, buttoned together and flung over the ridge pole. These were stretched taut and pegged down tight, making a snug dry shelter. All the boys had to do was to crawl in, pull up their other blanket, and go to sleep.

And this they did, just as soon as they had finished cramming in their supper.

The smell of broiling bacon wakened Brick early the next morning. It was hardly daylight and the stars were still out, but the camp was astir, or rather what was left of it, for the canoes and the two escorting braves were gone. Bear Hunter was crouched over the fire, and by both sight and smell, breakfast gave warning that it would be ready in a few minutes. Brick stuck his elbow into Teddy's ribs.

"Come on, get up," he said. "It's time to eat."

The Able-seamen scrambled out, washed in the chill water of the lake, and warmed away their shivers in front of the fire. Joe showed up with a pail of wild raspberries, and they had breakfast. Then they made up their blanket rolls, slung their packs, put out the fire, and started.

Without a word the party struck off into the forest, Aba-ka-mas in the lead. Brick came next, then Teddy, with Bear Hunter bringing up the rear. Their course was south, toward a distant mountain chain. This was the raised sand ridge of the relief map that Bear Hunter had drawn with his stick on the beach near the council fire. There it hadn't looked like much, but now in the clear morning air, its jagged peaks and sheer cliffs jutted sharply through its pine covered slopes. Brick would have liked to ask some questions.

How far were they going? How soon would they get there? How would they cross the mountains?

But he didn't. He followed blindly. And he soon found that if he did even that, and did it well, he would have his hands full. The Chief walked in an even regular stride. His gait had a queer sort of sag to it, and his head was thrust a little forward. His carriage was just short of erect and his knees were always slightly bent. He never hurried, but neither did he ever rest.

At first the boys followed without much trouble. But Aba-ka-mas moved with the steady lope of a plains pony that ate up mile after mile, and after a while it became a decided effort to keep pace. Each step was a deliberate forcing of one foot after the other. They grew tired and hot, and sullen and resentful of stones, roots, or patches of soft ground. The distance was bad enough, other obstacles were a studied insult. And then suddenly they both got their second wind. The going became easier. They breathed deeply and freely, and moved with steady swinging strides.

At the end of three hours, they were at the base of the mountain chain. Here the Indian called a halt. They drank from a nearby stream and threw themselves down and slept. They rested half an hour. At noon they repeated the rest and ate a little food—some cold corn pone, some colder and more tasteless fish left over from breakfast. The march began again. The way led up and up, and the trail grew rougher and rougher. Twice they swam rivers—cold swift mountain streams that bit into tired and aching muscles but washed away fatigue.

Suddenly they came out on the top of the divide, and mountain and forest dropped away before them. Off in the distance was the shine and sparkle of Georgian Bay, dotted with green-wooded islands. And from here on, their progress was easier. Down hill to begin with, and a fresh breeze from the lake to cool them off.

And wasn't Brick glad of that! The Indians were as fresh, or as tired, as when they had started. You never could tell by looking at them. The miles they had come! The heights they had climbed! There was no outward effect. Every hardship was born in stolid, indifferent silence. But for the boys, the last two hours were almost more than they could stand. Each thought he would drop with weariness. Time after time, Brick thought he would have to quit.

And then . . .

"No, I'll keep on a little longer. But when we get to the top of that next ledge—I'm through."

Then he would struggle on another forty or fifty rods. A patch of sunlit glade would appear a short way ahead.

"I'll make that," he would say to himself. "And then I'm going to lie down and die."

But he didn't, and now the end was in sight. In two hours more they were down out of the mountains and working through a pine forest that fringed the shore. For a mile or so they skirted the beach, and then turned back inland again, letting the forest close about them. Joe was looking for something, and suddenly he found it. He stopped and held up his hand. Bear Hunter immediately moved around the boys to the head of the file and joined his Chief.

The something was a trail that came down out of the mountains and led toward a point that jutted out into Georgian Bay. Together, the Indians bent and examined some blurred footprints. Faint as they were, they made a definite track, and to the scouts' eyes, as easy to follow as a well marked city street.

Aba-ka-mas motioned the boys to him.

"Follow us," he said. "But don't talk. And lie down when I tell you."

The Indians spread out on either side of the foot tracks, and the little party moved cautiously down the point of land. The boys lagged a short way behind, but kept Joe always in sight. For a half mile they crept through the woods, carefully watching each step they took. To tread on a dry stick would break it, and the snap would ring out in the silence like a shot. Suddenly Joe stopped again and waited for the boys to come up. Then he pointed toward the tip of the point.

"Down," he whispered. "Base Number One is just ahead. Bear Hunter and I will scout it."

The Able-seamen dropped into the underbrush and wriggled behind a tree. Then carefully, so as not to rustle the bushes, Brick made a little opening and looked out.

There was nothing in sight—nothing living or moving, that is. The Indians had vanished, instantly and without a sound. But perhaps fifty yards farther on, and on the shore of the lake, was an old building at the landward end of a half-ruined dock. The shack, for the building was little more than that, could be anything—an old fishing station—an abandoned lumber camp. But a line of freshly painted buoys marked a channel from the dock edge to deep water. Somebody was using it, and a furtive, secretive air about the whole place fairly shrieked aloud that the use was not a lawful one. And why keep open and mark that channel? Certainly not just to show the passage to a deserted shore.

Brick watched interestedly, holding his breath. Where were the Indians? What were they doing?

Suddenly Joe answered both questions for him by coming around one corner of the shack. He appeared openly and without any effort toward concealment. Bear Hunter showed up around the opposite corner. He had something white in one hand, and as he joined his Chief, he began an explanation, pointing to the white object and gesturing toward the shack. Joe looked back at the woods where he had left the boys. He whistled and waved his hand.

"Come here," he called.

The Able-seamen did, on the run. There was no need for caution now.

"What is it?" asked Brick as he came up.

"Is anybody here?" asked Teddy in the next breath.

"No," said Joe; "they've gone. But someone was here yesterday, or maybe the day before. Do you know this?"

He held out the white object.

Brick took it. It was a white sailor's hat, similar to the ones worn by the crew of the *Gull-Flight*. He turned it over and looked inside. Under the band were two initials, stenciled in ink. Brick recognized them.

He turned to Aba-ka-mas.

"It's Katy's," he said.

"Katy's!" said Teddy wildly. "How did she get here?"

The Indian Chief didn't answer him directly.

"We go to Little Current," he said. "Bear Hunter takes the trail for Base Two."

CHAPTER XV

OVER THE stern rail of the *Gull-Flight*, Katy and Spinach watched the Chief's canoe fade down the reach of Drowned Man's Cove. Soon it dwindled to a dot, and at last even the flash of the sun on the paddle blade winked and went out, swallowed in the shadows cast by the mountains on either side. Aba-ka-mas and the Able-seamen were gone.

Katy turned to her cousin.

"I wonder when we'll see them again?" she said.

"I'm not wondering about that," said Spinach. "It's what's apt to happen in the meanwhile that bothers me. And what *we're* going to do."

But neither of them had time for much questioning of the future, for the sudden roar of the ship's motor shattered the quiet of the Northland morning. Startled, the girls looked around. Dominick was busy knocking out the shore props, and Sailor Bill was walking aft to the wheel. The *Gull-Flight* had sprung to life.

"Mates on the dock," said the Blue Nose. "Let go the shore lines."

Katy and Spinach clambered out on the rock ledge and

251

freed the mooring lines from around their fir trees. Then they scrambled back aboard, and none too soon either, for Morgan had come up from the engine room and stood by the clutch level.

"Slow ahead," said the Skipper.

The schooner's nose swung away from the landing and headed for the entrance to Drowned Man's Cove. They were helped through the narrows by the natural flow of the current which swept them past the end of the sand bar and out into Georgian Bay. Here Sailor Bill set a course that paralleled the frowning cliff that had seemed such an impassable barrier when they were heading toward it two days ago. But there was no thought of getting up sail. Already two of the crew had gone, and soon only the Skipper and the Chief Engineer would be left aboard. For by the looks of him, Dominick was getting ready to leave and take the Mates with him.

"Bear a hand!" he called. "We'll get the *Bonny* ready."

"You mean we're going to leave the *Gull-Flight?*" asked Spinach.

"That very thing," said the Blue Nose. "How else would we help find the smugglers?"

Then they were busy. Everything came out of the little cutter. Oars, masts and sails—spare line, life preservers and tiller—all came out for a thorough inspection and then were put back again. Next they began loading her up for the trip. Katy and Spinach fairly staggered under the weight of two huge duffel bags which they hoisted up to where Dominick sat perched in the *Bonny*.

"For Heaven's sake, what's in those?" asked Katy, grunting and puffing, as she passed them up.

"Gear," said the Blue Nose. "Pots, pans, and provisions. Smugglers or no smugglers, we may as well be comfortable. And we don't have to do our own carrying. The *Bonny* will do it for us."

For the little cutter could easily be loaded with everything to make them more than comfortable when they made camp for the night. There were folding chairs and a canvas-topped table. Nor did the girls have to sling their own blanket rolls. Each had a sleeping bag, waterproof canvas on the outside, soft mattress, wooly blankets and pillow inside. Finally all was ready and Dominick jumped down out of the cutter to the deck.

"And just in time, I'm thinking," he said. "It looks as though we'd shove off any minute."

For in the meanwhile, the schooner had kept on along the rock cliff. After the first hour its towering height began to dwindle to a more easy slope, petering out finally to a rock point. Even this gave way at last to a sand spit, and the *Gull-Flight* came to a stop outside an offshore bar that almost blocked the entrance to a pair of bays that cut back inland for several miles. They were wider than the cove they had left in the morning, and dotted with small wooded islands. But they were wild enough—not a dock or a house in sight—and the forest came down to the water's edge on all sides. The schooner might easily run aground on the shoals and bars, but in the little *Bonny,* the bays could be explored from end to end.

"Well, here we are," said the Skipper. "Lower the cutter into the water. We'll stand off out here. Work through the first bay this afternoon, and if you see anything suspicious, come back to the ship at once. Otherwise, you can sleep ashore."

"Aye aye, sir," said the Blue Nose. "We'll camp tonight where you can see our fire. Tomorrow, we'll explore the next bay."

They all lowered away on the *Bonny,* and soon she rode in the water. Sailor Bill stood looking down over the rail, sizing up the little craft and its equipment. Dominick went below for a minute. Just as the Skipper was helping his nieces over the side, the Blue Nose came back on deck. In his hand was a 303 bolt-action rifle, a regular Army pattern.

The Skipper looked at it.

"See here," he said, "I'd rather you didn't take that. You can't handle a whole band of smugglers alone you know, and I don't want the girls mixed up in any shooting. They're only along to make this voyage look like a family cruise."

Dominick stopped still as though he had just remembered something. He looked at the girls standing there waiting to climb down into the cutter. Then he handed the rifle to the Skipper.

"*Mon Captaine,*" he said, "you're right. I almost forgot that our Mates were so young."

For the best part of two hours they sailed the cutter down through the mouth and well into the first bay.

Katy was posted up in the bows where she kept an eye open for shoals and bars as well as watched the shore. Spinach had the sheet lines amidships and Dominick, the tiller. They were skirting the right-hand beach opposite the rugged peninsula which separated the two bays, and working in as close as they dared, sailed the *Bonny* clear to the end of the bay. But they saw nothing. Nothing human, that is, just the wilderness of pine scrub and an endless stretch of yellow sand beach.

"We'll run out and look over that large wooded island," said Dominick. "They might operate from there."

But nobody was there either, nor ever had been apparently, for even the wild game was bold and unafraid. A porcupine stared at them impudently, and refused to move from a dead branch on which he sat. A grouse drummed and thundered from the dry wash of an old creek bed. From a patch of reeds, a mallard led four or five of her ducklings on an experimental swim, and was in no way frightened by the cutter moving along offshore. Three or four gulls left huddles of eggs nestled in among the sun-warmed beach pebbles—circled and screamed a few insults at them—and returned to their nests.

"Well, we haven't seen anybody so far," said Katy.

"Not yet," said Dominick. "But we'll work across to the other shore and out toward the mouth of the bay. Then if nothing turns up, we'll camp for the night."

They put the *Bonny* about and made several short tacks. Handling sail and sheet kept them busy for a while, and nobody said much. Finally they got over to the east shore and began to work along it. Nothing there either, just the sand beach and the endless pine forest. Spinach got sick of the profitless search and said so to Dominick. The undercover agent's eyes twinkled.

"And what would you do if we suddenly came on Scarface standing on the shore? And suppose he had a rifle in his hand?"

Spinach hadn't thought of that.

"Well, I really don't know," she admitted after a minute.

"What *should* we do?" asked Katy. "Before we get back to the *Gull-Flight,* I suppose we may do that very thing."

"Yes," said Dominick, "and when it happens, it's a very innocent pair you want to be. Just two girls on a cutter trip in charge of one of the ship's hands."

"Let's keep on supposing," said Katy. "What if he shoots that rifle?"

"At us," said Spinach. "I don't have to suppose about that. I know I wouldn't like it."

"He won't," said Dominick, "not if you act your part. No one's going to kill an innocent tourist, just for the fun of it. But he may be suspicious—and if he tells us to get out—why that's just what we'll do. And without any back talk. We'll do our arguing afterward."

"I'm not going to do any arguing, either before or after," said Katy. "At least not while he has the rifle."

"You won't have to," said the Blue Nose. "Not today anyway, for there's nary a smuggler in this bay. We'll make camp for the night and start our search again to-morrow. Here's as fine a place as any."

The "fine place" was the sand beach at the tip of the peninsula that separated the two bays. Here, their camp-fire could easily be seen from the ship, and Sailor Bill would know that they were safe and that so far, his searching party had seen nothing suspicious. It would also be a signal to him to move the *Gull-Flight* so as to be able to watch the far side of the entrance to the second bay. For if anyone attempted to run either in or out of it in the night he would certainly give their campfire a wide berth and try to escape or enter along the upper shore. And there, the Skipper and Morgan would be ready and waiting for him.

A few more minutes and the *Bonny's* nose bumped the sand bottom of the beach at the point. The girls trimmed in on the sheet lines and Dominick helped them lower the sails and unstep the masts. Then he jumped out and waded ashore, and with a few tugs and pulls dragged the cutter far enough up the beach so the girls could step ashore.

"What do we do first?" asked Spinach. "I've never made a camp in the wilderness before."

"Wilderness, is it?" said Dominick. "In an hour from now we'll be so snug you'll think you're at home in your own parlor."

First they unloaded. Then Dominick picked out two trees a little ways apart and lashed the upper edge of the *Bonny's* foresail between them, about shoulder high.

Then he carried the lower edge out and back a couple of yards so that the canvas was taut, and pegged it down tight. This made a canvas wall that sloped like a roof. It would not only keep out the cold night wind, but would reflect the heat from their fire downward, and in case of rain, would shed water like a duck's back.

"Now," said Dominick, "we can build our fire and get supper ready."

And apparently supper was to be a very elaborate affair. No Army mess tins or birch-bark plates for them. First the folding table was set up between the fire and the tent wall, and spread with a white cloth. Then it was laid with glassware, china and cutlery brought from the *Gull-Flight's* lockers. And they had comfortable canvas chairs to sit on. Nor were their cooking arrangements of the rough and ready type, with an Indian crouched in the smoke of the fire, trying to juggle a frying pan over the coals.

"It's grand chefs you are, in the ship's galley," said Dominick to the girls. "None better. But if you'll bring me those duffel bags, maybe there's a trick or two I can show you about cooking in the open."

And many were the tricks that he had. For when he got through rigging his fire it was as convenient as any modern gas range. On either side of the fire pit he drove a forked stake, with a taut wire strung between. From this he suspended his pots and kettles, over the blaze where they got all the heat but none of the smoke or sparks. Then out of the bags came a small sheet-iron oven and a well-charred fish plank. In a bucket was a dressed whitefish, caught the night before and packed in ice. After larding the fish with thin strips of salt pork he placed it, together with a tin cup half full of water, on the plank and popped the whole thing into the oven. Then deep into the fire pit it went, to be covered with hot coals, and steam and bake for an hour.

When everything was ready Dominick served it with a flourish—in courses—true French style. First the soup. Then the vegetables—whole hominy boiled with pieces of salt pork, sliced eggplant dipped in flour and fried in bacon grease. Then the planked whitefish, brown, juicy, and steaming hot, served with boiled potatoes mashed to a fluffy creaminess. Dominick had coffee, and the girls cocoa.

Afterward they built up the fire and sat around it. The Blue Nose lit his pipe and smoked away in perfect contentment. Katy and Spinach decided to go for a stroll down the beach to shake down their supper. When they came back their two bedding rolls were spread out under the canvas fly, heads away, and feet toward the fire.

"Hop in," said Dominick. "Tomorrow will be a long day as we want to make an early start."

"What about you?" asked Katy. "Where are you going to sleep?"

"There's room enough under the tent for all of us," said Spinach.

"I'll sleep in the *Bonny*," said Dominick. "And it won't be the first time I've curled up in a ship's small boat. But suppose I take a walk myself now, and give you a chance to tuck in."

And tuck in they did, each shucking off a uniform and into a pair of flannel pajamas. Then in between the warm blankets on the soft mattress and pillow; and when Dominick came back he was greeted by a pair of curly heads and two pairs of bright eyes shining over the tops of the sleeping bags.

"So there you are," said the Blue Nose. "Snug as a bug in a rug."

"Good night," said the girls a little sleepily.

"Just one thing," said Dominick. "And I almost forgot it."

He went back to the dunnage bags and got out the bag of salt. Loosening the neck string so the salt would pour, he made a complete circle of the sleeping bags, dribbling a trail of salt as he went.

"What's that for?" said Katy, curious, though only half awake.

"To make you have sweet dreams," said Dominick. "Go to sleep now, and not another word."

He didn't tell her that it was to keep out snakes. For not even to crawl in where it was warm, would a snake cross that protecting circular trail of salt.

WITHIN an hour after sunup the next morning they had breakfast, struck camp and launched the *Bonny*. There was a fresh breeze blowing toward the land, and as they rounded the point and turned into the second bay, the little cutter heeled over and fairly flew along. Dominick switched places with Katy and was up in the bows which left to the Mates the actual handling of the boat. Spinach had the sheet lines amidships again and her cousin, the tiller.

Yesterday, the Blue Nose hadn't taken the trip into the first bay very seriously. Apparently he hadn't expected to find any trace of the smugglers, and more than anything else, was intent on enjoying his sail in the cutter. He was almost boyishly delighted at the prospect of making a shore camp and had a wonderful time cooking supper. But this morning he had a very business-like air about him. He had brought along a pair of glasses, and from his place up in the bows, searching the shore line carefully as they swept along. He continually snapped orders back to Katy telling her when to ease off or change course so that he could make a closer inspection.

"Run out to that island," he said, pointing toward the middle of the bay.

Katy put the tiller down and Spinach trimmed in the sheets. The cutter swung up to a close-hauled port tack. Dominick searched the island through his glasses.

"All right," he said after a few minutes. "Nobody there. Ease off and work back along the shore line."

They kept on, in toward the head of the bay. Nobody said anything for some time, Katy and Spinach intent on the handling of the cutter, and Dominick on his scrutiny of the wooded shores. Suddenly the Blue Nose stiffened, something like a bird dog coming to point. He was looking away from shore, ahead, and off to port.

Two or three miles away something that looked like a line of stakes stuck up out of the water. There was a sort of pattern to the way they were placed, as though they might be channel markings. And they led inland, toward the end of the bay.

"Run out to them," ordered Dominick.

As the cutter drew near they could see that they did mark a channel, a tortuous winding one, for to every other stake or so, was fastened a white bull's-eye with black crosses which were ranges to show the way through the twists and turns of the channel. As they swept up to the first stake, Katy luffed up a little and brought the *Bonny* almost to a standstill while the undercover agent examined the range marking.

"I thought so," he said. "Fresh paint. Somebody is using the channel. We'll follow them in," he added grimly.

The ranges led directly away from the open waters of the bay and soon began to wind in and out through a maze of small islands. Within a half hour their course became so twisted and the islands cut off so much of the breeze that they had to drop the sails and take to the oars. Dominick and Spinach did the pulling and Katy the steering. Suddenly they rounded an island and the channel markings straightened out. An open passage led to a dock.

They ran in and tied up. The top of the dock was several feet above their heads and the stringers were half rotted away. But a number of timbers had been recently replaced and a rough ladder led down to the water. It was brand new, built of raw peeled logs, and the nails which fastened it together hadn't even had time to rust. Dominick got out of the boat and climbed the ladder. Katy and Spinach followed him up. There hadn't been anyone in sight when they ran in under the pier, and nobody was around now. But at the shore end of the half-ruined dock was a weather-beaten shack with a much trodden path leading toward it.

"Follow me," said the undercover agent. They moved down the footpath.

In spite of the well-worn path, the shack had a deserted vacant look. A pine-slab door with rusty strap-iron hinges had been let into its front wall, and on either side were shoulder-high cross-barred windows. The panes were dirty and smeared with spiderwebs. They were old ones, with dried skeletons of half-eaten flies tangled grotesquely in their broken meshes. In an effort to look out, someone had tried to wipe one of the panes clean, and a few spots of clear glass blinked from the center of a circular smudge. The morning sun shone on these and was reflected back in a crooked blurred leer.

They went up to the door. "I suppose it's locked," said the Blue Nose.

It was. By a shining brass padlock hooked through a hasp, and some new wire staples had been driven in over the hinges. But the door jamb was half rotten and the hinges rusty and weak. Dominick stepped back a pace or two, and then charged the door. He struck it with his shoulder and the fastenings gave way. The door fell inward, slamming down on the floor and raising a cloud of dust. They went through the opening.

Inside was a single room, raftered across the top of its peeled log walls, and with a smooth pine floor. At the far end was a rough stone fireplace with a flagged hearth. Three of the four walls had been punched through with windows and the sun filtered through the dirty panes in slanting shafts of light wtih dust motes dancing through them. Dust was everywhere. On the window sills, between the chinks of the wall logs, and on the floor.

But someone had been using the room, and very recently too. For there were patterned squares on the floor along the walls that were free of dust, as though things had been piled there. A clean circle marked the sharp outline of a barrel head. A clear rectangle showed where a box had rested, and in another place was a queer design in the shape of a bearskin hearthrug. A pile of raw furs had been there. And footprints led everywhere, crossing and recrossing from all sides of the room.

Dominick examined all these telltale signs closely. Then he went over to the fireplace and sifted some of the dry powdery ashes through his fingers. He jerked his hand back quickly, for the ashes were still hot and burned his fingers. Someone had had a fire there, and within the last few hours.

"Stay here," he said to the girls, "while I look around."

He walked back to the doorway, and the Mates watched him clamber over the broken-in door. Then he went through the opening, his square figure blocking out the light for a second, turned, and disappeared around the corner of the house. The girls looked at each other.

"Now what?" asked Spinach. "Do you suppose he'll find anybody?"

Katy didn't answer for a minute. It was hot in the shack, and stuffy; and the pressure of the tight sailor's hat clamped across her brow was giving her a headache. She took it off, walked over to the fireplace, blew some of the dust off the mantel, and laid the hat down. Then she turned to speak to Spinach. But she didn't. Instead, she stared through the window in the side wall, fascinated, and struck silent by what she saw.

Dominick was walking past, back toward the front of the building. Only his head and the upper part of his body showed through the window, but something in his gait frightened her. He tramped along steadily enough but he was staring straight forward, and his chest was thrust out in front of him as though something were poking him in the small of the back. In a second she saw what it was, a rifle, held by another man who was prodding the Blue Nose along. They passed by. Then followed a third head and shoulders, framed sharply in the window. Katy recognized this one.

It was Scar-face.

She gulped and tried to warn Spinach. But the words

wouldn't come, and she only succeeded in making some half-strangled noises. But she *did* point toward the door.

Spinach thought that her cousin had suddenly gone crazy. But her gaze followed the outstretched finger.

"What's the mat . . . ?" she started to ask.

Then it was her turn to be struck dumb.

Dominick came in the door. Or rather, Scar-face flung him in by the scruff of his neck. The other man covered him with the rifle.

"I'll teach you to break down doors," said the leader of the smuggler band. "What are you doing here? How did you get here? And who are you anyway?"

Then he saw Katy standing by the fireplace. There was no doubt that he knew who *she* was.

"So—ho!" he said. "The girls off the schooner! And just what are *you* doing here?"

Katy did some fast thinking. Her brain must not lag, nor her voice falter now.

"I'm sorry about the door," she said, "perhaps we can pay you for it. We thought this was just an abandoned shack. I told him," pointing to Dominick, "to break in. It really wasn't his fault. He has to obey orders, you know. I'm Mate aboard ship, he's our foremast hand."

The man with the rifle started to say something. Scar-face snarled at him.

"Shut up," he said. "I'll run this."

Dominick spoke up. "I'd have told you all that if you'd given me a chance," he said. "We were taking a sight-seeing trip in the ship's cutter. It's the first time in the

North Country for the girls, and they want to see every-thing. We ran across your ranges and followed the chan-nel in under the dock. We had no idea you were using the shack."

"He's ly . . ." began the man with the rifle.

Scar-face glared at him. "I told you to shut up," he said.

Then he faced Dominick again.

"Where's your boat now?" he said.

Dominick told him.

"Untie her and shove off," said Scar-face. "We don't want tourists nosing around. You've been here. Now get out."

"And don't come back," said the man with the rifle.

At last he had gotten his word in.

SAILOR BILL saw the *Bonny* coming out of the bay and worked the *Gull-Flight* in as close as he dared to pick them up. As the schooner lost way and drifted alongside, Dominick flung up his bowline and the Skipper made it fast amidships. Then he lowered the falls to the davits and they hooked them on. They all scrambled on deck and helped hoist the cutter out of the water. Then Cap-tain Williams faced his searching party.

"Well?" he said.

The undercover agent placed his hand on Katy's shoul-der.

"It's a grand little Mate we have," he said. "And it's thanks to her quick thinking that we're back safe."

"What happened?" asked the Skipper.

Dominick told him everything they had done since leaving the schooner the afternoon before.

And then Sailor Bill said a funny thing, in almost the same words that Aba-ka-mas was going to use the next day.

"We'll go to Little Current," he said.

CHAPTER XVI

RENDEZVOUS AT LITTLE CURRENT

FROM WHERE the *Gull-Flight* picked up Dominick and the Mates in the *Bonny*, it was only forty or fifty miles to Little Current. Straight miles, that is, as the crow flies, which meant travel by land down the Cloche Penin-sula, a passing of the Southwest Gut, and on across the Great Cloche Island. And of course the ship couldn't go that way.

"Not even with the engine full on," said Morgan. "The *Gull-Flight's* no prairie schooner."

Nor could they even take the most direct water route. For the meeting with Joe College, and their own part in the smuggler chase had taken them along a lonely and badly charted shore. Sailor Bill had never been there before, and Dominick not for many years. In the coming dark and through such dangerous waters, neither dared pilot the ship. For to run aground now, or have any other accident, meant disaster to all their plans.

"So we'll play safe," said Sailor Bill. "And work back out the way we came in, along the cliff, until daylight fades. Then we'll stand off a few miles into Georgian Bay and put the hook down for the night."

269

"Aye," said the Blue Nose. "In the morning we can run out to where we can get a bearing on a lighthouse or two. Then we can lay our course to Little Current."

They took full advantage of the long northern twilight, and not until about ten o'clock did they drop the anchor. There they rode secure for the night, several miles back on the course which had brought them to the entrance to

Drowned Man's Cove. The girls went immediately below to turn in. The Skipper, Dominick, and Morgan were each to stand a two-hour trick on anchor watch.*

So it was early the next afternoon before they sighted Little Current, and not until about four o'clock were they

---

* *Anchor Watch.* At night, when a ship rides at anchor in an open roadstead, some one is always on duty. His job is literally to "watch the anchor"—to see that the ship does not drag it along the bottom. Of course he also keeps an eye on everything else in general and sees that the riding light stays lit. . . . To "put the hook down" means to drop the anchor. —KATY.

close enough to signal to the railroad bridge that crossed the narrow strait which joined the North Channel to Georgian Bay.

"Two long, and two short," said Sailor Bill.

Katy pulled the whistle lanyard.

T-O-O-T, T-O-O-T . . . TOOT, TOOT, went the whistle.

The draw swung slowly open.

They were bucking a stiff westerly breeze, which was piling down the water from the North Channel into the Narrows, and causing a three-mile tide rip; so that today the current in the strait was anything but "little." With motor full on, they clawed through the starboard draw opening and tied up to the public dock near the main street.

The bustling little town was a sharp contrast to the wilderness in which they had spent the last four days. A great passenger packet on her way to Mackinac and the "Soo," had put in that morning. Most of her trippers were ashore on souvenir hunts, or taking in the sights. They crowded the stores, eyeing the half-Indian, half-frontier offerings of the Hudson's Bay Company, and jammed the telegraph office till no one could get either in or out, much less send a message.

Camera in hand, several of them came down to the dock and stood looking the *Gull-Flight* over. They were very much interested in the trim ship and her natty crew.

"May we come aboard?" asked one of a pair of obviously vacationing schoolmarms.

"Certainly," said Sailor Bill politely, helping them over the rail.

Dominick looked much disgusted.

He had that immense disdain that all salt-water men show tourists, the world over. So he lit his pipe and went up on the foredeck. There he sat on an up-turned bucket, back to the pier, and gazed with a very detached air on a patch of forlorn and scraggly weeds that formed an island just across the strait. The view couldn't have been very interesting, but it served his purpose. He was let severely alone.

The visitors went through the ship. They were full of "oh's" and "ah's" at the snug comfort below, the roominess of the deckhouses, and the sturdy handiness of the rigging. They asked a thousand questions, and swarmed over Morgan's engine room until he too was disgusted, and joined Dominick on the foredeck.

"May we take your pictures?" one of them finally said to the Mates. "Here, in front of the thing you steer with."

"And will you put your hat on?" asked the other of Katy. Like your cousin. We'd like to show the folks at home how you both look in uniform."

Katy clapped her hand to her head . . . A scene flashed before her eyes . . .

A bare room in a shack at the end of a half-ruined dock in the wilderness. A dust-covered mantelpiece. The headache that had made her take off her hat and lay it down. The drama with Scar-face and the man with the rifle. Their forced and hurried exit.

The hat was still there!

And Sailor Bill was grinning.

"I wondered when you'd miss it," he said. "Go below and get your spare. . . . Then pose for the ladies."

IN THE morning the passenger packet had gone, and so had her throngs of tourists. Little Current settled back to its normal affairs, that of supply for cruising yachts and passing lake traffic, rail head and shopping center for the summer residents of Manitoulin Island. A few automobiles of rather ancient vintage, and a truck or two, grunted and rattled up and down the hilly dirt streets. A shopkeeper took down his night shutters and put up his awning. A boy laid the dust before the store by sprinkling the street with a hose, and another on a bicycle came down to the dock. This one had a bag slung over his shoulder.

"News-paper-r-r," he shrilled, cycling past the yachts tied up at the pier.

Dominick bought one, and carried it in to where they were all having breakfast in the deckhouse. Everyone took a page or two, looked it over, and passed it round. World events seemed detached, far off, remote from the business at hand, and somehow not very important. The smuggler chase had become such a part of them, they had thought it, lived it for so many days, that other happenings were of little interest. Finally Sailor Bill threw down his part of the paper impatiently, and got to his feet.

"Morning of the fourth day," he said to Dominick. "Joe

College and the Able-seamen should be here anytime now."

"It's glad I'll be to see them," said the Blue Nose. "But it's more we know than they, I'm thinking. And I hope the Chief has his tribe with him. So we can start back after Scar-face. I'd like to borrow an Indian hunting knife and do some scalping of my own."

So far, Morgan hadn't had a very exciting part in the adventures. But he felt himself to be an important cog in the machinery that was grinding the early clues to a patterned close. So he put in his oar.

"While we're waiting, we had better fill up with gasoline," he said. "Even this engine won't run without fuel, and we've been using it pretty steadily."

"Good idea," said Dominick.

"And how about your end of it?" asked Sailor Bill to the Mates. "You're shipkeepers again. Our supplies must be getting low."

Katy looked at the lists she and Spinach had gotten up the night before. "We need ice, meat, butter and milk, fruit and fresh vegetables," she said.

"Go get 'em," said the Skipper. "Morgan, how about petting that engine of yours a little? We can't risk any breakdowns. Dominick and I'll clean up the ship."

Morgan threw his uncle a look, reproachful, and not entirely unmixed with scorn. But he went below.

"Come on, Gyp," said Katy. "You haven't been ashore since Aba-ka-mas scared you off that rock ledge. With all that crowd in port last night, we had to keep you locked up."

The little dog barked and thumped his tail against the bench on which his mistress was sitting. When she opened the screen door of the deckhouse he ran to the ship's rail and jumped off on the dock ahead of them. He sniffed around under this and that, and trotted up to have a look at the yacht tied up in the next berth. He decided that compared to the *Gull-Flight,* she didn't amount to much. So he came back. After all, wharves throughout the world smell pretty much alike, and there wasn't anything particularly different about this one. Then he formed a sedate escort for Katy and Spinach on their way uptown.

Even in the butcher shop, where the size of Katy's huge order entitled him to at least one raw mutton chop, he behaved himself well. He sat up on his haunches in the clean sawdust in front of the counter, and took only a polite interest in what was going on.

But he had one fall from grace.

That was on the way back to the ship, a side foray after a cat he saw sitting in a blank doorway on the other side of the street. His last cat chase had been back in Grosse Ile at the start of the voyage, and he had won that one. But this was no Southland tabbie. She was a North Country wildcat, and a Canadian one at that, and not inclined to take any lip from Yankee visitors.

"Phs-i-z-zt," went the cat.

"Yo-w-o-l-p," went the dog.

He had cornered her after a wild dash across the street. Then before Katy and Spinach had time to rescue him, a gray snaky paw had snicked out, and a set of sharp claws had raked a cruel slash across a tender nose.

That was enough for Gyp.

He didn't think much of the North Country anyway, and even less of the animals that lived in it. And every time his nose picked up a scent, the pursuit led him into trouble. So he beat a dignified retreat. But the new sore spot on his nose made him do a lot of thinking.

First there was that queer smell on the rock ledge, he remembered. Scared me a little, but turned out all right. Wonder when that Indian will show up again? But that porcupine! Whew! That was a bad one.

The memory of those quills still hurt.

And now this cat! That was worse still. When would the family quit this foolish barging around in the wilderness and get back to civilization?

THE rest of the morning was spent in ship chandlery. The storm off Kettle Shoals had taken a certain amount of toll, and the daily wear and tear of wind and water had worn off paint here, and frazzled a line there. A new canvas cover for the *Bonny* was cut, sewed along the edges, and lashed down tight. There was about a half a ton of ice to be loaded in, and this meant a complete rearrangement of food stores. Several bags of charcoal were taken aboard. Some chipped hard coal was piled along side the galley range. Now an ever-glowing fire could be kept against the chill Northland nights and mornings.

Dinner time came and went.

They had the meal at the hotel. Katy and Spinach were glad to be free of cooking, but experience had made them critical of the skill of others. The dishes were greasy and the food lukewarm. The service was indifferent and the surroundings gloomy. There was a stale smell of meals devoured and forgotten long ago.

"I wish we'd stayed aboard," said Sailor Bill.

"I don't," said Spinach. She was thinking of the endless chain of crockery that fed into the galley sink after every meal.

"Why don't we go back?" said Dominick.

They did, and waited through the long afternoon. The street along the wharf quieted down for the night. Night of course, meaning six o'clock, and time for the storekeepers to knock off. But there were still four hours of daylight.

They waited through two of them.

And then suddenly Katy saw them coming. They were walking single file across the railroad bridge, the Indian leading. At least someone was in the lead who might be Aba-ka-mas, but she had to turn the glasses on him to be sure.

For he was almost buried under packs and blanket rolls. His own were slung across his shoulders and those of the Able-seamen heaped on top and tied around his body. He bent a little under the weight, but carefully cradled in the crook on one arm was a rifle, the gift of Captain Williams four days ago. His own stride was sturdy enough but the boys straggled out behind, stepping carefully but much more wearily over the open ties of the trestle.

The whole party fairly screamed fatigue. Twice through the telescope, Katy saw the boy bringing up the rear trip and fall. The Chief went back and helped him up. Then he would stumble on again. The rear boy was Teddy. And by the looks of him, Brick wasn't much better off. Each time that Joe went back to help Teddy, the redheaded Able-seaman sat down. And it took a lot of prodding to get him on his feet and going again.

Dominick wanted to go ashore and help them the rest of the way. But Sailor Bill wouldn't allow it.

"No," he said. "They've gotten this far, and I think they'd rather finish under their own steam."

So the rest of the crew of the *Gull-Flight* stayed aboard and watched their ambassadors to the Indian tribe struggle through the last leg of their journey. They climbed wearily down the stepped pier of the railroad trestle and made their way along the water-front street toward the schooner. Other people, still hanging around the shops and dockside, stared at them curiously as they trudged by.

An over-burdened guide? Two almost exhausted boys? And why was the Indian carrying that express rifle?

But the unspoken questions were not answered, and the little party plodded doggedly along. They were still about a block off from the ship when Brick happened to look up, to see the Skipper and his other shipmates lining the rail as reception committee. He grinned at them and waved his hand in tired salute. Then he said something to Joe and Teddy, and the three of them visibly quickened their pace. The journey was at an end.

But their clothes were in tatters, grimy and sweat stained from the hard going of the trail. Uniforms so bright and new when they started off, were weather beaten and faded from fording streams and sleeping out in the heavy night dews, and the combination of slashing rain storm and blazing mid-day sun had bleached and shrunk them almost to rags. There was a welt across Brick's cheek from the slap of a bough springing back into place in the thick brush, and a raw scratch from a thorn bramble started at Teddy's knee and ran raggedly up his leg to the bottom edge of his shorts. Their feet were blistered and sore, and both limped as they came over the gangway.

Aba-ka-mas didn't look any different than he ever had. Possibly fatigue had sunk his eyes more deeply in his head than usual, but there was the glitter of the chase in them, and a glow of satisfaction at its nearing end. Without a word he dropped the packs and blanket rolls to the deck. Then he snapped open the breech of his rifle, looked through the barrel for dirt or dust, snicked the bolt to again, and handed it to Dominick to stow away. He turned to Captain Williams to make his report.

But Sailor Bill wouldn't listen.

"Not now," he said. "Later. After we've taken care of the boys."

The Able-seamen stumbled down the companion stairs and into the galley where a red-hot fire was burning in the range. Dominick pulled off their clothes and popped them both into a steaming shower. He let them soak for a while, and when they came out, nearly took off what hide they had left with a rough turkish towel. Then he fed them a bowl of scalding meat broth, and warmed a pair of blankets before the stove while they ate. Two minutes later they were sound asleep in their bunks.

The Blue Nose stood looking at them, snoring away, and dead to the world.

"The poor lads," he said, as he shut their stateroom door. "A hard trail it must have been."

Then he went up on deck.

When he got there he found all hands gathered in the after-house, where charts of the North Channel and the west end of Georgian Bay were pinned to the navigating table. Joe College had been talking, and using a pencil too. For he had traced out the route he and the boys had taken since leaving the ship in Drowned Man's Cove. And like Bear Hunter, with his stick map on the sand beach of Reservation Lake, Aba-ka-mas had made two final crosses which located the smuggler bases.

Dominick fired some questions at him.

"Who was Bear Hunter? How well did he know the country? What was it that was being smuggled? Did they ever try to get Chinese across the line? Was the railroad always used to bring in the contraband? Why did Scar-face work from two such widely separated bases?"

At first the Chief answered in English. Then he lapsed into Chippewa, and so did Dominick. For the next few minutes the air fairly crackled and snapped with guttural grunts and hisses as question and answer flung back and forth. Finally the Blue Nose turned to the Skipper.

"So it's not back to the shack we'll be going," he said. "I'm sorry for that. We know the lay of the land there. But if the birds are flown, we'll hunt up their new nest."

Sailor Bill had also been doing some figuring. With dividers and parallel rule he had laid off a course on the chart, and made some calculations with a pencil. He finished his work and turned to face the crew.

"We'll start now," he said. "And we'll use both sail and engine. If we don't run into a head wind, tomorrow afternoon should see us dropping anchor off Base Two."

"The motor's ready," said Morgan. "And we've plenty of gas and oil in the tanks."

"The supplies are all aboard," put in the Mates.

"When should Bear Hunter arrive?" said Sailor Bill to the Chief. "It won't do us much good to get there ahead of him."

"He'll be there," said Aba-ka-mas grimly. "I told him to take no rest on the trail."

"Cast off then," said the Skipper.

THE Able-seamen didn't wake up until after noon the next day. Both were stiff and sore, but that wasn't what roused them. Physical ills and ship's noises bothered them not at all. The bustle of getting under way, the tramp of feet over head only lulled them to deeper slumber. The roar and throb of the motor, the hoarse shout of orders, the slap of halyard against a spar and the rattle of blocks and the creak of straining sail—all these were but sweet company to a dreamless sleep.

What got them up was hunger—a ravenous gnaw that clawed at their vitals. And there was nothing sudden about their coming awake. It began slowly, with the first smells of a cooking meal. Brick turned over and took a deep unconscious sniff. Then he punched his pillow and dropped off again. But the odor of browning roast and steaming vegetables persisted. He stirred uneasily. Finally came the click of knives and the clatter of forks on plates.

The crew was at dinner, and that was too much.

He snapped awake and prodded at Teddy in the upper bunk.

"Come on!" he yelled. "Get up!"

They tumbled out, and fairly slavering at the mouth, clawed into their clothes. Then they tore out into the cabin where Katy and Spinach were waiting for them. When the rest of the crew finished dinner the Mates had left the boys' places set, and in a minute the table was again piled with food. It was just as quickly unpiled, down the throats of the Able-seamen. Each of them had three helpings of everything and four mugs of cocoa. Nor did they waste any time in conversation, but tended strictly to the business of stuffing themselves full. Finally, when neither could cram down another bite, they pushed the plates away and sat back. Now they were willing to talk.

"Let's have it," said Katy. "The whole story."

"And begin at the beginning," said Spinach.

They did. With Brick doing most of the talking and Teddy putting in his oar only when his cousin was out of breath. They began with the start from the ship in Drowned Man's Cove. The hours of paddling, the portage, the reservation, and the night in Joe's cabin. Then the council next morning and Bear Hunter's stick map. The start by canoe again, the camp, and the trail across the mountains. Finally the story brought them to the shack at the end of the half-ruined dock, and the finding of Katy's hat.

"How did it get there?" asked Brick.

"And what were you doing there?" added Teddy.

Katy told them. Of the trip in the *Bonny,* of their own camp, and how they discovered the shack at the end of the pier. And of the encounter with Scar-face and his gunman.

"You know," she said, "at first I was ashamed at forgetting that hat—leaving clues behind us that way. But now I think it was a lucky mistake."

"How come?" said Brick. "Sherlock Holmes would never do a trick like that."

"Perhaps not," said Katy. "But when *you* start from Reservation Lake, fifty miles away, and find a hat *I* left on a mantlepiece in the wilderness, it proves that we were both in the same place. And that the shack really is Base One."

"What of it?" said Teddy. "The smugglers were gone when we got there."

"That's just it," said Katy. "Dominick was only waiting at Little Current for reinforcements before going back to capture Scar-face. He might not have believed that there even was a Base Two, and we would have gone off on a wild goose chase."

"Well?" asked the Able-seamen together.

"Silly," said Spinach. She was backing Katy up and getting even for that remark about Sherlock Holmes. "We'd have gone back by boat and sent you and the Indians overland. How would you like to back-track over yesterday's trail?"

"I wouldn't," said Teddy. "That was awful."

"Do you know what we did?" asked Brick. "The minute we found your hat we started off. Bear Hunter led for two hours and I never saw anybody walk so fast. Then we cut off toward Little Current. We kept on until it was pitch dark and you couldn't see your hand in front of your face. That was when that bough slapped me across the cheek. Then Joe called a halt and we just flopped down where we were. The Chief made a fire I guess, and rolled us up in our blankets. Because that's where we were when he woke us up before daylight."

"Then we started again," said Teddy. "All day long— through the brush, around swamps and over hills—we forded creeks and swam rivers. We'd have never made it if Joe hadn't carried our packs."

"That's a terrible man," said Brick. "Both of them. Those Indians never seem to get tired."

"Well, you won't have to go through that sort of thing again," said Katy. "You're back on the *Gull-Flight* now, and in an hour more we should drop anchor off Base Two."

"Then what?" said Teddy.

"We don't know exactly," said Spinach. "Bear Hunter will have something to say when he comes aboard. But Sailor Bill, Dominick and the Chief have been holding little meetings all morning. Morgan has been running his engine and we've been doing the steering. They've worked out some sort of plan, for they're getting the *Bonny* ready to launch again."

"I wonder what the plan is?" said Brick.

"Let's go on deck," said Teddy.

"And find out," said Brick.

CHAPTER XVII

CLOSING IN

BUT DURING the fourteen hours the Able-seamen had lain in exhausted sleep, much had happened. For the arrival of the armed Indian Chief and the two almost spent boys had caused considerable comment in the little town. Evening though it was, with all the shops closed and the bustle of the day over and done, several idlers were gathered about. These came down to the dockside and collected about the ship's gangway. And they were full of questions.

"Where away, Mate? Been long in these waters? Who's your guide? What are you doing up here?"

These were only a few that were flung at them. Dominick answered some, the crew others. And not very directly, it must be admitted, hardly even truthfully. Who they were—where they were going—and what they intended doing when they got there—well, that was entirely their business, and quayside courtesy had its limits. So the curious got little information.

But Sailor Bill was worried. Anyone could see that. Suppose some of the gang were in town, hanging about to pick up what they could. If they put two and two to-gether, a warning might be sent on ahead. And that would never do.

So the Skipper decided to play safe and delay his going until he could slip away quietly with none to tell whether the schooner headed north or south. He moved around to each of the crew, giving them their orders separately, and in a low tone.

"Go below," he said, "one at a time. Just as though you were turning in for the night. But stand by. Don't get undressed. We're leaving the minute the coast is clear."

So it was nearly midnight before the *Gull-Flight* cast loose her moorings at Little Current and nosed out into the inky dark. Like a wartime blockade runner, she slid away from the glitter of the town lights, and with port-holes covered and engine throttled down, picked her way carefully through the buoys and beacons that marked the narrow and twisted strait. They were headed toward the free and open waters of the North Channel. But Sailor Bill at the helm needed some help.

"Go up on the foredeck," he ordered the Mates. "Keep your eyes open for approaching ships. There isn't much traffic through here, but until we lose sight of the town, I want to run without lights."

Then he turned the wheel over to Dominick and ducked into the after-house to take a squint at the chart. Back on deck, he gave the wheelsman the course.

"We'll keep to the north of the Low and Picnic Is-lands," he said.

In a few minutes they were in behind them, so that they formed a screen between the ship and the mainland. Now, no one could see them, and the Skipper ordered Morgan to the top of the forward deckhouse.

"Rig the light," he said. "Keep it on the channel markings. We don't have to run blind any longer."

Morgan climbed up and took off the hood to the searchlight. He snapped on the connection, and the powerful beam stabbed out a bright path over the dark water. It lit the way ahead, darting from buoy to buoy, and showed them through the narrow and tortured passage between island and shoal. They left the steamer track for a while, and a few hours later were free and clear and into the North Channel.

From here on, they had wide water, and also daylight. The morning broke clear and fine, with scarcely a ripple of breeze. Over the bows the stars winked and went out, and the sunburst danced and sparkled in the diamond-clear air, bathing the ship in a wash of golden light.

But Sailor Bill looked disappointed and even impatient at the still beauty of the morning.

"We've sixty miles or more to go," he said. "And I'd like a little wind—provided it doesn't blow right up our nose."

But when it came, an hour or so later, it *was* right up their nose. It blew strongly—dead ahead—and slowed them down to four or five miles an hour. And of course it kicked up a sea so that the *Gull-Flight* bucked and pitched. Under the drive of her engine she buried her nose, and flung sheets of water aft, which the crew tried to duck as best they might. But they were soon wet down, as thoroughly as though they had stepped in and out of a shower bath. Oilskins didn't help much, and Katy and Spinach were glad to knock off deck work and go into the saloon to get breakfast. Here at least they had the shelter of the closed cabin windows.

In a few minutes the meal was ready, but only the Skip‚ per and Dominick came in to eat it.

"The Chief's below," said Sailor Bill, "still asleep. Save some breakfast for him. Morgan's on steering trick. He can't come in until I relieve him."

Over the top of the charthouse they could see him, ducking slaps of spray, and tugging and straining away at the wheel to keep the schooner on her course. And he didn't look any too happy about the punishment his engine was taking. When they rode up the crest of a sea the propeller came half clear of the water, and the engine would race, and try to tear itself to pieces. When they slid down the slope, the screw would bite in and kick them along until they met the thrust of the next wave. Then with the motor groaning and pounding, they would shudder up the next slope, and the whole performance would begin all over again.

The Skipper stood it as long as he could. Then he threw down a half-eaten piece of toast and pushed his coffee cup aside.

"We'll set some sail," he said. "She'll be steadier that way. Even with going off on a tack, we'll make better time."

They really didn't tack at all. They set the main and two jibs, and bore off just enough to allow the wind to fill the sails, heeling them over slightly and keeping them fine and steady. The North Channel was wide here, with plenty of open water, so they began a series of long slides, ten or fifteen miles to a leg. First they slipped off a little to port—then over to starboard—zigzagging across the true course. Under both motor and sail the log showed nine, ten, and even eleven miles to the hour. Actually they gained a net average of about eight, which was much better than clawing slowly through head seas under power alone.

About ten o'clock, Aba-ka-mas appeared on deck, up from the fo'c'sle where he had been asleep for nearly twelve hours. He came directly to the saloon.

"Morning," he said briefly. "Any breakfast left?"

There was, and Katy and Spinach gave it to him. He ate sparingly, a couple of pieces of toast and a little bacon. But he drank cup after cup of strong black coffee, smoking away on a cigarette in between.

"No," he said, when Katy offered him more bacon and an egg, "not now. Indians think it bad to eat much the first meal after long trail. Drink lots of water—lots of coffee. Then maybe two, three hours later, have good dinner."

For him, this was a long speech, and after it he lapsed

into a glum silence, staring moodily out of the cabin windows and puffing away on his cigarette. Katy and Spinach fidgeted around. In the backs of their heads were many questions they would like to ask the Chief, but neither quite dared. Finally Spinach broke the ice.

"How is Bear Hunter going to get aboard ship?" she asked.

"And how are we going to capture the smugglers?" said Katy.

"He swim out," said Aba-ka-mas briefly, answering the first question. "I see Captain now. We talk about plans. You go below—fix good dinner."

Then he got up and stalked through the saloon door, walking aft to where the Skipper and Dominick were standing near Morgan at the wheel. The girls knew he was master of the trail, a king in the winderness, and chief of his tribe; but both had rather a sneaking hope that he might prove somewhat of a landlubber aboard ship. He wasn't. He balanced himself easily, swaying to the rise and fall of the deck, and as sure footed in the tangle of rigging and gear as he was in dense thicket or woodland trail. More than that, he seemed to know just where he was. Neither shore was quite out of sight, and there were several islands in plain view. Two or three looks around, and he had the ship's exact position spotted.

The Mates looked at each other. Then they burst out laughing.

"Getting anything out of him is worse than prying open an oyster with a button hook," said Katy.

"Brick and Teddy must have had a noisy time of it," said Spinach.

"If they did," said Katy, "they talked to each other. But come on—we'll start that dinner. When they get their plan worked out, we'll hear about it."

Nor did they hear anything until the entire crew had been fed, and Brick and Teddy had stormed from their stateroom, ravenous enough to eat the cover off the table. So it was nearly three o'clock when the four of them got to the deck. The schooner was heeled over a little, but fine and steady on what was to be her last port tack before anchoring off Base Two. The sheet was trimmed flat so that the main boom was barely outboard, and the engine was running, full on. Under both sail and power, the *Gull-Flight* was tearing along at a great rate. Morgan had the wheel. No one else was in sight.

"Where is everybody?" said Katy.

"And where *are* we?" asked Brick. It was the first time he had stuck his nose into the open since the evening before, and now the great mainsail hid everything off to starboard.

"Go forward of the mast," said Morgan. "Take a look for yourselves. We're going to drop the hook before long."

From midships, over the starboard rail, they had a clear view. The schooner was working in, so as to just clear the upper end of a long wooded island. It formed the right of the entrance, to what at first glance looked like a land-locked bay. The island had a queer shape, something like a fishhook. The hook end was away from them, reaching in toward the north shore of the channel. The shank was long and narrow, bending seaward to end in a bald rock knob that resembled a closed fist.

Katy and Spinach looked it over. Then they immediately christened it Fishhook Key.

They were headed past the knob of the key toward another island, perhaps two miles farther on. This one ran almost at a right angle to the shore and was high at its inner end, but tapered down to spindle off in a seaward spit that continued in a line of sand humps with blue water in between. The humps were covered with gulls that flashed white in the sun as they wheeled and turned, their screams and cries carrying down wind to the schooner. Later, and for lack of a better name, they called it West Island.

There was a third island that came slowly into view as they cleared the knob of Fishhook Key. It was crescent shaped, with its back toward the mainland.

"Ile de Croissant," said Katy, remembering the description of Parisian breakfast rolls in her French books.

"And we'll name the whole place 'Smuggler Bay,'" said Teddy.

For the three islands *did* form a bay. Not a very sheltered one if the wind happened to blow from the southeast, but this afternoon, calm and unruffled with the clearest of water and sand and clay bottom that looked dangerously near the surface. Apparently the Skipper and

Dominick thought so too, for they appeared suddenly through the door of the saloon, followed by Joe College. The Blue Nose had the lead and line in his hands and went up into the bow to take soundings. Smuggler Bay was too isolated and remote to have the depth of its waters shown on any chart.

"Slow ahead," said Sailor Bill to Morgan. "And luff up. We'll drop the sail."

They all bore a hand, and the main came down with a run. Dominick gathered in the jibs himself. Then as the schooner swung slowly back on her course and crept along with the engine barely turning over, the Blue Nose made his first cast.

"Three fathoms," he sang back.

"A little farther," said the Skipper.

They went on in, perhaps another quarter of a mile, almost to the middle of the bay.

"Way enough," said Sailor Bill.

Down went the anchor. And then to Morgan, "Kill your engine."

The *Gull-Flight* had arrived off Base Two.

"Now," said the Skipper a minute later. "The thing to do is to make our position here look as casual as possible. Just a pleasure craft anchored out for a little fishing, or perhaps a shore excursion or two."

Soon they all were busy. With the heavy bow anchor deep in the sand and clay bottom, they let the schooner settle back on a long length of forward chain. Then with the dinghy, they carried out the light kedge anchor and dropped it well astern. Afterward they moored the small boat safely under the ship's counter. Then for the first time on the trip they swung out the boat boom, rigged the head rope, and dropped a ladder down so that it dangled just above the water. The *Bonny* was lowered and rowed around to ride at the boat boom. Sail covers

THE BOAT BOOM

and deck awning came next, and finally the riding light was hoisted to the main truck. At last the Skipper cast an approving eye over the *Gull-Flight*, her position in the bay, and her general air of leisure and comfort.*

* Here are some new nautical terms: A truck is the wooden cap at the top of the mast. It is usually pierced with holes so that a halyard can be rove through. A ship's counter is that part of the stern which under-curves to meet the water line. A boat boom is a spar swung out from the deck, usually amidships and at right angles to the hull. A head rope is a line rigged above the boat boom. You hang on to it so as not to fall off when you run along the boom. . . .—Katy.

"There," he said, "snugged down tight. Now all of you come into the saloon."

They did, with Sailor Bill leading the way. The forward house looked much different now than it did a few hours ago when Katy and Spinach left it to go below and get dinner. Then it was a breakfast room. Now it was a combination arsenal and military headquarters. On the Skipper's bunk lay two Springfield Army rifles, flanked on either side by clips of service ammunition. The Chief's express rifle and belt were there too, and at the head of the bed, the butts of a pair of forty-five automatics glowered from under the flaps of their leather holsters. On the table was pinned a large sheet of blank white paper, and beside it were pencils, a compass and dividers, and both straight and parallel rules. A pair of binoculars hung from a peg under the cabin windows that had a shoreward view.

The eyes of the Mates and the Able-seamen nearly popped from their heads. It was the first time they had seen the ship's armament.

"Wh-a-t!" began Brick.

Sailor Bill piped him down.

"Time for talk later," he said. "When Bear Hunter comes aboard, then we'll have a council of war. It'll be dark in an hour, and before that I want to make a map of this bay—at least as much of it as I can see from here."

He worked rapidly, all of them looking on, and with Dominick and Aba-ka-mas putting in a low word now and then. First he squared off the paper, and with the compass laid off North, East, South and West. About the middle of the paper, and toward its lower edge, he made a line about a half an inch long and running exactly East to West.

"There," he said, "that's the *Gull-Flight.*"

Then on the sill of the cabin window that looked toward the shore, he laid the compass, adjusting it so that its East and West paralleled the line that represented the *Gull-Flight.* This was his direction finder. There was no instrument to calculate exact distances. For these, he must rely on his own judgment.

Never going out on the deck where he might be seen by a hidden watcher on the land, he worked entirely by focusing the binoculars through the cabin windows. First he would search through the glass at the islands and shore, note their bearings from the ship, and then walk over to the table. For three quarters of an hour he beat a path, back and forth, from cabin window to table.

Finally bits of disconnected curved lines joined each other. A definite outline began to take form, and at last a map of Smuggler Bay, with all its confines and reaches and exactly as it appeared through the ship's windows, was transferred to the paper. It was drawn to scale, quite accurate in direction and close enough as to distance. Sailor Bill drew back and looked it over.

"There," he said, "Base Two—at least all we can see of it. When Bear Hunter comes aboard we'll fill in what is hidden behind the islands."

Katy had been intent on what Sailor Bill was doing. So

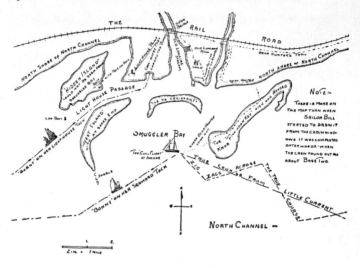

had the others. But all the while she had realized, although quite unconsciously, that she had been waiting for something, getting more and more tense all the time. At the mention of the Scout's name, she knew what it was.

"Why of course," she said out loud, "we really can't do anything until he comes."

"Comes? Who's coming?" asked Brick. "And where is he coming from?"

He too had been feeling something of what had bothered Katy, and not knowing exactly what it was either.

"Bear Hunter," said Spinach. "Our scout."

"How will he get out to the ship?" asked Teddy.

"Swim," said Katy, remembering what Aba-ka-mas had said when he first came on deck in the morning.

"And he'll try it before long, I'm thinking," said Dominick. "It's getting dark."

"Look at Gyp," said Sailor Bill suddenly.

They did—everybody—and stopped talking while they were doing it. An instant silence clamped down on them, replacing the cheerful buzz of talk of the minute before. The gloom of falling dark thickened with each passing second as they waited—and watched. The dog had stiffened to a point, his nose toward the open saloon door. His ruff was rising, his fangs were bared, and the muscles under his jowls writhed and crawled. In a minute more he would have snarled. It was the old familiar warning of the coming of a stranger, silently and unseen.

Aba-ka-mas spoke to the dog quickly, in Chippewa, getting up from where he sat and crossing the cabin to lay his hand on Gyp's shoulder.

The dog quieted.

"What is it?" asked Katy in a whisper.

"Bear Hunter comes, I think," said the Chief. "Go and look."

Katy went to the saloon door. She looked out, at the blank expanse of empty deck, and at the companion-way where they had rigged the boat boom. The cabin lights had not been turned on as yet, and it was lighter outside than in. The ship's rail was outlined sharply against the gray water. She saw nothing—nor was there a sound. Then came a faint scraping noise, and the rigging that held up the boat boom quivered a little. Then it was still.

Katy shivered, though there was no chill in the air. She hardly dared breathe.

Suddenly from over the side, a hand flashed up and gripped the rail. It was joined by its fellow. A black head of hair followed. Then a dark scarred face and a pair of powerful shoulders. Finally there arose a naked coppery torso, and with a vault over the rail, came an Indian stripped to his leggings and moccasins. Water streamed down his legs and made a dark pool on the white deck planking. He shook himself, flinging the moisture from his face and hair, and leaned over to wipe down his leggings. The he took off his moccasins, one after the other, emptied them out, and put them back on.

Katy watched, fascinated, and was startled when Aba-ka-mas made some guttural noises over her shoulder. These were answered by the Scout who immediately moved toward the saloon door and came in to where they all were.

"Bear Hunter," said the Chief, introducing him.

"Get his story," said the Skipper briefly.

A three-cornered conversation followed. Dominick being perfectly at home in Chippewa joined in freely, and he and the Chief interrupted often as the Scout told what had happened since leaving Joe College and the Able-seamen on the trail from Base One. Finally the Blue Nose moved over to the table on which was pinned the Skipper's unfinished sketch. He took up the pencil so as to give Sailor Bill the story and complete the map along with it.

"But we'd better have some light," he said. "It's too dark now to see."

"You're right," said the Skipper; "and it would look suspicious for us to lie here without them." Then, "Cabin, saloon, deck and riding lights," he told Morgan.

The Chief Engineer left and soon the flood of light came. Sailor Bill turned to Dominick.

"Now go on," he said.

"Bear Hunter followed the shore to a point about five miles east of here. Then he struck back to the railroad. Soon it crossed a creek and he worked back down it to the beach. That would be about here."

Dominick turned and drew in the railroad track, the creek, and the shore of the mainland eastward past the far end of Fishhook Key. Then he took up the story again.

"He saw nothing, nor anybody, and went back to the railroad. About a mile west of the creek he came to a drawbridge over a sizable stream, used in the old days to float logs down to the North Channel. There was a rowboat tied up under the trestle, and a well-marked trail down the east bank of the stream. He left the boat there and followed the trail. Soon he came to the wreck of the old logging mill. Beyond that was a shack, and at the mouth of the stream, a dock. All very much like what we saw at Base One."

"Now sketch in what you've told us so far," said Sailor Bill.

Dominick picked up the pencil and made a considerable addition to the map. Afterward he went on.

"The mouth of the stream is wide and choked by a pair of low sandy islands, which probably weren't there when the loggers were using it. Across the stream at the tip of a point is an old lighthouse, or rather just the skeleton of it. It sits on a hump of sand overgrown with turf and brush. I suppose it shows a westward passage out, for there is deep water between the dock and Ile de Croissant."

"Did the Scout see anybody?" asked Sailor Bill.

"No," said Dominick. "But he says someone has been there—not long ago—just as we found at Base One. The place only looks deserted, if you don't look too closely."

"Did he cross over to the lighthouse?" said the Skipper.

"There wasn't time," said Dominick. "All this took place this afternoon. He had just gotten to the dock at the mouth of the stream when he saw the *Gull-Flight* come into Smuggler Bay. So he left and went back along the shore. He crossed to the lower end of Fishhook Key, worked along it to the knob, and waited for twilight. Then he swam out to the ship."

"Sketch in the west bank of the logging stream, the point and the lighthouse," said Sailor Bill.

When Dominick had done so, the Skipper looked the map over carefully.

"All right," he said. "Here's what we will do. Chief,

you and Bear Hunter swim back to the Key, and cross to the mainland. Go back to the drawbridge and wait. I think the smugglers are here, hidden out somewhere. But I'm not sure, so you stay at the bridge until noon tomorrow. In the morning, Dominick and I will go ashore in the dinghy and hide in the woods close to the shack. You find us. We'll bring your rifle along and Bear Hunter can have an automatic. Let him fasten the belt around his head. That way he can keep it dry while he swims over."

"Ugh," said Bear Hunter.

"We go," said Aba-ka-mas.

"Go over the seaward rail," said Sailor Bill. "We've got our lights on, and you might be seen from the shore."

The Chief took off his shirt so that he stood in leggings and moccasins, the same as his scout. Then the two Indians slipped out of the saloon door and over to port. Silently, stealthily—almost like a pair of ghosts in the gloom of the evening—they dropped over the rail without a splash or sound. Katy and Spinach walked casually down the after-deck as though for a stroll, and watched from under the awning. Slanting away from the quarter deck toward Fishhook Key was a streak of moonlight, bright against the dark water. Across it before long came two black dots, moving slowly toward the land. An arm flashed up as though in farewell.

Then they were gone.

CHAPTER XVIII

CAPTURED

THE GIRLS went back to the saloon. Inside, the Skipper and Dominick were bent over the map, talking eagerly. Morgan was leaning over the table too, taking in all that was being said and very much a part of the elder group. Brick and Teddy sat on the bunk, swinging their legs over the edge and left pretty much out of the proceedings. Katy sized up the situation at once. So did Spinach. It looked as though their part of the adventure were over, and neither liked the idea. Instinctively they ranged themselves at the side of the Able-seamen.

"What about us?" asked Katy. "All of you grownups have a plan for tomorrow. Can't we do something? We're your able crew, you know."

Sailor Bill eyed his nieces and nephews. He was thinking things over.

"Yes," he said after a bit, "if the four of you can handle the *Bonny*. Morgan must stay with the ship."

"Why not?" said Katy. "We sailed her all over Back Bay. These waters aren't any different—except they're not salt."

"Brick and I can handle canvas," said Teddy.

"That leaves me as extra hand," put in Spinach, "to help in emergency, or be up in the bow as lookout—or anything."

"What do you want us to do?" asked Brick, getting down to cases.

"All right," said the Skipper, with a business-like air. "The first thing in the morning I want you to sail around those sand humps. In behind West Island. Find out if there's a passage there, to Lighthouse Point, and whether or not they have it marked. We can stop them if they try to escape through Smuggler Bay, but if there's another way out I'd like to know it. Take your lunch and explore around. But keep away from the dock and the shack. Don't even cross the logging stream. I don't want you mixed up in any trouble."

"That'll be easy," said Brick.

"We'll be careful," said Katy.

"It will be fun," said Spinach.

"What about bed?" asked Dominick, his blue eyes twinkling. "It's nearly midnight and tomorrow will be a busy day, I'm thinking."

THEY all turned in, but nobody did much sleeping. Katy and Spinach talked in low tones, and over their heads they could hear Sailor Bill trampling about. From the sounds he made, he never once lay down. And with daylight, it became increasingly difficult to stay in bed. Finally the sun's rays slanted in the open porthole, and reflected from the dressing-table mirror to flash in Katy's eyes. That was enough. She looked at the clock. It was working on toward seven.

"Turn out," she said to Spinach. "There's breakfast to get, and four lunches to pack."

"What's it like?" asked her cousin. "The day, I mean."

The day was all right, bright and clear, with just a snort of breeze out of the west. Smuggler Bay was still and smooth, but to the south of them and out in the channel, there was plenty of wind. They could see that by the rifle and sparkle to the water. Fine weather—with a bit of North Country snap in the air.

THE *Bonny* had been drawn up under the boat boom so that the ladder led down into her. The masts had been stepped, but the sails were still furled. Katy ran out along the boom and was first down into the cutter to take her place in the stern sheets; Brick came next; then Teddy; and lastly Spinach, who stayed up in the bow. Lunch in a good-sized hamper was stowed amidships. Then they all looked up to Sailor Bill for final orders.

"Whenever you're ready," he said from the deck of the schooner. "But remember this. There can only be one Skipper aboard ship, big or little. Katy, you're it. The rest of you obey orders."

"It's a good crew I've got," she said.

Then, after a look around, "We're ready now, I think."

"Cast off then," said Sailor Bill. "Drop astern of the schooner before you get up sail. Then head out to the channel. Give the sand humps off West Island plenty of sea room. Keep on out—and work to windward until you see a clear passage in. You should make it in two tacks."

Dominick freed the painter, and flung it down to Spinach who coiled it in the cutter's bow. The wind was causing an eastward drift, and in a minute the little craft slid aft along the *Gull-Flight's* side and cleared the stern.*

"Raise canvas," ordered Katy. "Foresail first."

Up it went, was cleated down and sheeted home. The breeze caught it and the cutter heeled over, swinging her bow around and heading out toward the North Channel.

"Now the main," she said.

That too ran up, and under the pull of both sails the *Bonny* gathered way. Sailor Bill and Dominick stood watching them over the *Gull-Flight's* rail. The little cutter danced and bobbed along with a very business-like air. Katy held her close up, and the crew trimmed and flattened until they had a nice balance. Then they bore away, south and west, on a course well outside the shoaling sand humps with their burden of screaming gulls. West Island would soon have to give up the secret of what lay behind it.

The Blue Nose smiled, and tender admiration lit up his tanned and weather-beaten face.

"It's a grand crew we've got," he said. "None better, I'm thinking. And it's devil-a-bit they've been stumped by anything that's turned up yet."

---

* A "painter" on a ship is not a man with a brush. It's a piece of line, fastened to the bow of a small boat, and used to tie her up with.—SPINACH.

"I'm glad they're away, just the same," said Sailor Bill. "Out where they can't get hurt. I don't think there's anything behind that island, and by the time they explore around and get back, I hope to have this all over."

"Then you figure the smugglers are somewhere around," said Dominick.

"Yes," said the Skipper. "And it's time we began making things hot for them. Put the guns in the dinghy. You and I are going ashore."

In a half hour the *Bonny* was opposite the sand humps, but well to the seaward of them. West Island had something of a curve or hook to its outer end, so angling off as they were, it was three or four miles farther before they could see what lay behind it. Spinach, from her place in the bows, had a better view than the others and she had nothing else to do but look. And she kept her eyes peeled, sharply.

"There it is," she cried suddenly. "It's a passage, all right."

Wide and clear, and reaching in generally from the south and west to Lighthouse Point, was an open strait. To the left of it as you went in was another island, low, sandy, and covered with scrub trees. From Smuggler Bay, it was entirely hidden behind the high banks and forests of West Island.

"Could a boat get in or out?" asked Katy.

"I should *say* it could," said Spinach. "From the looks of it, you could take an ocean liner right up to the lighthouse."

"Do you see anything," asked Katy, "anything that would make you think they were using the passage? Like a line of buoys or channel markings?"

"We're pretty far out," said Spinach. "But there *is* something—off the lower end of that new island. Maybe it's just a rock though."

"Why don't we run in and see?" asked Brick, practical again. "That's why we're on this cutter trip, you know."

"We will," said Katy, "as soon as we make a little more westing. I don't want to have to go tacking about in that passage."

Nobody said anything for a while, and the cutter drove on. Lighthouse Point and the two islands drew farther and farther away. The Able-seamen fretted the sheet lines and kept looking hopefully aft at Katy. She didn't say anything either. She minded the helm and coaxed the *Bonny* along until she thought she had beaten upwind far enough to make the passage back in one leg.

Then . . .

"Ready about!" Loudly and clearly came the command.

Down went the helm. The sails flapped idly for a second, and then the booms whacked over. The cutter came around and headed back for the land—dead on Lighthouse Point. The passage was squarely ahead—a fair reach in, with the wind a little aft of their port beam. They had only about a seven-mile leg to shore.

"Now," said Katy, when they were settled away on their course, "here's the plan. Spinach, you keep your eyes ahead for shoals or rocks. Brick, you keep an eye to port. Teddy, you look off to the lee. That will be the shore of West Island. And all of you keep your ears open. We're still sailing, you know. If I have to give an order, I want you to hear it."

Three miles farther on and they were back to the sand humps, but on the opposite side of them this time. Soon they swept in behind West Island. There wasn't much to see for its coast line was regular and even, coming down sharply with blue water right up to the beach. Probably this was just as well, as Teddy had to duck and squint under the canvas to see anything at all, for the sails were swung to starboard and nearly hid what view there was. Spinach and Brick had clear vision, she ahead, and he to port.

"That *is* a buoy," said Spinach suddenly from the bow. "But maybe it's an old one, and has nothing to do with the smugglers."

Ten more minutes and it was almost abeam. Brick watched it swing up to them. It was a red can buoy, new, brightly painted, and floating high in the water. Someone had moored it there, recently, and with the definite purpose of marking a channel.*

"That's not an old one," said Brick.

Then his eye caught something else, a little ahead, and on a bulge of land on the hidden island. It was a white target on a pole about ten feet high. The white face of the target was crossed with black markings for daylight

---

* The beam—or abeam is the side of the boat amidships.—Katy.

use, and a halyard was rove through a ball at the top of the pole. A lantern could easily be hoisted there at night.

"What's that?" he asked.

"What's what?" said Katy.

Brick told her.

"It's a range," decided Katy, after she had looked it over. "Spinach, keep your eyes open. We're coming to a bend in this channel. That bull's-eye is in line with something else."

They sailed on, perhaps another hundred yards, until they drew almost abreast of the white target. Then they could see that a passage *did* open out, eastward from the main channel in. It reached away—past Lighthouse Point and Ile de Croissant—crossed the wide mouth of the little logging stream, and swung by a dock that projected from its east bank. On the end of the dock stood a pole, and fastened part way up the pole was another white and black crossed target. In line with the one on the hidden island, the two formed a range.

"There it is," said Katy. "A marked, deep-water passage to a dock. Just as at Base One."

"Shall we go over?" asked Spinach.

"Let's," said Brick.

"No," said Katy. "Remember Uncle Bill's orders. We were told to keep away from the east bank of that stream. What we *can* do is to explore that lighthouse. It looks deserted enough, but we can find out whether it's been used lately."

They swung into the passage, careful to keep one bull's-eye dead ahead, and the other, squarely astern. The new course was practically down-wind, and the breeze was pretty stiff for the narrow unfamiliar channel. Besides, it was only a scant half mile to the lighthouse, and at the rate the shores were tearing by Katy had no chance to size things up, figure out a landing place, or put her mind to much of anything except the handling of the cutter. So she decided to reduce sail.

"Drop the main," she said to Brick and Teddy. "Spinach, you take the foresheet while they do it."

There wasn't room enough in the narrow channel to luff up, so it was a ticklish job. But the Able-seamen managed it, and the boat slowed down. Now Katy had a chance to look the lighthouse over. Its blank face stared at them as they swept by.

From the summit of a turf knoll at the tip of Lighthouse Point, rose a circular bit of stone masonry. This formed the base for a half-rusted steel tripod, which had mounted at its top a square lamp box with the side glasses long broken and gone. There was no sign of either lens or reflector. The lamp box had a roof-like cover, and to the under side of this was screwed a pulley with a bright new line rove through it.

Katy started at this discovery. A lantern could be hoisted there!

There was something queer about the turf knoll. It looked natural enough as you approached it from the west, but from the logging stream side you could see it was man-made—probably a good many years ago by piling up earth. From the knoll rose the roof and one wall of a stone hut, and a row of tiny windows peered from above the sod line. These had complete command of the stream, and the buildings and dock on its other side.

More like a line of loopholes than windows, thought Katy.

From where they now were, they could see that the bit of masonry with its tripod mounting was really a round stone tower. It was at the seaward end of the building, but very much a part of it. In the old days it could easily have been the watch tower of a fort.

"I wonder what's inside that," said Spinach.

"Let's go and see," said Brick.

"Here's a good place to land," said Teddy.

The "good place" was a little bay that cut in at the east side of the lighthouse. It was sheltered somewhat, and had a sand beach.

"All right," said Katy. "Trim in the sheet as we make the turn. When we hit the beach, let it run. Spinach, you jump out and make the painter fast."

Katy threw over the tiller and they came up to port. Brick hauled frantically in on the sheet, trimming the sail so as not to spill the wind and let the cutter lose way. The *Bonny* drove on toward the beach. The water shoaled rapidly and the line of white sand drew near. Then they struck.

"Let go the sheet!" yelled Katy. "Spinach, out over the bow!"

Brick let the sail run, and Spinach jumped for the shore. She didn't quite make it and landed ankle deep in the water, almost falling down. The Able-seamen got out too and grabbed the *Bonny's* bow. Then they dragged her high and dry and Spinach took a turn in the line around a half-buried tree trunk. Katy left the tiller and scrambled to the beach. Then she went to see what kind of knot Spinach was using to make the cutter fast, for she wanted the boat secure but in a condition to cast off quickly. It was all right, a half hitch and a round turn. She left the mast standing with the sail furled, and the boom laid along the thwarts—all ready to shove off in a hurry. Then she turned to her crew.

"Now, we'll look the place over," she said.

The little cove where they had landed cut in so as to be almost behind the lighthouse and knoll. So for the first time they could see the landward face of the building. Katy looked at it carefully. Earth had been piled up there too, and the turf came up to another line of tiny windows. There was no door, no entrance of any sort.

"That's funny," said Katy. "I wonder how they get in and out."

"Maybe from the west side of the point," said Teddy. "We haven't looked that over yet."

"Why don't we then," urged Brick.

They did, and the party split up to do it. Katy and Brick went around to seaward, past the light tripod; and the other two circled the landward end. By the time they met on the far side, they had had another surprise. For

not only was there no entrance, but apparently the hut
had no west wall. The turf came up high and smooth,
so as to cover the roof almost to the ridge pole, and all
that showed above ground was the round stone tower
staring vacantly out to sea.

The cousins looked at each other. What to do next?

"Wait a minute," said Brick.

He walked away from them, toward the shore of the
point opposite to where they had beached the *Bonny*.
The land continued high and nearly level in this direction, with only a gentle slope, but ended in a bluff that
dropped away sheer to the water. Brick climbed down.
In a minute they heard a yell.

"Come here," it said.

Their crew mate was out of sight, down under the
bluff. The rest of them left the stone building on the
run and soon dropped over the bank. In a minute they
were standing beside him. He was examining a timbered
opening that led underground, something like the entrance to a mine. There was a heavy door fitted with a
hasp and staple so it could be closed with a padlock. The
lock was missing and Katy gave the door a push. It
swung inward on a dark tunnel shored with heavy
beams. Where the tunnel led wasn't hard to guess. Here
was the entrance to the stone fort.

The rest of the crew were for barging right in. But
Katy held them back.

"No," she said. "Spinach and I broke in another place

—Base One. That looked deserted too, only it wasn't. Let's look around. We don't want to walk into an ambush."

Some scrub brush grew around the entrance and it hadn't been disturbed much. A faint footpath, which was anything but well trodden, led toward the water's edge, perhaps ten feet away. If anyone were using the tunnel they were careful about it, and went there but seldom. But there must be some telltale signs, and Katy found them, a few marks in the sand at right angles to the beach. Just as though someone had landed a boat there, nose on.

"Those might mean anything," said Brick, after they had examined the marks. "Lots of people come here. Fishermen, campers, all sorts of people. They don't have to be the smugglers."

"I wish I were sure," said Katy.

"We can make sure," said Teddy, "by going through that tunnel."

"And walk right into their arms?" asked Katy.

"If we do," said Spinach, "we can tell our old story, about being sightseers. It worked before. It will again."

"I wish I could be sure of that too," said Katy.

"Uncle Bill told us to explore around," said Brick, putting on the final pressure. "Why don't we do it?"

Katy looked at her crew. They eyed her back, flushed with excitement and eager for the venture. Well, maybe she was overanxious. She made up her mind.

"All right," she said. "I'll lead the way. Keep together, and keep your heads. If we have to any talking— let me do it."

They recrossed the narrow beach, back to the timbered entrance in the bank. The door to the tunnel still hung open, and from outside, they could see a few feet into the passage. Its ceiling was solidly planked, but the supporting beams were widely spaced so that between each was a deep niche. The hard dirt floor went in perfectly straight, with only a slight upward slope.

Katy drew a long breath and looked around. It might be her last sight of the bright day, the blue water, and the sunny beach. "Follow me," she said.

Then she went in.

For several yards they moved rapidly until the thickening gloom of the passage slowed them down. Every step took them farther from the fading light of the open door behind, and the way grew blacker and blacker. Finally they could not see at all. Nor was this the friendly dark of a ship's deck at night, with the stars overhead, and the cheer of a wink and flash from an off-shore light. It clamped down on them—thick, oppressive—and their eyes strained into it.

Katy groped on for a few feet and then stopped. Immediately she was bumped into by Spinach who was next in line. *She* in turn was hit by Teddy, who was stumbled into by Brick who brought up the rear.

"What's the matter?" whispered Spinach. In the

choked black of the tunnel her question hissed sharply, and echoed back and forth.

"We'd better link hands," said Katy. "We mustn't get separated." Her voice was as low and controlled as she could make it.

The human chain crawled on. Suddenly its leader walked smack into one of the side beams of the tunnel, but thanks to the joined hands, the others stopped without piling up. Katy hadn't changed direction, she knew that. So they must have come to a turn in the passage. With her free hand she reached out, found the beam and groped across it to the next. There *was* a slight bend, to the left and they felt their way around it. Then the tunnel straightened, but the floor was no longer level. It sloped upward, sharply, and the others sensing the rise hung back so that she had to pull them along.

Suddenly Katy stopped again. Not because she had run into anything, or seen anything—that was impossible. But there was a thickening of the dark—a blind instinct that told of a hidden barrier ahead, and a sure knowledge that the tunnel bore was at an end. She stood still for a second and then decided to go on. Something whacked her across the shin and she leaned down to feel what it was. It was a step—two steps—and at their top, a shut door.

Now what!

Katy fumbled for Spinach's shoulder and when she found it, drew close and whispered in her cousin's ear.

"Stay here," she said. "And keep quiet."

Then she mounted the steps and pressed her ear against the door. There wasn't a sound—or was there? It was hard to tell, what with the pounding in her heart and the roaring in her ears. Behind her she could hear her crew mates breathe. From the noise they made, you might as well turn loose a steamboat whistle. On the other side of the door it was still, ominously so. There was a suspended silence as though someone were listening—and waiting. It was too quiet. The very absence of all sound was in itself a warning. Katy decided to go back, collect the others and go away from there—on through the dark passage to the bright day.

But she never had the chance.

Suddenly, behind them, was a blinding flash of light. It came from an electric torch in the hands of a blurred shape that stepped from one of the niches between the wall beams. At the same instant the door at the top of the stairs was pulled violently inward and daylight streamed into the tunnel. In the doorway, and framed sharply in its panel of light, stood a man. It was Scarface.

"Come in, my young friends," he said sneeringly. "We've been waiting for you."

And then, harshly to the shape at the dark end of the torch, "Herd 'em along."

"Get going," said the shape.

For a second Katy had a wild desire to turn and run, but her common sense quickly told her that would be useless. They couldn't get away, and one false move would destroy all chance of brazening through their guise of innocent tourists. So she stepped through the door into the single room of the stone hut, and the rest of the crew trailed after her. The vague shape at their rear turned out to be the gunman they had seen at Base One, and he slammed the door to as he followed them in.

One look at Scar-face and her heart sank. He wasn't going to be taken in a second time.

"Line 'em up along the wall," he said to his gunman. "Under the windows. We'll find out about this, right now."

"I told you we should have mussed 'em up," said the gunman. "This is the third time we've met 'em. That don't happen up in this country without it means something."

"Shut up," said Scar-face. "They won't make a fool of me again."

While they were being "lined up" Katy had a chance to look around. There were the four stone walls with the line of high windows on two sides. The door to the tunnel was the only entrance provided you didn't count the opening through the round tower at the far end. That served two purposes, chimney for the flagged hearth underneath, and a way up to the lookout. For a ladder of iron rungs led up the inside of the masonry and could be climbed to the top. Boxes and barrels were set about on the floor and a pile of raw furs flung down in one corner.

Katy had seen this sort of thing before—at Base One. What took her eye was an object squatted beside the hearth under the tower. At first glance it looked like a huddle of blue denim. Then it moved, or rather turned its head. A pair of slanting beady eyes glittered from a yellow dished face. Straight black hair was gathered in a knob at the nape of its neck. Its hands were shackled together and fastened to ankle irons by a short length of strong chain. It could move, but not stand upright. The huddled shape was a Chinaman—midway between the Orient and illegal entry into the United States.

"Well, what about it?" said Scar-face angrily. "Are you going to stand there dumb, and spend the afternoon looking around this room?"

"What about what?" answered Katy. She wanted to try a bluff, but she was getting angry too. "Suppose you answer. Why are you keeping us here?"

"None of your lip," broke in the gunman. "Any more of your sass and you'll get smacked flat. Answer the boss."

"What do you want to know?" asked Katy.

"Why is that schooner out in the bay?" said Scar-face. "We saw her come in yesterday. Who's aboard? And what are you brats snooping around here for?"

"My uncle and cousin," said Katy, "and our foremast hand. We're on a yachting trip. And we're not brats, and we're not snooping. We were playing at being explorers, in the ship's cutter."

"We didn't know this was a smugglers' base," put in Teddy, trying to help and not realizing what he was saying.

The instant the words were out of his mouth, he could have bitten off his tongue. Scar-face turned a brick red, and the veins on his forehead stood out with rage. He put his hands on his hips and glared at them.

"So that's it," he said. "I thought you were too damned innocent to be true."

"I told you," said the gunman.

"Tie 'em up," said Scar-face. "We'll get to the bottom of this. Rope the girls together. Keep the boys apart."

The gunman went to an open packing case and got out several lengths of stout line.

"Turn around," he said to Katy and Spinach. "Back to back. And put your hands down at your sides."

First he made a running noose in one end of the line and roped the girls together. Then he turned the rest of the line round and round their bodies, so that from shoulders to knees they were bound up like thread around a spool. The other end he fastened in a knot between them, at the small of their backs, so that neither could reach it. Finally he kicked their feet from under them and threw them to the ground. Five minutes later Brick and Teddy were trussed up and tied to convenient ring bolts, each on an opposite side of the room.

"What about the Chink?" asked the gunman. "He can get around. He might let 'em loose."

"Sack him up," said Scar-face.

Katy never forgot the scene that followed. The gunman walked over to a corner of the room and picked up a large canvas sack, something like an oversize mail pouch. The minute the Chinaman saw the bag he began to whimper in a scared way, wriggling and sidling off toward the opposite corner. Knowing what was coming, he groveled in the dirt and whined with fear.

"Stick him in," said Scar-face. "And hurry up about it."

The gunman seized the Chinaman by the hair, close up near the scalp, and threw him down. Then he twisted the hair knot, forcing back his head. Clenching his right fist he swung hard on the Chinaman's jaw, knocking him cold. The yellow man stiffened out, kicked and jerked for a minute, and then lay still. The gunman calmly drew on the sack, from the feet up, stuffing in the arms and tightening the pull cord around the neck. Then he eyed his prostrate and unconscious victim and kicked him brutally. The Chinaman's head lolled limply from side to side.

"Oh don't!" cried Katy.

"Shut up," said the gunman. "One more squawk and that's what you'll get. That goes for the rest of you too."

"Come on," said Scar-face. "I want to meet that uncle of theirs."

The smugglers had a final look around the room. Then Scar-face walked over to where the girls lay bound on the floor and examined their lashings. And he wasn't any too gentle about it either. Not even bothering to stoop down, he rolled them over with his foot, so that Katy's face was ground into the earth and she got dirt in her eyes and mouth. His gunman waited for him. Then each of them took a rifle and went to the tunnel door. Scar-face had his last word.

"If that uncle of yours is nosing around our dock or cabins," he said, "it'll be his last trip ashore."

The door slammed, and the children were left alone with the sacked-up and unconscious Chinaman.

CHAPTER XIX

DEATH ACROSS THE STREAM

THE SILENCE during the next few minutes was terrible. Katy lay on her side on the floor and her back-to-back position with Spinach brought into view the far end of the room where the sacked and unconscious Chinaman lay.

Thoughts raced through her head. . . . If the smugglers can do that to him—how will they treat Uncle Bill and Dominick?

But Aba-ka-mas and Bear Hunter were somewhere in the woods, above the smugglers. So at least it would be four against two. But the two were fore-warned and armed—armed with modern high-powered rifles that could snuff out a man's life from behind a tree. If Scarface and his gunman once got across the logging stream without being seen by the Indians, they could hide in ambush and pick off the Skipper and Blue Nose at leisure. . . . If there were only some way to warn them!

The way was found—quickly, and from an entirely unsuspected source.

"Katy," said Brick suddenly.

"What?" she answered.

By craning her neck, she could see him. He was tied to a shoulder-high ring bolt anchored in the wall. A short piece of line was lashed around his ankles, and another about his wrists which were crossed behind his back. The end of the wrist lashing had been led up through the ring bolt, and the Able-seaman drawn close. He must have been uncomfortable, but there was enough slack in the line so that he could strain forward and even wriggle a bit.

"Remember back at Sarnia?" he said.

"Sarnia!" said Katy. "What's Sarnia got to do with this? I'm trying to figure out a way to get a warning to Uncle Bill and Dominick."

Her answer was short, and somewhat impatient. She was a little annoyed with boys anyway. Teddy's entirely thoughtless and somewhat stupid remark had gotten them into their present mess, and now here was her brother prattling away about a town six hundred miles behind them.

"That's what I'm talking about," said Brick. "Remember Dominick saying how he hoped the next time he saw Scar-face, that it would be at the end of a line—bound up tight?"

"Well?" said Katy.

"And how, when I offered to tie the knot, Dominick asked, 'Did I know how?' And that it must be a secure one. One that an eel couldn't slip out of?"

"Go on," said Katy. She was getting interested.

"And that it must be a square knot? That a 'granny' wouldn't hold?"

"You mean?" asked Katy.

"Yes," said Brick; "those smugglers weren't so smart. I think I can get loose."

"Try!" said Katy desperately. "Oh, if you only could!"

The Able-seaman squirmed and twisted, and strained forward. The lashings cut into his wrists and hurt cruelly, but when he stood quiet and upright again, he had gained a little slack. There wasn't enough, so he tried again. This time he could just touch the knot. It was stubborn, and he couldn't get purchase enough to work at it successfully.

"Once more," said Katy. "You've got to get loose!"

Brick lunged forward, with every ounce of strength he had. The granny knot slipped a little—maybe only part of an inch—but enough so that he could pick away at it. The thongs had cut off the circulation in his hands so that his fingers were numb and clumsy, and his progress slow and fumbling.

Katy watched anxiously. Could he get away in time?

But he made it, finally. The granny knot let go with a run, and the wrist lashings came loose. He rubbed his numbed arms and fingers and leaned down to free his ankles. Then he went over to unbind the Mates.

"Never mind us," said Katy. "Run! Back out through the tunnel! The smugglers have a ten-minute start, and every second counts."

"What shall I do?" said Brick.

"Keep to the shore," said Katy. "Go round the seaward end of the lighthouse until you come to the logging stream, but stay on this side. If you see any of our party, yell! Above all, don't get caught."

"Where do you suppose the smugglers are?" asked Brick.

"I don't know," said Katy. "But they will probably cross upstream a ways, and work down through the woods on the opposite side. They may run into our Indians—and I hope they do!" she added.

"I'll try," said Brick. "If there's any way, I'll get word across."

He slipped out the tunnel door. The road back wasn't as scary as the way in—nor as dark—for the doors at both ends were open, and he made it almost on the run. Clear of the entrance, he turned left, skirted the shore of the point past the lighthouse and knoll, and hugged the beach all the way. Soon he came to the cove where they had landed the *Bonny*. Its far shore led outward toward a stubby point at the mouth of the logging stream, and Brick looked across. He could see the dock, the shack, and the old lumber mill, but nothing else. The two grassy islands that choked the mouth of the stream held his vision head-high, something like looking over a field of grain, and he couldn't tell whether the dinghy had been drawn up on the beach or not. No one was in sight, so he decided to work up the west bank of the stream, above the shack, and perhaps as high as the

lumber mill. From there, he could see anybody that tried
to go up or down.

He moved along warily, for perhaps two hundred
yards, keeping out of sight as best he might, and ducking
from tree trunk to clump of brush, and crawling across
the open spaces. At last he saw a likely spot—a rise of
ground that ended as a high bank over the stream, with
a line of bushes at its very edge.

"If I can make that," he said to himself, "I can see
everything, and still keep hidden."

He crawled across the last bit of bare ground on his
stomach, and wriggled under the bushes. Then with his
hands, he made an opening in the brush and looked out.

From where he lay, the old lumber mill was about
opposite. The shack was about two hundred feet farther
down, and the dock below that. The grassy islands no
longer blocked his view. The first thing he spied was
the dinghy, drawn up on the beach a few feet beyond the
far side of the dock. So he knew Sailor Bill and the
Blue Nose had landed. The scene was set. Could he
bring its action to a favorable close? To do it, he must
see the *Gull-Flight's* shore party before the smugglers did.

There was no one in sight. Around the buildings and
dock, the forest had been cleared, making a rough half
circle of open ground. For a few feet in, the trees had
been thinned, so that the cleared circle was fringed by a
sparse scant woods. Beyond that, the wilderness clamped
down. Somewhere in it, Brick knew were six men,
working in pairs—three separate parties.

He lay there, under the bushes, sizing up the situation.

Sailor Bill and Dominick were moving north from the shore—he knew that. The Indians were coming south from the railroad track. So the smugglers must be in between. And they were due for a surprise. They

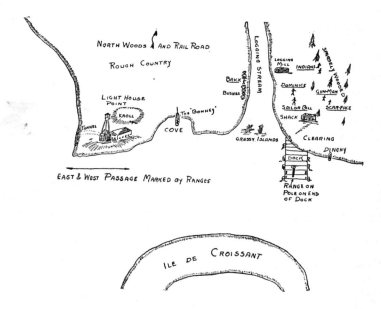

thought they were looking for two men. They would have to deal with four. And two of the four were behind them.

Brick wriggled and squirmed impatiently. He knew he must get his warning across the stream, and that every second counted. But there was nobody to warn. The clearing and its buildings lay deserted—silent—and he wished someone would show up. But nobody did—for several minutes.

Then it all happened.

Suddenly the little clearing was filled with men. All of them had rifles in their hands, ready for action. Sailor Bill and Dominick came out of a door in the lumber mill and walked toward the shack. At the same instant, and a little to the rear, Scar-face and his gunman stepped from behind trees into the open. Then two shadows appeared. They glided swiftly from tree to tree until they cleared the fringe of forest. Aba-ka-mas and Bear Hunter were hot on the rear of the smugglers. Only Sailor Bill and Dominick were unconcerned. Each other pair was intent on the men in front.

Brick jumped to his feet, waving his arms and yelling. "Uncle Bill!" he cried. "Look behind you!"

His wasn't the only yell. Instantly, an Indian war whoop split the air. Then four shots rang out.

It took a second for Brick to realize what had happened. When Sailor Bill heard his nephew's shout, he whirled, saw the armed smugglers, and dropped to the ground. Scar-face snapped a quick shot at him—and missed. The gunman spun to the sound of the war cry, saw the Indians behind him, and let drive at the Scout. Bear Hunter pitched forward on his face. Then Aba-ka-mas fired. The Chief's bullet knocked the gunman half way round. He let go his rifle, clutched his middle, and started to sag. Then his knees bent, and he crumpled into a sprawled heap.

Brick's shout had saved his uncle's life. Scar-face was clawing at his breech-bolt to eject the empty shell for another try when Dominick let him have it. The shot was lucky—for the smuggler. Instead of hitting him, it struck his rifle, splintering the stock and knocking the piece out of his hands. The bullet whined off over the woods in a screaming ricochet. Disarmed himself, the smuggler saw his gunman a lifeless huddle on the ground. That took away any fight he had left, and he put up his hands.

"I surrender," he said.

"You're lucky to have the chance," said Dominick. "Turn around and look at that Indian Chief. I've a notion to leave you to *his* tender mercies."

Aba-ka-mas had bent over the fallen scout. He had turned him over—gently—and pressed an ear to his heart. There was no use. Bear Hunter was dead. The Chief rose and looked at Scar-face. Then he took a step forward. His eyes had a glassy stare, and he moved like a panther stalking its prey. He had reverted to tribal savagery, and it took but little imagination to picture a scalping knife or tomahawk in his hand.

Scar-face turned white and backed away, toward Sailor Bill and Dominick, still keeping his hands over his head. The Blue Nose spoke several sharp phrases in Chippewa. The Chief started, shivered a little as though coming out of a trance, and without a word turned back to the dead Bear Hunter.

Sailor Bill covered Scar-face with his rifle. "Keep coming," he said. "Backwards. The way you are. . . . Now stop," he added a few seconds later.

"Snap." A pair of steel cuffs bound the smuggler's wrists.

"Now sit down," ordered Sailor Bill. "Dominick, you hold him here. I want to find out about the children, where they are, and how Brick got on that bank across the stream—Thank Heaven he did though," he added.

"That damned kid," said Scar-face.

"That'll be enough from you," said Dominick. "Another word, and I'll let the Indian have you."

Sailor Bill turned to Brick on the opposite shore. "Stay where you are," he shouted. "I'm coming over."

The Able-seaman watched his uncle wade out into the stream. The bottom dropped away. To knee depth at first—then waist high, and soon the Skipper had to swim. He turned on his back, held his rifle high to keep it dry, and kicked himself across with his feet. So it was perhaps five minutes before he climbed the bank and stood dripping beside his nephew.

"How did you get here?" he said. "And where are the others? Are they safe?"

"They're safe," said Brick, ignoring his uncle's first question. "But they're tied up—along with the Chinaman."

"Tied up!" said Sailor Bill. "Where? With what Chinaman?"

"In the stone hut," said Brick. "Under the light tower. I don't know much about the Chinaman either."

Sailor Bill looked at his nephew. He wondered if the Able-seaman weren't just a bit off in the head. From where they stood, brush and scrub pine hid the knoll, the hut, and even the cove where they had beached the *Bonny*. To say nothing of the Chinaman. So what Brick had just said hardly seemed to make sense.

"Go back to the beginning," said the Skipper. "Tell me what happened. When I saw you last, you were in the cutter, headed out around West Island. I sent you there to keep you out of trouble. Apparently you didn't."

Brick told his story. When he had finished, Sailor Bill laid his hand on the boy's shoulder.

"You did a real job," he said. "All of you. Without your help neither Dominick nor I would be alive. We figured that Scar-face was somewhere around, but on the other side of the stream. So we rigged the outboard and came ashore in the dinghy. We should have waited for our Indians to find us. But we didn't. We searched the shack and the old lumber mill. When we were inside the smugglers came across unseen. But that part of it's over. The thing to do now is to free the rest of you—and find out about that Chinaman. Suppose you lead the way to the hut. I'll have Dominick join us there."

He turned and shouted to the Blue Nose on the opposite shore.

"Take the dinghy. Bring Scar-face with you. I want to talk to him. Go round the point to the far side of the lighthouse. There's an entrance to a tunnel there, and we'll be inside. Tell the Chief to stay where he is, on guard. We'll be back for him later."

Sailor Bill and the Able-seaman watched to see how Dominick would make out. Scar-face was a dangerous man, and by now, desperate as well. To the charge of smuggling would be added the crime of murder. The murder of Bear Hunter—if not by his own hand, then certainly by one of the gang. And his was the deliberate shot at Sailor Bill. No denying that, and there were four witnesses to it. So handcuffed though he was, he might well break for freedom. True, Aba-ka-mas was near. But he sat alone—apart—a mourning figure, crouched over the dead body of his scout.

None of this seemed to bother Dominick. He grabbed the smuggler by the back of the shirt collar and jerked him to his feet.

"Get going," he said. "Down to the dock. And if you know what's good for you, don't try to get away."

Scar-face shuffled off and Dominick trailed him. At the water's edge the Blue Nose ordered him to stop. Then he unlocked the handcuffs and stepped back. With rifle at the ready, and finger on the trigger, he had complete command of the smuggler and forced him to do his bidding.

"Launch the dinghy," he said. "Never mind the motor. Get out the oars and row over to the dock. I'll go aboard there. And if you still think you can get away —go ahead and try it. I'd as lief take a pot shot at you as not."

The Skipper watched the proceedings for a minute. Then he laughed.

"I guess we needn't worry," he said. "Where is this hut of yours?"

Brick led off—through the brush—not following the shore this time, but cutting straight across the point past the landward end of the half-buried stone hut. Sailor Bill eyed the line of loopholes that served as windows, but made no comment. A minute more brought them down under the bluff, on the beach, and to the mine-like entrance to the tunnel.

"Hm-m-m," said the Skipper. "So here's where you went in. Well there's nothing the matter with your nerve."

The door to the passage hung open and they raced through. Sailor Bill led, drawing his sheath knife as he ran along, and a second later they burst into the hut. Katy and Spinach still lay on the earth floor, bound back to back. They had struggled and rolled and kicked to get free, but outside of dirt in their eyes and mouths, and a whole lot more in their hair and on their uniforms, they weren't hurt much. Teddy was in far worse shape. The lashings that fastened his wrists behind him were cruelly tight, and had cut off the circulation so that his hands were swollen and puffed to a purplish black. Worse than that, he had been drawn up so close to the shoulder-high ring bolt that he had had to stand on tip-toe to keep his weight off tortured arm and shoulder muscles. His head drooped, and in trying not to cry, he had bitten his lip until the blood came. He couldn't have stood it much longer without fainting.

Sailor Bill cut him down in a hurry. Then he rubbed the boy's swollen arms and legs and ripped off his shoes. Returning circulation brought its thousands of pins and needles that pricked and burned, and in spite of himself, Teddy blubbered a little. His uncle patted him on the shoulder.

"There, there, Old Boy," he said. "It won't last long. Run around a bit."

By the time the Skipper could turn to help the girls, Brick was already at their bonds, working away at the knot tied in between them. Sailor Bill hurried the process by slashing through the cords with his knife—and then to his great surprise, Katy burst into tears.

"Uncle Bill, Uncle Bill!" she cried, getting to her feet and running to him. "You're safe—and we were so afraid!"

Captain Williams hugged his nieces tight. "Don't cry," he said. "It's all over, and we're all right."

"We heard the shots," said Spinach. "We were so worried—and scared. Was anyone hurt?"

Sailor Bill hesitated. Then he decided to tell them the truth.

"Yes," he said gravely. "Bear Hunter. Shot and killed by the gunman. And revenged instantly by Chief Aba-ka-mas. Scar-face was captured. Dominick is bringing him here."

"Will Joe College come too?" asked Katy.

"No," said the Skipper simply. "He is watching by the body of his dead brave."

Suddenly there came a queer noise from the tower end of the room. It was a combination of squeak and bird-like chirp. Sailor Bill whirled and saw the sacked China-man. He was conscious now—probably had been for some while—but had kept perfectly still until he had figured out for himself that the new presence in the room had a kindly intent, and came as a friend. He happened to lie, or had wriggled around, so as to face the room. Only his head stuck from out of the sack. The slanting black eyes were alive and curious now, and from his mouth came a series of cackles in a high singsong voice. He was talking away at a great rate in his native Can-tonese.

The effect was funny. A comic relief from the stark tragedy of the past hours, and Katy burst out laughing. Then she felt ashamed.

"The poor thing," she said. "Let's get him free. To be in that sack all this time."

"And knocked out first," said Brick.

"So there's your Chinaman," said Sailor Bill. "How did he get here? And why is he in that sack?"

Brick started to explain, but he didn't get far. He was stopped in the middle of the first few sentences by a noise in the tunnel. They all heard it, and even the Chinaman ceased his cackle. It was Dominick, prodding Scar-face through the passage and speeding him along with an oc-casional well-aimed kick.

The two of them came in. The smuggler's arms were hand-cuffed behind him again. The Blue Nose, with his rifle carried easily in the crook of an arm, had complete command.

"Hello," he said. "Here's our little guest. What do you want with him? He'll be glad to answer any questions—You'd better," he added to Scar-face.

The crew of the *Gull-Flight* stood in a group in the middle of the stone-walled room. It never dawned on Dominick that until a few minutes ago, its younger members had been bound and held as prisoners. So his interest was all for the hut. His eyes traveled from box to barrel, and over to a bundle of furs.

"So here's their base," he started to say. "And a good hideout it . . ."

He never finished the sentence. Suddenly he saw the Chinaman lying on the hearth under the stone tower. A glance took in the whole story. No need for the undercover agent to ask the reason for the sack. He knew. And he turned to the smuggler.

"Running aliens too," he said. "Well—Immigration will be as glad to see you as Customs, to say nothing of the Prosecutor for the Crown. Where are the weights?"

Scar-face nodded sullenly toward one of the boxes. "In there," he said.

Dominick went to the box. He opened the lid and rummaged down through some loose piles of cordage. When he raised up, he had both hands full. In one was a set of arm and leg irons similar to those the Chinaman wore. In the other, a short piece of heavy bar-iron weighing perhaps forty pounds.

"Poor Chink," said the Blue Nose. "He'd never come up with those."

"What does it all mean?" asked the Skipper.

"Rules," said Dominick, "of the sweet game of Chinaman running. From the time they leave their own country, they're at the mercy of the runners. They come over in the hold of some tramp steamer, barreled up like fish, or maybe two of 'em in a crate with air holes punched in the bottom. When they come ashore, some railroad 'brakie' is bribed to stow them away on a trans-country train, or they're boxed up again and shipped as freight. Finally they land at some place like this. Then they're ironed and sewed up in a sack weighted with one of these —holding up the piece of bar-iron. Some dark night a boat calls and they start the run across the lake. If they're lucky—they land. If not"—and the French in Dominick expressed itself both by shrug and gesture—"*Fini le Chinois.*"

"You mean!" said Katy.

"Yes," said Dominick, "if they run into the Coast Guard, or if for any reason the landing plan goes astray —plop—overboard goes the Chinaman, sacked and weighted, to the bottom of the lake. The runner doesn't care. He has already been paid."

"I wouldn't want any of that," said Brick, "especially when you start off with a clip on the jaw. Let's get him out of that sack."

The Chinaman wasn't pleased. You could tell that, by the furrows in the brow and the wrinkles in the nose of his otherwise expressionless yellow face. Brutal as Scar-face had been, and friendly and kind as the crew of the *Gull-Flight* now was—he knew the game was up. Back to China he would go, shorn of all hope, and minus the thousand or more dollars passage money. The promised land lay across a border he could never cross.

While the Chinaman was being freed from his sack, Sailor Bill had been doing some thinking.

"The boat," he said suddenly to Dominick; "isn't it likely to come tonight—to call for the Chinaman? Shall we wait and see whether we can bag any more of this gang—or get out now?"

"Get out now," answered Dominick. "There's more than two in this operation—no doubt. But Scar-face is the leader. We've enough on him for a hanging party—and he'll hang all right. But he'll talk first—we'll see to that. We don't know their night signals and the boat will hang off shore and wait for those. She won't come in that blind channel without them. I move we go—now."

"What about Aba-ka-mas and the two dead men?" said Sailor Bill. "And Scar-face, and the Chinaman, and any evidence you want to take back. The *Gull-Flight's* no ocean liner, you know."

Dominick turned to the crew.

"Mates," he said, "and Able-seamen, too, you've never failed us yet. Can we count on you once more?"

"What do you want us to do?" said Katy quietly.

"Go back in the *Bonny*. Out behind West Island—the way you came in. Take the Chinaman with you. We'll leave the chains on him, and you mustn't let him get away. There are two or three other things in this hut I want to send along. You'll have all the smuggling and alien-running evidence. Can you get it safely aboard the schooner?"

"Suppose the Chinaman tries to break for freedom?" asked Sailor Bill. "Our crew's rather young, you know."

"He won't," said Dominick. "He can't swim in those chains, and he can't run. Besides, he's so scared he can hardly move."

"There's still the smuggler, the Indian, and the two dead men," said Sailor Bill, not quite convinced.

"We've the dinghy," said the Blue Nose. "We'll take Scar-face to the ship. You stay aboard. I'll come back with canvas hammocks for the bodies. In two trips, I can bring everything out. It will take the cutter that long to get around West Island."

"We can do it, Uncle Bill," said Katy.

"Let's go," said Brick.

"One more thing," said Dominick, "we'll fix this place so no smuggler can ever use it again."

"How?" said Sailor Bill.

"Dynamite," said Dominick. "There's a case of sticks over there. They've been using it to blow up streams to get a cargo of fish for their smacks. That's illegal too.

But what of it, if you need a disguise in a hurry. So it's good-bye to this hut and the old light tower. We'll leave the shack and the mill on the other side of the stream. Hunters and fishermen can use those."

"It's a good idea," said Sailor Bill.

CHAPTER XX

FOR THE next ten minutes, Dominick busied himself mightily. First he herded Scar-face and the Chinaman into a corner of the room. Then he handed his rifle to Sailor Bill.

"Keep 'em there," he said.

The Blue Nose hunted around until he found a tarpaulin which he spread on the floor. Onto it went something from each barrel and crate, plus a couple of pelts from the pile of raw furs. This was the smuggling evidence. Then he went to the box of dynamite sticks and made up several charges of a half dozen cartridges each, burying them in the wall masonry. One of them he fused with a long piece of cotton line, and led the end through a window.

"We're ready," he said at last. "We'll light the fuse from the outside. Look around. It's the last anyone will ever see of this room."

"Don't forget the Chinaman," said Sailor Bill.

"I won't," said Dominick. "It's quite a party we'll hold for Scar-face—smuggling—alien running—and murder. He'll hang, all right."

"Let's go," said Sailor Bill impatiently.

The Able-seamen grabbed the bundle of contraband and lugged it through the tunnel door. The rest followed. Outside, Dominick took charge of Scar-face again and hustled him down to the beach where the dinghy lay. The others turned left, toward the *Bonny.* The Chinaman shambled along with them, awkward and hampered by his chains and equally voluble with his plaints to get them removed. At least that's the way his clucks and cackles sounded. But it didn't do him any good.

"I'm afraid to let him loose," said Sailor Bill. "Once aboard the *Gull-Flight,* we'll give him the run of the ship. And feed him up. He looks as though he hadn't had a square meal in a month."

They got the cutter afloat and the tarpaulin stowed amidships. In sign language, the Chinaman was told to climb in and lie down on it. But he couldn't—or wouldn't—understand, and finally the Skipper grabbed him and hauled him in. They were ready to go.

Sailor Bill cast his eye up at the wind. It was dead ahead, blowing down the narrow channel past Lighthouse Point. There was no chance of getting up sail until the cutter turned southward into the reach of West Island Passage.

"Better let Dominick tow you out," he said, " you can't tack around in here. Don't even try."

So they waited for the dinghy, and before long its put-put was heard coming round the point. Dominick was sitting in the bow, rifle across his knees, facing the smug-

gler. Sailor Bill motioned for the tow. The Blue Nose
gave Scar-face the necessary orders, and looked as though
he enjoyed doing it.

"For once you're some use," the crew heard him say.
"Make their painter fast. And look alive. One false
move, and you'll get it." He gestured toward his rifle.

Of all the unwilling hands, Scar-face was the best example ever. But he was afraid to disobey. So he backed the
dinghy down and hooked on to the bow of the cutter. A
few minutes later they had been towed to the entrance
of West Island Passage, and the dinghy let go. The boats
drew apart.

"Keep your eye on the lighthouse," yelled Dominick
above the clatter of the outboard. "You'll see some fireworks."

The crew got up sail. As the cutter gathered way the
range pole on Hidden Island slipped by, and the can
buoy drew abeam. On their left was the regular shore
of West Island with its white beach and boundary of blue
water. Nothing looked any different now than it had in
the morning when they sailed so gaily in, the day's adventures still ahead. The death of two men—the capture of
the smugglers—the race against the coming of the rein-
forcing boat. None of these had any effect on the North
Country. It lay there, calm and serene—indifferent to
human struggle.

"What about the fireworks?" said Brick. He too had
heard Dominick's farewell remark.

B-O-O-M!

The explosion came as though in direct answer.

The startled crew looked astern and the Chinaman tried to crawl under the tarpaulin. The stone tower leaped into the air and then settled back in a cloud of dust and a haze of yellow smoke. The light tripod toppled lazily forward and the lamp box fell into the water. A flight of gulls rose screaming, and some frightened animal crashed off through the brush on Hidden Island. Echoes rolled back and forth, and when the smoke cleared, a rubble of broken masonry and a gaping hole in an earthen knoll were all that remained of the fortress-like hut that had been the hide-out at Base Two.

THEY sailed on for a while, and then, just as had Sailor Bill but for an entirely different reason, Katy cast her eye up at the wind.

"We've an hour or more to the schooner," she said, "provided the breeze holds. But it's getting late, and sundown may bring a calm."

"We'll be all right anyway," said Brick. "Once we get out where they can see us. If the wind drops, Dominick can pick us up in the dinghy."

"I hope he doesn't have to," said Katy. "He has enough to do as it is."

She was thinking of the job of ferrying out Aba-ka-mas and the two bodies. To say nothing of putting Sailor Bill and Scar-face aboard. The others fell silent. Perhaps they were thinking of the same thing. And of the voyage home, and of the strange cargo the *Gull-Flight* would carry: an Indian Chief—two dead men—a desperado in chains—and a chattering Chinaman to be delivered to the authorities for deportation.

But the breeze held. Instead of dropping toward sundown, it stiffened. The *Bonny* tore around the sand humps and swooped down on the schooner. They rounded the stern and came up under the boat boom. Sailor Bill was there, waiting to make their painter fast. Then while the Able-seamen were lowering the sails, the Skipper passed down the rope ladder.

"Heave him up," he said. "The Chinaman I mean."

It was easy to say, but hard to do. Each order had to be given in sign language, and the Chinaman was exceedingly dumb, or at least it seemed so to the crew who had to do the heaving. First they prodded him into the cutter's bow. He stumbled over the forward thwart, lost his balance, and nearly tipped the *Bonny* over. That scared him so that he sat down on the seat and wouldn't move until Brick hauled him off. Then they placed his hands on one of the lower rungs of the rope ladder, and pointed up at the boat boom.

"Up. Up," said the Able-seaman, jerking his thumb in the air.

The Chinaman didn't move.

"Show him how," said Sailor Bill.

Brick grabbed the ladder and scrambled up. Encouraged by this example, the Chinaman seemed willing to try, and with all of them either pushing or hauling, at last he made it. But the idea of having to walk along the boat boom to the schooner's rail was too much for him and he sat down again. Finally the Skipper picked him up bodily and carried him inboard.

The crew of the *Bonny* collapsed limply on the thwarts.

"That's worse than trying to get an elephant aboard," said Brick. "Next time we'll use a cargo whip."

"He's going to be handy around the schooner," said Teddy. "Especially if we run into a blow."

"I bet he gets sick," said Spinach. She was remembering her own experience off Kettle Shoals. .

Sailor Bill came back out along the boat boom. He had lugged the Chinaman below and locked him up safely in a stateroom.

"Now the things in the tarp," he said.

The bundle was bulky rather than heavy, and passing it up took only a second. Afterward they rowed around to the port davits and hoisted the *Bonny* aboard. The cutter crew scrambled to the schooner's deck and Katy looked eagerly around. Dear old *Gull-Flight,* she thought. It's nice to be back again. So much had happened since they left in the morning, and there were so many things she wanted to tell her eldest cousin. But the Chief Engineer was nowhere in sight.

"Where's Morgan?" she asked.

"And where's Gyp?" said Brick.

"The dog's in your stateroom," said Sailor Bill to the Able-seamen, "shut up, to keep out of mischief. And I don't want him trying to lunch off the Chinaman's leg. Morgan's in the fo'c'sle—on guard. Teddy, you relieve him. I'll show you what to do in a minute."

Suddenly Katy realized that the trip home was to be no pleasure cruise. It would be business—grim business— with everyone's job cut out for him, and strict attention to be paid it. The schooner no longer presented an air of leisure and comfort. She was stripped for action, awning down, sail covers off, and kedge anchor in. They were ready to cast off—in a hurry—the minute Dominick finished his last trip ashore.

"Come below," said the Skipper.

Katy started to walk over to the forward deck house. She had intended to go down the saloon stairs. But Sailor Bill stopped her.

"I wouldn't go through there," he said. "Use the after companionway. Through the chartroom."

A queer feeling prickled up the back of Katy's neck. "You mean?" she said.

"Yes," said Sailor Bill, "the body of Bear Hunter—on my bunk. Dominick has already made one trip. He's ashore now. To fetch the Chief and the gunman."

The Skipper led the way aft, down into the cabin, through the galley, and into the fo'c'sle. There sat Morgan, perched on the single port berth. He was swinging his legs and regarding Scar-face who was chained to a stanchion that supported the double bunks across the compartment. The smuggler's hands were cuffed in front of him—more comfort than he had allowed Teddy a few hours ago—but he was secure enough, and glowered sourly at his captors.

"Any trouble?" asked the Skipper.

"Nary a bit," said Morgan. "His language was pretty bad though." And then to the Mates and Able-seamen, "Hello, gang! I hear you're quite the heroes."

"Keep a decent tongue in your head," said Sailor Bill to Scar-face, "or you'll go into the hold. Watch him Teddy. If he tries to get away, yell."

The rest went on deck, and it wasn't long before they saw the dinghy coming out from shore. The Chief sat in the bow and Dominick had the tiller. Amidships was something white. As the boat swung alongside, the "something" proved to be a seaman's hammock, lashed shut at the ends, and sewn down the middle with a line of rough stitching. It contained the body of the second dead man, resting on a plank in its canvas shroud.

Sailor Bill swung out the dinghy davits to get it aboard, and he and Dominick made ready to carry it into the saloon.

Katy couldn't bear to watch. Neither could the others apparently, for Spinach and the Able-seamen followed her below. They let Gyp out, and the little dog barked and wriggled a frenzied welcome. But there were some new smells aboard, strange and tantalizing, and he worked through 'tween decks to investigate them. First he ran through the galley into the fo'c'sle and took a look at Scar-face. He disapproved—strongly—and growled to let everyone know it. A queer odor that drifted through from under the door to Morgan's cabin had him stumped for a while. So Katy opened the stateroom and let him in. There, on the bunk sat the Chinaman, chains and all, and the ship's mascot got another North Country shock. But he got over it, with a fine show of disdain.

"Don't think much of that," his air plainly said. "Not even worth a bite."

Then he ran up the stairs to the deck. There was something queer here—and horrible. The glad spirit went out of him. His ears flattened, and the stump of his tail tried to curl itself between his legs. His nose led him forward to the open saloon door, and he went in. He came out again, flying, and crossed to the schooner's rail. There he sat on his haunches, stuck his nose into the air, and howled. It was the first time he had met death, and a remote ancestry cried aloud into the sinking sun.

Katy swept the pup into her arms. Her own heart thumped, and her eyes were near to tears.

"Don't, Doggie. Don't!" she said. "It's bad enough as it is."

For the Mates, the voyage back was a nightmare—an evil dream of cooking and dishwashing. There were now ten mouths to feed, and eight of the ten were ravenous men who required constant stoking to repair bodies worn out with fatigue. For the crew stood watch and watch— four hours on, and four off. Sailor Bill took Morgan, Katy and Teddy in his, and Dominick had the Chief, Spinach and Brick.

The Able-seamen relieved each other in the fo'c'sle keeping an eye on Scar-face, and the Mates were always in the galley. The Chinaman didn't count. He roamed around generally, got in everyone's way, and was always hungry. So that really left only two on a watch to handle the ship. And that wasn't enough, what with the squalls, gales, flat calms, and generally vile weather they met all the way. So the tired watch below was continually being roused out to heave on this line, slack off on that, or help crack on or reduce sail.

They went out through Detour Passage—maybe sixty or seventy miles out of their way—north, from Base Two. The Skipper and Dominick talked it over first, and decided that it would be wiser to head for the nearest phone.

"I want the 'Mounties' there when we land," said the Blue Nose. "And some of Joe's tribe will want to be on the dock to form a funeral escort. So Little Current won't do. We'd get there before they could. We'll go back to Sarnia and meet everybody there."

It was nearly dark by the time they got under way. The weather thickened, and they immediately began to fight head winds. It wasn't so bad in the open water of the North Channel, but it was still night, rainy and raw, while they were working through the island-dotted Potagannising Bay. Daylight didn't come until they brought up opposite the little town of Detour. They stood off in the Passage while Dominick and Morgan lowered the dinghy and went ashore in search of a telephone. A misty half gloom hid the village so they saw nothing of

the glorious wealth of color that on clear days blazed from the garden of Father Papineau. Nor could they see the church, school or parish house of this famous mission, established long ago as a Jesuit outpost in the Northwest Wilderness.

The Blue Nose came back an hour or so later, and the dinghy was hoisted aboard. Sailor Bill looked at him enquiringly.

"All set," he answered.

They went on. South for a while, slanting off the westerly sweep of wind that howled through the Straits of Mackinac, and putting miles of water between them and the dangerous lee shores of Cockburn and Manitoulin. Sailor Bill took no chances of piling up on this graveyard of Great Lakes shipping.

Then they turned down lake, toward the journey's end. All that day they sailed on, with only occasional smudges of steamer smoke for company. As night fell the wind stiffened to a half gale, and by dark they were roaring along with two reefs in the main, and only one jib set. During a lull Katy went on deck for a breath of air. A watery moon peered through a rift in the flying clouds, and a troubled sea tossed and broke in giant combers. She caught Sailor Bill in the act of turning over the wheel to his watch relief.

"Don't let her come up," she heard him say. "She can take it. Keep her off—and lam her. Stick her nose into it, let her have it."

The "letting her have it" heeled them over and buried

the lee rail. Sheets of water slammed inboard, and runnels of flying spray pelted the deckhouses, and streamed
off the dripping oilskins of the wheelsman. Katy ducked
below again.

"The galley range wasn't so bad after all."

Morning came and found them working down into the
wedge of the lake. The Mates were up before dawn,
cleaning the galley fire, and setting out the breakfast coffee. A pot of porridge bubbled away, and bacon and eggs
in a frying pan began to sizzle and steam. Spinach was
slicing bread for toast, when a hail from Sailor Bill took
them both up top.

"Get the glasses and go forward," he said. "Take a
look, and tell me what you see."

The day had broken dirty and gray, and a wicked cross
chop of stinging sea made the way along the deck a peril-
ous venture. Land could be seen on both sides now—a
pair of low ridges that narrowed the open lake into the
mouth of the Saint Clair River. Two or three freighters
were making their way up or down, and smudges of
smoke from their stacks were snatched away by the wind
to roll off in ragged greasy streaks.

The Mates wedged themselves into the bows and fo-
cused their glasses ahead. The blurred horizon leaped
into sharp outline.

Fifteen or sixteen miles away was a tossing blob on a
sea of breaking whitecaps. This was an old friend—the
Lake Huron Lightship. Midway were two black dots
that bobbed into view on the tops of waves, only to sink

out of sight in the hollows. The dots were Coast Guard cutters coming out to meet them, and making heavy weather of it. Head seas flung against them and smothered them in clouds of flying spray.

The Mates made their way aft and reported.

"That's it," said the Skipper, "our escort. Get everybody up. They'll be alongside in about half an hour."

Dominick and the Chief were routed out. They came

THE CONVOY

out of their staterooms rubbing the sleep from their eyes, and the Blue Nose cocked an eye up at the cabin clock. His watch wasn't due on deck for another hour.

"What's up?" he said.

Katy told him.

"Och-one!" said Dominick. "What a wonderful sleep I was havin'. Dreamin' about breakfast. Will there be time now for a dowse of hot coffee before we have to go up?"

Katy gave them each a scalding cup and they drank it slowly, juggling the hot mug from hand to hand so as

not to burn their fingers. Dominick was his usual chatty
self, and the Chief as glum as ever. During the entire
voyage down he had never mentioned Bear Hunter, nor
gone into the saloon. He worked, slept, ate, and kept his
own council. What he thought, none of the crew knew.

"Well, we'll be going," said Dominick after he finished
his coffee.

The two of them climbed the companion stairs to the
deck. Katy and Spinach shoved the cooking breakfast far
back on the range top where it wouldn't burn, washed
and put away the breakfast cups, and followed them up.

The cutters were much nearer now and working toward
them, one a little way off to port, and the other to starboard. They were running through a cross sea and rolling worse than torpedo boat destroyers. As they came
abreast both circled widely, turned, and ran in the same
direction as the schooner. Katy saw a man come out of
one of the Guard boat cabins, get out a pair of glasses,
and look the *Gull-Flight* over. Apparently satisfied, he
waved an arm and the boats came close. The man picked
up a megaphone.

"Are you all right?" he trumpeted. "We've been looking for you. It must have been rather dusty coming down
lake last night."

"It was," said Sailor Bill; "but we're all right."

"They're waiting for you at Sarnia," said the man with
the trumpet. "We'll take you in."

One cutter forged ahead, and the other dropped astern.
The two of them formed a convoy.

"What's all this?" asked Sailor Bill a little nettled. "Do they think we can't make shore without help?"

Dominick grinned.

"It's to see we make the right shore, I'm thinkin'," he said. "It's quite a passenger list we have: a Canadian Blue Nose—an illegal Chinaman—a Canadian Indian Chief—to say nothing of a murderer, and the bodies of the men he killed in Canada. If all that landed in 'The States,' our governments wouldn't stop writing notes for two years."

Sailor Bill laughed.

"Maybe you're right," he said.

THEY were three or four hours out from the mouth of the river, and while the gale had let up a bit, there was still wind and sea enough to keep things lively. The Mates served the belated breakfast as the crew could eat it—in relays. Afterward they cleaned up and made things shipshape. Who might come aboard at Sarnia, they didn't know. But after a voyage with Sailor Bill, there was one thing they did know—that any order short of spick-and-span wouldn't do. So they worked away. After a while the schooner stopped pitching and rolling, and they knew they had entered the river. Soon came a shout of orders, a creak of blocks and the slap of canvas. That was the sail going down. Immediately followed the roar of the motor, and curiosity took the Mates on deck.

The schooner was working in toward the dock. Quite

a crowd was there, and things looked pretty exciting. On the pier head was a squad of Royal Canadian Mounted Police in charge of a sergeant. Two hearses were backed down and their stretchers pulled out on the stands. But the most interesting thing was the line of Indians from Joe's tribe. These were drawn up in double row, and their feathered headdresses and bright blankets made a

INDIAN GRAVES AND RELICS —

brilliant ceremonial spectacle. They were come to bear away the body of their dead scout, and take him back for burial in the queer hut-like cluster of graves near the shore of Reservation Lake.

In spite of considerable preparation, the scene that followed was exceedingly short.

Two of the "Mounties" took the *Gull-Flight's* bow and stern lines. The sergeant came aboard and stood talking with Sailor Bill, Dominick and Aba-ka-mas. One of the hearses backed down to the gangway. The driver and his helper carried out the body of the gunman and loaded it in. Then they drove off.

Katy couldn't bear to look while this went on.

Then four of the Indians trundled up the second stretcher and stood, one at each corner. The others came aboard and went into the forward deckhouse. Aba-ka-mas said something to Dominick in low-voiced Chippewa.

"Now?" said the undercover agent.

"Yes," said the Chief.

Then he went ashore to stand at the head of the bier.

Captain Williams motioned to his crew. Then he led them to the dock where they took up a position a little to the rear of Aba-ka-mas, and a bit to one side. The sergeant formed his men in a squad and called them to attention. The Indians who had gone aboard came off again, bearing the body of Bear Hunter and laid it on the stretcher. The sergeant stepped forward, spread a Union Jack over the still form, and came to a salute. There was silence for a minute.

That was all.

The Indians wheeled the stretcher stand to the hearse. The car moved slowly off, and the tribal escort followed it to a waiting train. Aba-ka-mas and Sailor Bill shook hands in farewell.

Then the Chief turned to Dominick.

"My Brother," he said, "it is finished. Now I go."

Katy unashamedly wiped away a tear.

"Poor Joe," she said.

"Poor Bear Hunter," said Spinach.

Dominick laid a hand on each of their shoulders. "Death comes often in the North Country," he said. "His was quick and without pain."

SLOWLY the crew went back aboard. Then the sergeant brought his men over the side and formed them on the after-deck.

"Where's the Chink, and this Scar-face of yours?" he said.

Dominick told him, and handed over the keys to the locked stateroom and the smuggler's chains.

"My box too, if you will," he added. "It's packed and ready in the fo'c'sle."

"Right," said the Sergeant.

And then to his men, "Go get 'em."

The Chinaman came up first, chattering and clucking and tripping over everything, and as awkward as ever. The trooper who had him in charge was grinning as he steered him over the gangplank. Next came Dominick's sea box and ditty bag. A couple of Mounties took them off. And lastly Scar-face, cursing and struggling in the hands of two of the police. They heaved him up to face their officer, and held him erect whether he liked it or not.

The Sergeant took a look at him.

"Scar-face, eh!" he said. "That wasn't the name you

went by up near Slave Lake. We've been hunting you for two years. To answer to the murder of that 'breed' trapper. You'll hang all right."

And then to his men, "Take him away."

The Sergeant wheeled and saluted the Skipper and Dominick. Then he followed his troops over the side.

So there they were. The voyage was over and done. The adventure was ended and the smugglers brought to book. All that remained was the short trip home, and the good-byes to Dominick. And that didn't take long.

The Blue Nose was cheerful about it, and perfectly matter-of-fact. He shook hands with everybody and clapped the Able-seamen on the back. It was a good hearty cuff that about knocked them overboard.

"Stout fellows," he said.

To Morgan went special praise. Both for the motor and the Chief Engineer. "Never a miss—from either the engine or its master."

And then he came to the Mates. He stood off a minute, and then gave them each a great hug. His eyes shone as he held them at arm's length.

"A grander pair of Ship's Officers never was," he said. Nor better camp mates—and cooks!" The French in him came to the surface. *"Ou-la-la."* It was the only way he could end the sentence.

The next instant he was over the rail, and busied flinging off the shore lines. Blue water widened between the dock and the schooner, and the ship headed out into the stream. The *Gull-Flight's* crew stood watching over the stern.

Their last sight of him was as the first. A gay figure on a dock—hands on hips, and head cocked a little to one side. A debonair spirit, undaunted by adverse circumstance, and undismayed by happenings unforeseen.

EPILOGUE

THE DINING ROOM in the old house on Grosse Ile looked much the same. And to Katy, standing in the window bay, just as she had that Spring morning before the cruise began, it seemed strange that it should. The stress of the voyage—the ever shifting scene—the excitement and danger of the adventure—were none of these to make even a mark on the serene old house? Outside, the advancing season had grayed the trees. Events had affected nothing within. What had passed was as a dream.

Yesterday they had tied up at Ferry's Dock, and Father and Mother were there waiting. Gyp was first off, bounding away and hardly stopping to bark a welcome. He dashed up the dock, and once actually ashore on his beloved Island, took a refreshing roll in the familiar dust at the side of the road. Then he shook himself, tried some experimental sniffs under this and that, and came back wagging his tail.

"Wuf," he said. "This is something like. Home again. No more of that crazy North Country for me."

Morgan, Spinach and Teddy had said their good-byes. A letter was there waiting for them—to hurry them off to a train for the East. Sailor Bill had an hour or two's work taking on supplies and casting about for a couple of temporary hands. Then he shoved the schooner off for the long trip back to salt water. What was left of the crew stood watching the ship disappear behind the high banks of the down-river channel cut. Soon the *Gull-Flight* was but a memory.

Katy sighed.

Well—that was that. The cruise was over, the ship had gone, and their gallant company was dispersed. But now, where was the family? It was more than time for breakfast.

Brick came in first. He too had slept uneasily in his unaccustomed shore bunk and had turned out before daylight. Mother was next, smiling at the pair of them, and disappearing through the door into the kitchen. Breakfast was to be something special this morning. Then came Father. In his hand was a long, official-appearing envelope that bore a Canadian stamp. He laid it beside his plate.

"Good Morning. Good Morning," he said. "Do I scrape a forelock, or dance a hornpipe? Or how does one begin the day aboard ship?"

"Jim," said Mother, coming back into the dining room, "you stop. On their very first day home!"

Breakfast began.

Katy kept one eye on the envelope, and winked violently at Brick with the other. The Able-seaman finally caught on. His itch to know what was in the envelope was as great as Katy's, but rather than let their curiosity become apparent, the crew of the *Gull-Flight* would rather be boiled in oil.

Coffee and orange juice were tipped into Father. The morning paper was finished along with bacon and eggs. Then after what seemd an endless wait, the envelope was at last picked up and sliced across the top with a butter knife.

Then Mother noticed it.

"Why Jim," she said. "What's that?"

"Hm-m-m," said Father, reading the letter.

"Come on, Dad," said Brick, who couldn't hold in any longer. "What's in it? Tell us."

Father passed the letter over to Mother.

"Why children!" she said a minute later. "What an honor! It says that all of you—the whole crew—are to come to Ottawa this Christmas Vacation. Each is to receive a watch for what you did this Summer."

"Gee!" interrupted Brick.

"And it's signed by the Premier," Mother went on . . . "As a small reward for heroic service to the Canadian Government."

"Now what do you think of that?" said Father.

THE END